"Elizabeth," he watched her intently, "how do you think of me? As Lord Falconer or as Adam?"

To his horror her eyes began filling with tears. "Don't ask that," she implored, raising her hand to cover his. "Please don't."

Panic filled Adam, panic and an overwhelming sense of aching desire. As a gentleman he knew he should release her, let her walk away and never importune her again. He should, but he could not.

"Why?" he demanded, slipping his hands down to gently cup her face. "I think of you as Elizabeth. My Elizabeth. My beautiful Elizabeth," and he covered her mouth with his own.

Her lips were soft and warm beneath his, and he was helpless to resist their sweetness. Fighting the desire exploding inside of him, he drew her closer, savoring the feel of her pressed to his hungry body. It took every ounce of will he possessed to keep from taking more, but he cared for her too much to risk frightening her. Reining in his passion, he slowly raised his head, his heart pounding as he gazed down into her flushed face.

"Adam." His name slipped breathlessly from her parted lips, and her eyes were slumberous as she lifted her heavy lashes.

"Ah, my sweet, the things you do to a man's resolve," he murmured, tracing a finger along the bow of her mouth.

Her cheeks grew rosy, but to his delight she made no move to end their embrace. "You also have a deleterious effect upon my good sense," she said, smiling sadly. "But this changes nothing."

"You are wrong," he disagreed, "___ ___ thing."

BOOK YOUR PLACE ON OUR WEBSITE AND MAKE THE READING CONNECTION!

We've created a customized website just for our very special readers, where you can get the inside scoop on everything that's going on with Zebra, Pinnacle and Kensington books.

When you come online, you'll have the exciting opportunity to:

- View covers of upcoming books
- Read sample chapters
- Learn about our future publishing schedule (listed by publication month *and author*)
- Find out when your favorite authors will be visiting a city near you
- Search for and order backlist books from our online catalog
- Check out author bios and background information
- Send e-mail to your favorite authors
- Meet the Kensington staff online
- Join us in weekly chats with authors, readers and other guests
- Get writing guidelines
- AND MUCH MORE!

Visit our website at
http://www.zebrabooks.com

THE SINISTER SPINSTER

Carolyn Madison

ZEBRA BOOKS
Kensington Publishing Corp.
http://www.zebrabooks.com

This book is dedicated to the memory of my mother,
Barbara Elizabeth Smith Overfield.

February 21, 1925–December 20, 2000

With love always.

One

"Gad, but I am bored!" The young dandy gave a theatrical sigh, glaring out the library window at the curtain of steadily falling rain. "Does *nothing* ever occur in the country?"

Adam Darrach, Marquess of Falconer, glanced up from the book he'd been reading, his tawny eyes flashing in annoyance. He'd been enjoying the quiet, tucked away amongst the books and fine paintings, and he couldn't like having his peace disrupted by a pack of indolent care-for-nothings.

"Many things, Derwent," he said, his voice edged with cold disdain. "Birth, death, struggle, and triumph; it is all there if one but takes the time to look." *And possesses the wits to see,* he added in silent derision. Geoffrey Derwent and the rest of his useless set were proving a sore trial for him, but unfortunately he had no choice but to suffer their company. This visit to Derring's country estate was his last chance to secure the cagey earl's support before the arrival of the Czar and his court.

"I meant anything *interesting,*" Derwent qualified, tossing back his exquisite mop of gold curls. "We've been here for three days, and not one scandalous things has occurred. It is not to be borne!" He turned to the young man sprawled in a high-backed chair.

"Wills, you are our host's son," he said, gesturing dramatically. "It is your duty to see we are properly entertained. Do something!"

The pimply-faced youth's thick lips protruded in a sullen pout. "What do you suggest?" he demanded, in an equally petulant manner. "Can't hunt; the blasted rain's seen to that. And if it's bedroom sport you mean, you can jolly well forget it. The only maids m'mother hires are plain as mud and twice as thick. They shriek like the very devil if you so much as pinch 'em."

"Aye, that's true," the third dandy, Charles Colburt, said, rubbing his hand. "And they bite as well."

Adam remained silent, his lean countenance showing no trace of the cold fury he was feeling. Half the country was in desperate want of the most common necessities, he brooded, and all these worthless sots could do was whine about the maids rejecting their vile advances. He wished he had the raising of them for a few weeks. Or better still, he wished he might turn them over to his friend, Viscount St. Jerome. His lips lifted in a rare smile at the thought of the terrified dandies being put through their paces by the hard-faced former sergeant in the Rifles. If they managed to survive the experience, there might even be some hope for them.

"When are the rest of the guests to arrive?" Derwent paused in front of the mirror to admire the impossibly high points of his starched collar. "Perhaps there will be some sport to be found there?"

"The first group is set to arrive tomorrow after luncheon," William said in a glum tone. "Mama is already in high alt, running that new companion of hers ragged and planning every manner of entertainment. But I shouldn't bother looking there. Tiresome virgins for the most part; dandle with one of them and it's the parson's mousetrap for you."

"Only if you're caught," Colburt smirked. "And there's

always the mamas. Some of them ain't so bad, and more willing than you might think."

The crude observation put paid to the last of Adam's patience. He was about to administer a blistering scold on the proper conduct of gentlemen when the door to the library opened, and a slender young woman with her light brown hair drawn back in a tight bun started into the room. At the sight of the four men lounging about, she came to an uncertain halt.

"I beg your pardon, sirs, my lord," she said, her thin face pinking with embarrassment. "I thought the library was deserted. My apologies for disturbing you." And she made to withdraw.

"Pray do not leave on our account," Derwent drawled, turning to study the woman with a look Adam couldn't trust gleaming in his pale eyes. "Come in, by all means."

A panicked expression crossed the young woman's face. "No, that's all right," she said, backing toward the safety of the hall. "I'll come back another time. Good day."

"Oh, but we insist!" Charles Colburt rose to his feet and began advancing on her with predatory intent.

Genuine alarm had the woman's misty blue eyes going wide. "No, really, sirs, I—"

"Get in here, Mattingale," William barked, his face reddening in temper. "Do as you are told, or I shall have Mama turn you off without a character. We'll see how soon you manage to find another position given *your* reputation!"

The young woman jerked at the threat but remained where she was, her eyes downcast and her hands clenched at her sides.

More furious than he could remember being in years, Adam surged to his feet, his powerful body rippling in a subtle show of strength. He sent each of the other men a deadly glance and then turned to the woman standing in the doorway.

"It is quite all right, Miss Mattingale," he said, his deep

voice gentle as he offered her a smile. "These gentlemen and I were just leaving. Our apologies for keeping you from your duties." And he stepped around her, opening the door wider before turning back to the three dandies. It took but a single lift of his jet black eyebrow to bring them dragging after him.

He closed the door behind them and then led the way to the small study he remembered from an earlier visit. When he had secured that door he turned to face the other men, all trace of the gentleness he'd shown Miss Mattingale quite gone.

"I am going to say this but once," he said, pronouncing each word with icy menace. *"Gentlemen* never impose themselves on those who are weaker or lack the means to defend themselves. You appear to have forgotten that. Forget it again, and it will be my pleasure to put a bullet through you."

William sulked, Derwent pouted, and Colburt gave an incredulous laugh. "Oh, come, Lord Falconer, do you expect us to believe you'd call us out for trifling with a companion?"

Adam studied him with cold contempt. "Yes."

"But that's ridiculous!" Charles blustered, clearly stunned. "She's a *companion,* for heaven's sake, and one whose reputation is not all it should be, if what Wills says is true."

Adam turned to the first dandy. "Derwent, what am I called in the shooting clubs?"

" 'Six-shot Falconer,' " the younger man provided, looking decidedly ill at ease.

"And why am I called that?"

"Because you can hit six out of six targets in under two minutes, including reloading time."

Adam gave that a second to sink in, and then eyed each man in turn. "Six shots," he said coldly. "Six shots, and there's only three of you. Remember that." And feeling there was nothing left to be said, he turned and quietly left the room.

As soon as they knew themselves to be alone, the three remaining men collapsed onto the chairs.

"Gad, I need a drink," Derwent said, fanning himself with his hand. "Wills, ring for some brandy, won't you? The marquess has quite overset my poor nerves."

"You don't think he means it, do you?" William asked, after doing as he'd been bid. "He can't mean it. I am his host's son. Can't kill me. It would be bad form."

"Oh, he meant it, right enough," Colburt muttered, looking murderous. "Stiff-rumped prig. It's not as if we meant the wench any harm; just having fun was all. She looks as if she could use a bit of sport. And what was that crack about her reputation?" he asked, turning back toward William. "Never say that fiercely grim mama of yours hired a fashionable impure to keep her company?"

"If only," Wills mourned, shaking his head. "No such thing, though. I merely meant Miss Mattingale's family's a bit odd. Travel everywhere, and her father writes those dull and dusty tomes no one can make any sense of. Only reason Mama hired her was because she was bosom bows with her grandmother, and the old gel begged Mama to give the chit a position. Papa didn't like it above half, I can tell you," he added darkly.

"Indeed, and why is that?" Charles asked, intrigued. His pride was still stinging from Lord Falconer's reprimand, and he was eager to make someone pay for the blow he'd taken.

William gave a derisive snort. "Thinks she's a French spy," he said, his lips twisting in a sneer. "Can you imagine anything so foolish? Female don't say but two words half the time, and goes skittering about like a demmed mouse the rest of it."

"Why should he think she's a spy, and a French one at that?" A footman had delivered the decanter of brandy and several glasses, and Derwent was wasting little time in helping himself.

"Because she's lived in France for any number of years, and she's only just come from America," William answered, cocking his head to one side as he considered the matter. "Her papa's still there, and Father has forbidden her to write him so long as our soldiers are busy killing one another. Shouldn't be surprised if she ain't defying him, though. Saw her sneaking into town the other day, and I'll wager it wasn't just to take the air, as *she* said."

"That's it!" Colburt exclaimed, slapping his hand on the arm of his chair. "It's the perfect answer!"

"Eh?" William blinked at him owlishly. "What is?"

"The answer to poor Derwent's ennui, of course," Charles said, cleverly keeping his plans for revenge private. "We shall start a rumor Miss Mattingale is in reality a notorious French spy!"

"What?" This from William.

"Charles, that is inspired!" Derwent beamed his approval.

"Don't be daft," William said, for once the voice of reason. "No one would believe it! Not of that milk-and-water miss!"

"Ah, but only think, dear Wills," Charles purred, all but rubbing his hands in glee. "Who else would make the perfect spy but the last person anyone would suspect?"

It took a few moments for William to chew over that. "But if we tell people she's a spy, then that means we suspect her," he said, showing a heretofore unrevealed facility for logic. "And if we suspect her, then how can she be a spy? Besides, wouldn't want people thinking my father would keep a Frenchie spy tucked under his roof. Think of the scandal."

Charles thought for a moment. "Then what we will do," he said at last, "is to tell people we suspect there to be a spy in our midst. We'll . . . oh, I don't know, say some of your father's papers are gone missing. He's still a member of the Privy Council, isn't he?" He glanced at William.

"I suppose so." William lifted his shoulders in an indifferent shrug. "Carries a box of papers with him he keeps locked up in his study. And even if he ain't a member, Falconer is, I'll warrant. Papa said he's close to the prince, and he's helping him plan the fête for the Czar and his sister."

"Even better," Charles decided. "We'll hint some papers relating to the Russian court's visit have vanished, and that is why Falconer has come. We can get the other guests to try to guess the spy's true identity, tossing out just enough hints to make them believe what we want them to believe."

"Charles, I am in awe," Derwent said, leaping to his feet and sweeping low in an exaggerated bow. "You are brilliant; truly brilliant. I had no idea."

"I don't know," William said, annoyed to find he had a conscience after all. "May not care for Miss Mattingale, but that don't mean I want her taken up as a spy. They hang spies, you know."

But having come so close to savoring victory, Charles wasn't ready to quit the field. "Dunce, we won't let it get that far!" he said cuttingly. "If it gets too out of hand, we can always say it was all a hum, and the matter will be forgotten."

"I'm not certain . . ."

"Oh, don't be so tiresomely dull, Wills!" Derwent pouted at him. "This is going to be wonderful! Think of all the fun we shall have; planting notions in people's minds, raising a hue and cry, and then settling back to watch the others scurrying about chasing after mare's nests. How can you be so cruel as to deny me the one bit of enjoyment I have had since coming to this dreary place?"

Put like that, William did think it would be rather churlish of him to act the spoiler. Still . . .

"Tell you what," Charles interposed, taking William's measure. "We'll make it a wager, shall we? That way none of us can cry off."

"A wager?" William stirred with interest. "What sort of wager?"

"I'll wager a thousand pounds we can carry it off,"

Charles said, thinking quickly. "And you, Wills, shall wager a thousand we cannot. How's that?"

"We would bet against each other?" William wanted to be certain he understood correctly. "That don't sound quite aboveboard."

"Of course it is," Charles assured him. "It's perfectly acceptable. So long as we don't cheat, of course."

"Cheat?"

All of this plotting and scheming was proving harder than Charles anticipated. He was trying to think of some way to explain when help arrived from an unexpected quarter.

"Slowtop," Derwent said, with exaggerated patience, "if we tell anyone this is all a game, and that there are no missing papers and, therefore, no French spy, *that* would be cheating. To carry off our wager in an honorable fashion we have to take a vow here and now that under penalty of forfeiture we can never, ever reveal the truth." He looked at Charles. "Is that not right?"

"Aye," Charles said, nodding. "Exactly so."

"Then," Derwent said smugly, "are we agreed?"

"Aye," Charles repeated, and glanced expectantly at William.

William nodded. "Aye," he said reluctantly. "We are agreed."

"Filthy, useless, parasitic fops!" Miss Elizabeth Mattingale's aquamarine eyes flashed with temper as she paced up and down the narrow confines of her small room. "Stupid, small-minded little nothings! How dare they treat me so!"

It wasn't often Elizabeth allowed herself to lose her temper; but then, it was seldom she was offered such deliberate provocation. She'd heard several of the maids complaining of the grabbing and pinching they'd encountered from Mr. Derwent's London friends, and had done her best to keep out of their way. Thank heaven Lord Falconer had been there, she thought, breathing a mental sigh of relief. She shuddered to think what might have happened had she been forced to deal with the wretches on her own.

The memory of the decisive way the handsome marquess had routed the younger men filled her with reluctant admiration. She'd met him the first night he'd arrived from London, and at the time had thought him quite the coldest man she had ever encountered. Having had the opportunity to observe him in action, she now considered him one of the most dangerous men as well. She knew she would not wish to make an enemy of his lordship; something told her he would be a merciless opponent.

After taking a few more minutes to compose herself, Elizabeth splashed some cool water on her face and went back downstairs to the drawing room. Her new employer was just as she'd left her, pouring over another of her endless lists. She glanced up when Elizabeth opened the door, her thick brows meeting in a disapproving scowl.

"There you are, Miss Mattingale," she said, sounding as if Elizabeth had been gone for days instead of a mere quarter hour. "Did you find the book I wanted?"

Since her hands were plainly empty, Elizabeth thought the answer to that rather obvious, but she kept such thoughts to herself.

"No, my lady, I did not," she said, returning to her chair. "Are you quite certain you left it in the library? I looked everywhere."

The countess pursed her lips. "I am *almost* certain I did," she said, tapping her finger against her chin. "Although I suppose I may have left it in my sitting room just as well. Ah, well, it is of no moment. I didn't need it after all."

Elizabeth choked back a cry of fury. She'd risked a pawing, if not worse, for some foolish book about the peerage, and now her employer decided it was of "no moment"? She eyed the pot of tea setting on the table in front of Lady Derring before giving a wistful sigh. However tempting it might be to upend the contents over the older woman's head, it was best she resisted the impulse. She'd only just secured this position, and Grandmother would be quite put out if she lost it in less than a sennight.

"I thought of holding a Roman ball for Robert's birthday," Lady Derring said, the matter of the missing book already forgotten. "Classic themes are always best, don't you think?"

An image of the portly earl in a toga, his balding head draped in laurel, flashed in Elizabeth's head and nearly proved her undoing.

"Indeed, my lady," she managed, albeit in a somewhat strained voice. Her vivid imagination was her greatest gift as well as her greatest curse, her father had once told her, but lud, how dull life would be without it.

Lady Catherine cast her a suspicious look. "Are you all right, Miss Mattingale?" she asked sharply. "Your voice sounds queer."

"A tickle in my throat, ma'am," Elizabeth assured her, hiding a smile behind her teacup. "I shall be fine in a moment."

"And so I should think," the countess replied with a grumble. "People who fancy themselves invalids are tiresome beyond enduring. For myself, I have always enjoyed the best of health."

"Yes, my lady," Elizabeth repeated, wisely not mentioning that only yesterday Lady Derring had laid claim to the most delicate constitution in the shire.

"So, it is decided, then." As usual, the countess was oblivious to Elizabeth's wry tone. "A Roman ball for his lordship's birthday, and a costume ball for the first week. Now"—she picked up her quill and frowned thoughtfully—"all that is needed is something truly spectacular for the last evening our guests are here. Something that will be all the talk when we all return to London." She looked at Elizabeth, clearly expecting her to pull some wondrous idea out of thin air.

Elizabeth didn't disappoint her. "All things Russian

seem to be quite the thing at the moment," she said, re-membering the gossip she'd overheard between her grand-mother and their neighbor. "A ball with Russian foods and music should prove quite entertaining for your guests."

"A Russian ball?" The countess stirred in interest.

"Yes," Elizabeth said, warming to her theme. "We could serve salmon and other delicacies, and vodka for the gentlemen."

"Vodka?" the countess asked, clearly unfamiliar with the term.

"A potent drink that is much favored in Russia," Eliza-beth explained. "Rather like whiskey in Scotland."

"Well, if it is popular in Russia, then we must by all means serve it here," the countess said, her dark brown eyes sparkling with enthusiasm. "And you are right about the popularity of all things Russian. The last edition of *La Belle Assemble* did have several fashions that were *à la Russe.*" She paused and cast Elizabeth a speculative look.

"You seem rather knowledgeable about Russia," she said, her tone frankly suspicious. "Never say *you* have been there?"

"As a matter of fact, my lady, I have." It was all Eliza-beth could do to keep the smugness out of her voice. "My parents and I spent two years in St. Petersburg while my father was writing a book on the history of one of the more prominent families. Prince Zaramoff, as I recall."

"A prince?" Lady Derring gasped, all but clapping her hands in glee.

"Yes, my lady." Elizabeth hadn't the heart to tell the older woman such titles were common in Russia, and every other person of note was either a prince or a count of something.

"When was this?"

It took Elizabeth a moment or two remember. "Three . . . no, four years ago," she said, remembering her sadness at leaving the stunning beauty of the port city. "It was shortly before my mother took ill and died."

"And you know a prince; fancy that," Lady Derring said, ignoring Elizabeth's mention of her mother. "What was his name again?"

"Zaramoff," Elizabeth provided, smiling at the memory of the jovial prince with his huge mustache and booming laugh.

"Zaramoff." Lady Derring was tapping her chin again. "I know I have heard that name before, but I can't think where. Ah, well." She shrugged. "It hardly signifies, I suppose. But your idea for a Russian ball is excellent, Miss Mattingale, thank you. See to it, won't you?"

Elizabeth thought of the work involved in arranging such a ball and gave the teapot another wistful glance. "Yes, my lady."

Dressing for dinner that evening, Elizabeth took special pains with her appearance. From her limited knowledge of men, she knew the three dandies who had attempted to accost her would now regard her as a challenge, and would do their best to set up a flirtation with her. Since she couldn't expect Lord Falconer to spend his entire stay rescuing her from their importuning, she would have to find some other means of dissuading them.

After donning her plainest gown, Elizabeth reached for one of the starched caps she'd purchased when she'd decided to become a companion. She hated the thought of wearing one, for if she had any vanity it was her hair. It was the same warm golden-brown as her mother's hair and, unbound, it flowed almost to her waist. Still, if it came down to wearing a cap or being mauled, she knew which fate she preferred. Sighing, she bound up her hair and stuffed it beneath the starched square of muslin.

By hurrying, Elizabeth managed to be the first to arrive in the dining room. Her employer let it be known that she expected Elizabeth to make herself useful whenever possible, and that meant seeing to things that were normally the province of the hostess. She'd just finished checking the seating arrangements when she heard a noise behind her. Thinking it was the housekeeper coming in for a chat, she glanced casually over her shoulder. The sight of Lord Falconer, dressed in a black velvet jacket and cream satin breeches, had her starting in alarm.

"Oh, Lord Falconer," she said, bobbing a hasty curtsy. "I beg your pardon, sir, I hadn't heard you come in."

"There is no reason you should have," he replied, the deep voice she remembered devoid of any expression. His black hair was brushed back from his forehead, throwing the sharp bones of his face into prominence. It was a handsome face, she thought, but cold. She brushed the thought aside and gave him a polite smile.

"Is there something I can do for you, my lord?" she offered in the diffident tones she had spent days perfecting. Companions were expected to be diffident, and although she'd yet to perfect the skill, she was determined to succeed.

"No, thank you, Miss Mattingale," he said, his golden eyes remote as he studied her. "I only wanted to make certain you had recovered from this afternoon's unpleasantness. Should it happen again, I want you to come to me at once. I shall attend to the matter for you."

"How? By calling them out?" The question slipped out before Elizabeth could stop it. She bit her lip in mortification, but it was too late to call the words back.

He smiled; not the gentle smile he'd given her earlier, but something hard and deadly. "Yes, that is precisely what I will do."

Elizabeth wasn't certain how to respond. Thanking someone for offering to kill another human being seemed wrong, but good manners dictated she say something. She thought for a moment.

"Hopefully it won't come to that, my lord," she said, then, because she thought that sounded rather abrupt, she added, "Thank you for your concern. It is very kind of you."

He studied her for several seconds before inclining his head with regal hauteur. "You are welcome, Miss Mattingale," he said. "But I mean what I say; I want you to tell me if anyone bothers you."

Sensing his implacable determination, Elizabeth's sense of curiosity was piqued. "Why?" she asked, thinking not only of her employer's younger son and his equally pestilent friends, but also of many of the other members of the so-called aristocracy it had been her misfortune to encounter. Men who felt their wealth and titles entitled them to behave however ill they desired to those they considered beneath them. And, of course, to such men everyone was beneath them.

The marquess continued regarding her, his expression revealing nothing of his thoughts. "Because I am a gentleman," he replied, as if somehow privy to her thoughts. "I was raised to believe that means more than a mere accident of birth; it means I have an obligation to protect those who are under my care." His gaze sharpened as it met hers. "I take my obligations very seriously, Miss Mattingale."

Elizabeth was surprised to feel her heart pounding in her chest. Disconcerted, she blurted out the first thing to pop into her mind.

"I am not under your care."

He raised an elegant eyebrow. "Are you not?" he asked softly. "I shouldn't be so certain of that if I were you." While she continued gaping at him, he smiled again, offering his arm with a low bow. "If you are ready to join the others in the drawing room, Miss Mattingale, it would be my honor to escort you."

TWO

Adam awoke the following morning to bright skies and birdsong. After two days of pouring rains, the sight was enough to have him leaping out of bed and ringing for his valet. With his host's permission he'd had his latest purchase from Tattersall's sent down, and he was itching to take the full-blooded Arab gelding for a proper gallop. By rushing through his breakfast and morning ablutions he was soon on his way, whistling beneath his breath as he started down the main staircase. His good mood vanished at the sight of the three men making their way up the stairs toward him.

"Lord Falconer." Geoffrey Derwent gave him one of his annoying smirks. "Off for a ride, are you?" he added, indicating Adam's green jacket and doeskin breeches with a sweeping gesture of his hand. "How ambitious you are. 'Tis scarce twelve of the clock."

"I thought to ride out to the ruins," Adam replied, eyeing the three warily. He'd come to think of them as the enemy, and he'd learned from St. Jerome never to trust an enemy.

"Heavens, the thought of such industry quite fatigues me," Derwent sighed in his die-away fashion. "I must now repair to my rooms and rest, lest I show the ladies a haggard countenance. Come, Charles." And he minced away, leaving Colburt to trail in his wake. To Adam's annoyance William remained behind, shuffling his weight from one foot to another as he stood blocking Adam's way.

"Is there something you wish, Mr. Carling?" Adam asked, taking care to show no emotion as he tugged on his riding gloves. The lad was up to something; all that remained was discovering what that something might be.

William's face reddened. "No," he began, and cleared his throat. "That is to say," he continued, his gaze fixed on his feet, "a moment of your time, my lord, if you would. There is something I should like to discuss with you."

Adam kept his surprise hidden behind a mask of indifference. "As you wish," he said coolly. If the lad was about to stammer an apology, he would take great delight in reminding him that it wasn't he who was owed an apology.

He followed the earl's younger son down the stairs and into the elegant drawing room the countess had set aside for her guest's use. A bouquet of lilacs and tulips in a crystal vase was set on the polished mantel, and he wondered if Miss Mattingale was responsible for the charming arrangement. He doubted his flighty hostess possessed the wits to do something so original.

William stood in front of the fireplace, his hands clasped behind him. "I was wondering, sir, if you've spoken with m'father this morning," William asked, still not meeting Adam's gaze.

So that was it, Adam realized, his lips twisting in well-bred scorn. The young whelp was terrified he had tattled to his papa. He needn't have worried. Adam wasn't one to carry tales, although he had no intention of letting William know that.

"No, I've not yet had the pleasure," he drawled, deliberately infusing a note of unspoken menace in his voice. "Why? Is there anything you wish me to say?"

William jerked, his gaze flying up to meet Adam's before he lowered it again. "No, no such thing," he said, shuffling. "I was only wondering if you'd seen him, and how he seemed to you."

The question took Adam aback. "How should he seem?" he asked, frowning in thought. The earl wasn't the most loquacious of men, but as he himself had often been accused of being as closemouthed as a clam, he didn't consider that to be a failing.

"I don't know," William admitted. "I'm almost certain it's all a hum, but one never knows." He lifted his head to send Adam a strained smile. "Sorry to have bothered you, my lord," he said, bobbing his head in apology. "Enjoy your ride."

The odd conversation was much on Adam's mind as he rode over the hills and down to the sea. Had it been anyone else, he would have suspected them of deliberately planting the uneasy doubts in his mind, but he didn't think William possessed the cunning. Derwent did, most assuredly, and he didn't trust Colburt so much as an inch. Perhaps there was nothing wrong with the earl, perhaps there was. In any case, it would do no harm to ask. With the Czar's ambassadors due to arrive in London within a week, it was best not to leave even the smallest detail to chance.

Relieved he'd decided upon a course of action, Adam threw himself into the ride. He spent the next hour riding hell-for-leather across the countryside, taking Shalimar over hedgerows and fences as he raced away from the house. Along the way he lost his hat and the veneer of smooth sophistication he wore as easily as other men wore their fine lawn shirts and elegant velvet jackets. With his black hair tumbling about his forehead and his cheeks flushed from wind and the sheer pleasure of riding, he looked little like the man who had set out from the Hall. The knowledge pleased him on same basic level, and feeling quite satisfied, he turned Shalimar around and started for the stables.

On impulse he decided to ride through the village instead of the fields, with the idea of stopping for a pint of ale at the tiny inn. He had just dismounted and was about to toss the reins to a linkboy who'd run up to greet him when the door to the milliner's shop across the lane opened, and Miss Mattingale stepped out. The hatbox swinging from her arm explained her presence, and he wondered if she had come in one of the estate's many carriages. When she turned and began walking in the direction of the Hall, he had his answer. His lips thinning in fury, he remounted his horse and set out after her.

"Miss Mattingale," he called out, urging his horse into a trot. "Hold there!"

He thought she hesitated for a moment, but when she turned to face him a smile of cautious welcome was pinned to her lips.

"Good day, Lord Falconer," she said, dropping a graceful curtsy. "You are up and about at an early hour this morning. Did you enjoy your ride?"

"Very much so," he replied, taking in her maroon cloak and gown of cream-and-gold-striped cambric in disapproval. Although the sun was quite bright the wind was sharp, and the thin cloak looked inadequate to the task of keeping her warm.

"How did you get into the village, if I may ask? Surely you didn't walk?" he queried, thinking that when he spoke with the earl he would also drop a flea in his ear about the shabby way his wife was treating her companion. As master, it was his responsibility to make certain those under his roof lacked for nothing.

"No, my lord," she replied, a spark of annoyance shimmering in her silvery blue eyes. "I rode in the gig with Mrs. Keys, the cook. But she is visiting her sister, who is the vicar's housekeeper, and rather than wait for her, I decided to walk back to the manor. It's such a lovely day, even though I fear it may rain again."

Adam was in no mood to discuss the vagaries of the weather. "It is over four miles to the house," he reminded her, angered at the thought of her walking that distance on what was certain to be muddy and slippery roads. He recalled his journey from London, when the horses had struggled through deep ruts.

"Only if one keeps to the road," she answered coolly. "If you cut through the meadows, it is less than half that. And I don't mind walking. Indeed, I quite like it." This last was added with a defiant lift of her pointed chin.

Adam's lips twitched as he resisted the sudden urge to laugh. The companion's recalcitrant nature put him strongly in mind of his friend's new wife, and he didn't doubt but that Lady St. Jerome would heartily applaud Miss Mattingale's attempts to put him in his place. But however much he might enjoy her spirited defiance, that didn't mean he intended letting her go blithely on her way. Reaching out, he cupped her chin in his gloved hand and tilted her face up to his.

"Miss Mattingale," he began, his lips curving in a wry smile, "you must know I won't let you walk back on your own. It would be a violation of all that I believe in, and I cannot allow it."

There was no mistaking the fury sparkling in her jewel eyes as she glared up at him. "Your pardon, Lord Falconer," she said, freeing herself from his grip and taking a deliberate step backward, "but I don't believe it is within your province to *allow* me to do anything. You are not my employer."

"No," he agreed, unaffected by her temper, "I'm not. But I still have no intention of letting you do as you propose. And you needn't bother casting daggers at me," he added, as her eyes narrowed even further. "Didn't I tell you I considered you to be under my care?"

For a moment he didn't think she would answer; then she gave a muttered exclamation. "Oh, for heaven's sake, you wretched tyrant! Have it your own way if you must." And with that, she turned and walked back toward the village.

Intrigued as much as he was amused, he trailed after her. "Where are you going?" he asked, easily matching his longer strides to hers.

"Back to the parsonage to wait for Mrs. Keys," she muttered, delicately lifting her skirts as she navigated the muddy lanes. "Although given the way she and her sister were gossiping, I shall be fortunate to see the Hall before next Sunday!"

Adam bit his lip to keep from chuckling at the acerbic observation. "You might take the gig now and send it back for Mrs. Keys in an hour or so," he suggested.

"Yes, as if I should put poor Dobbin and the groom to such bother," she grumbled, clearly unimpressed with his stratagems.

Adam slid her a thoughtful glance, considering several alternatives. Had he come upon her on the road or in the meadow, he could probably have taken her up behind him without risking too great of a scandal. Unfortunately he knew enough of village life not to suggest such a thing now. Pity, he thought with a rueful sigh. He would rather have enjoyed a few more minutes in the tart-tongued lady's company.

That was too close! The moment she reached the sanctuary of her room, Elizabeth flattened herself against the door, her eyes squeezing shut in relief. If she lived to be as old as Granny Dithers, she didn't think she would ever be half so frightened as she'd been when the marquess had surprised her coming out of the milliner's shop. Perhaps it was true what the Bible said about the guilty fleeing where no man pursued, she decided, moving away from the door and removing her cloak. But for herself, she'd never known five more uncomfortable minutes in her life. It seemed she would need to take even greater care if his lordship was going to be popping up when least expected.

After making certain her door was securely locked, she hurried over to her narrow bed and laid the hatbox upon the embroidered cover. The countess's newest bonnet, a hideous concoction of chipstraw and ceramic cherries, lay inside, but it was the box itself that concerned Elizabeth. Employing the greatest care, she ran her fingertips along the papered sides, stopping when she found the seam holding the pasted edges together. Slowly and skillfully, she peeled the paper apart, holding back a soft cry of delight at the letter she found secreted inside. One could say what one wished of the Gentlemen, she thought, lifting out the letter and smiling at the familiar handwriting. They were every bit as reliable as the post when it came to delivering the mail, and a dashed sight faster. She set the box on the floor, taking time to reseal the sides before sitting down on her bed to read the latest missive from her papa.

> *Dearest Daughter,*
> *Outrage upon outrage has been visited upon my adopted land. Only wait until I tell you of the foul crime our fine Army has committed against an innocent and unarmed populace . . .*

Elizabeth continued reading, her high spirits growing somber at what she read. From her father's last letter she'd known the war in America was going badly for the newly formed nation, but now it seemed matters were even more desperate than she'd believed. The letter listed a litany of atrocities and horrors committed by the British troops, and from the scratchy quality of the handwriting Elizabeth could tell her father was shaking with fury. He concluded the missive with the request Elizabeth had been expecting since he had announced his decision to move to America.

> *I know it was your mother's dying wish that you return to England, and I would never want you to act in a manner not in accordance with your conscience. But I must ask, Elizabeth, nay, I must insist that you leave a country which possesses so little in the way of honor, and join me here in Virginia. I am settled quite comfortably in Richmond, and can*

now afford to keep you in some comfort and style.
Join me, Elizabeth, but before you do, there is some-
thing I would ask of you . . .

"Miss Mattingale? Miss Mattingale?"

The timid knock on her door had Elizabeth biting back
a shriek of alarm. She folded the letter quickly, tucking
it underneath her spread before hurrying over to open the
door. One of the maids stood there, her plain face breaking
into a smile of relief when she saw Elizabeth.

"Oh, good, miss, you're here. Her ladyship is calling
for you. She's in a rare taking and asks that you come at
once."

"Very good, Ceila, thank you," Elizabeth managed a
weak smile. "Only give me a moment to retrieve her ladyship's bonnet, and I shall be right with you."

"Not o'nother one!" the young maid exclaimed with a
pert roll of her eyes. "Is it ugly as all the rest?"

"Heavens no!" Elizabeth, equally pert, assured her.
"It's even worse."

Elizabeth found her employer in the front hallway, barking out a final set of orders and consulting her lists.

"No, no, no, we cannot move the viscountess to the
Red Room, Jerrell," she said to the unflappable individual
who acted as her majordomo. "The woman has a dreadful
fear of flowers, and the suite overlooks my rose gardens.
We shall have to put her in the Chinese Suite, and hope
to heavens she doesn't break something."

She glanced up at Elizabeth's approach, her imperious
features settling in a scowl.

"And where have you been?" she demanded in impatient tones. "I have been calling for you for above an
hour!"

"My apologies, my lady, but I have only just returned
from the village," Elizabeth said, swallowing her temper
along with a considerable portion of her pride. "Is there
some problem?"

"I should say there is!" the countess exclaimed, her

annoyance with Elizabeth giving way to a childlike excitement. "A messenger from London has brought word that we shall be expected to receive a member of the Russian nobility. One of the princes attending the Czar learned of our house party and has taken it into his head to join us. Can you imagine?" she added, preening with self-importance. "A Russian prince, in *our* home! I shall be the envy of all our friends when we return to London for the festivities."

Elizabeth refrained from commenting on the other woman's unbecoming toadying. "Do you recall the prince's name?" she asked, frowning thoughtfully.

"Something unpronounceable," her ladyship replied with an indifferent shrug. "Why do you ask?"

"I was wondering if perhaps I might know him," Elizabeth admitted. "I met several members of the Diplomatic Corps while Papa and I were living in St. Petersburg. It is entirely possible I may have met this prince at some function or another."

"That's right!" The countess exclaimed, studying her with sharp-eyed interest. "I'd quite forgotten you claim to have lived there. I don't suppose you speak the language?"

Elizabeth recalled her struggles to master the impossible tongue. "After a fashion," she admitted, not willing to lay claim to an expertise she did not possess. "I shouldn't say I was an expert, but I did speak it well enough to get on with shopkeepers and the like."

"Then you must teach me a few phrases, that I might greet his highness properly," the older woman demanded, looking at Elizabeth expectantly. "How does one say, 'Welcome' in Russian?"

Elizabeth thought for a moment, and then said, *"Dabroh pazhaluvat."*

Lady Derring looked horrified. "Good heavens! Are you certain you are pronouncing it correctly? It sounds like gibberish to me."

"Quite certain, my lady," Elizabeth assured her, doing

her best not to take offense. "But I shouldn't worry if I were you. If the prince is in the Diplomatic Corps, then he is likely to be fluent in French. You may greet him in that tongue."

A sullen expression flashed across the countess's face. "I have never bothered learning the wretched language," she said in peevish tones. "The French are our enemy, after all." She eyed Elizabeth resentfully. "You speak it as well, I trust?"

For a brief moment Elizabeth was strongly tempted to teach the countess some of the more colorful epithets she'd picked up in her travels, but in the end common sense prevailed. "Yes, my lady," she murmured, and proceeded to teach her employer the most innocuous phrases she could think of.

The countess's mangled attempts at French were still ringing in Elizabeth's ears when the Earl of Derring emerged from his study. To her annoyance, Lord Falconer was at his side, and she noted with some surprise that he'd already changed out of his riding togs and into a maroon jacket of Bath superfine and gray kerseymere breeches tucked into the tops of his glossy boots. He looked every inch the haughty English gentleman, and Elizabeth could only shake her head at such a pattern card of perfection.

"Can't believe the cheek of this fellow," the earl was grumbling to the marquess. "I don't know him from Adam, and he thinks nothing of battening himself on me. Bloody irregular, if you ask me."

"Royalty, my lord, makes its own regulations," Lord Falconer reminded him, his cool voice sharp. "And as this particular royal is an intimate of the Czar's, you dare not give offense. The Alliance must be protected at all costs."

"I know that," the earl responded, scowling. "But I don't have to like having my home invaded by a mob of Cossacks without so much as a by-your-leave, do I? And I'll warrant the fellow doesn't even speak English. Everyone knows these Russians are half wild and half mad at best."

"Pray do not take on so, Robert," the countess scolded, reaching out to straighten her lord's cravat in a show of wifely impatience. "Only think of the honor his highness is according us, and what it might mean to your career. And as for conversing with the prince, you needn't worry. Miss Mattingale assures me she speaks the tongue like a native."

"Does she, by gad?" The earl peered at Elizabeth, as if only that moment aware of her existence. "Good afternoon to you, Miss Mattingale," he said, sketching a brief bow. "Mind you don't stray too far afield, eh? Might need you to jabber at the fellow so he don't slaughter us all. They do that, one hears."

"Robert!" Lady Derring laid a shaking hand to her throat. "You cannot mean so!" Before he could answer she turned to Elizabeth. "You must speak with him, Miss Mattingale, and make him promise not to do us harm!"

It was more than Elizabeth could resist. "I can certainly *try,* my lady," she said, allowing a note of doubt to creep into her voice. "But if his highness should take offense to even the slightest thing . . ." Her voice trailed off meaningfully.

The countess gave a shriek, but before she could engage in a fit of hysterics a massive carriage rumbled to a halt in front of the house. Several liveried footmen swarmed down from the top and pulled open the door of the heavy coach. A short, heavyset man with a flowing mustache and a large staff clutched in his hand stepped down first, but it was the taller, handsome man with piercing sky-blue eyes and dark gold hair who followed him who had the breath catching in Elizabeth's throat. Even as she was deciding how best to handle the next few minutes, the man with the staff swept into the hall, pounding the staff on the marbled tiles.

"His highness, Prince Peter Alexander Bronyeskin," he boomed out, and the Prince stepped into the hallway.

The earl moved forward to greet him, bending low in a polite bow. "Your highness, allow me to make you welcome to Derring Hall. You are most welcome here."

"Thank you, my lord," the prince replied, his voice deeper, cooler than Elizabeth remembered. "It is good of you to be so kind to a guest who has arrived without an invitation." He next made his bow to the countess, kissing her hand while she simpered and pinked in delight. He was turning to Lord Falconer when he saw Elizabeth, and his eyes widened in recognition.

"Elizabeth," he whispered. "Little queen, it is you?"

"Your highness," Elizabeth began, her greeting ending in a gasp of surprise when she was scooped up in a pair of masculine arms and swung in a circle.

She was deposited on her feet, and her cheeks enthusiastically kissed. *"Milaya,* what a delight to see you again!" the prince continued, blue eyes dancing as he grinned down at her. "And you are a guest here as well, yes? How happy that makes me! It is good to see an old friend when one is so far from home."

Elizabeth's cheeks bloomed with embarrassment. Not certain how to explain her current situation, she took a hasty step back from Alexi, noting the way his eyes flashed first with hurt and then with awareness.

An awkward silence followed, broken when Lord Derring hastily introduced the marquess.

"Lord Falconer, it is an honor to meet you," Alexi said, his smooth manner a world removed from that of the laughing, carefree young man Elizabeth remembered with such fondness. "I have heard of your prowess with the pistols, and I am looking forward to shooting with you. We shall have a contest, yes?"

Lord Falconer's response was equally as smooth. "It will be a pleasure, your highness, thank you."

Another silence followed, and then Alexi turned back to Elizabeth. "But where is your good father, Elizabeth?" he queried, showing an imperiousness she hadn't seen in him before. "I should like to pay my respects to him."

"He is in America, your highness," she replied, feeling more awkward than ever. "I haven't heard from him in some time." She hated lying to Alexi, but with the earl and the sharp-eyed Lord Falconer looking on, there was little else she could do.

"Ah," Alexi said after a delicate pause. "Then you will mention me when next you are able to write him."

That seemed safe enough, and Elizabeth gave a graceful curtsy. "I shall, your highness. He will be pleased you remember him."

The pause was shorter this time, but no less awkward. The countess was the one to break the silence, fixing Elizabeth with a look of pointed displeasure.

"Miss Mattingale," she said, her smile as sharp as her tone, "please inform Cook that the first of our guests have arrived and ask her to have tea sent to the drawing room. When you are done with that, I will need you to finish addressing the invitations for me."

The invitations had been sent out already, but Elizabeth didn't pretend not to take the countess's real meaning. She was not so subtly reminding her of her position, and making it plain her presence at tea was neither desired nor required. Burning with resentment and humiliation, she bobbed a low curtsy.

"Yes, my lady," she murmured, curtsying to the gentlemen before turning to make her escape. She'd taken but a few steps when Alexi reached out to lay a hand on her upper arm.

"What is this, *syestra?*" he demanded in Russian. "Is there something you wish to tell your Alexi?"

Aware of the avid interest of the others, she could only shake her head. "Later, Alexi," she promised in the same language, and then hurried up the stairs before anyone else could stop her.

What the devil was going on? Adam brooded, leaning back in his chair and studying Prince Bronyeskin with narrowed eyes. The man was coldly polite to his host and hostess, but beneath his imperious manner Adam could sense a black temper tightly leashed. As a rule Adam was a man who expected control in himself and appreciated it in others, but there was something about the prince he couldn't quite trust. He wanted to believe his suspicions were occasioned only by the secret letter he'd received from the Duke of Creshton, asking him to keep an eye on the prince, but he couldn't be certain.

"Has your highness been in England long?" the countess asked, beaming over her teacup at the prince. She'd been making a dead set at fixing his interest since they had entered the drawing room, ignoring his coolness and curt responses the same way Miss Mattingale had ignored her own appalling rudeness in the entryway.

The prince's blue eyes flicked over her in a manner that came within a hair of insolence. "A week, perhaps a few days longer," he said, his tone dismissing. "I was to accompany the Grand Duchess when she arrived in March, but matters in St. Petersburg delayed me."

"I fear my knowledge of your country is sadly limited," the earl said jovially, making a weak attempt at conversation. "Is St. Petersburg north or south of Moscow?"

"It is to the west," the prince corrected. "A beautiful city built by our emperor, Peter, some years ago. Many Russians, myself included, have homes in both Moscow and St. Petersburg."

"Moscow," Lady Derring said, leaning forward in avid interest. "Did Napoleon truly burn it when he was forced to retreat? Wretched man, it sounds precisely the sort of thing he would do."

The prince glanced at her, his expression frozen. "He burned it, *da*," he said grimly. "But only after we ourselves put it to the torch."

The countess hastily set her teacup to one side. "You burned your own city?" she echoed weakly, her hand fluttering to her throat. "But why?"

"To keep what they could from falling into the enemy's

hands, I should think," Adam answered, his wariness giving way to a grudging respect. "It must have been a difficult decision, your highness."

"It was a necessary decision," Bronyeskin answered, studying Adam with some interest. "You have been in the army, my lord? You speak as a soldier."

Adam was pleased by what he knew to be a compliment. "No," he admitted, shaking his head with genuine regret. "I was the last of my line and so not allowed to purchase a commission, but I have many friends who had the good fortune to serve. And you?"

The prince gave a brief nod. "I have served as well," he said, his quiet tone telling Adam all he needed to know.

The conversation ended with the arrival of the other guests. Lord and Lady Derring went to greet the new arrivals, leaving Adam alone with the prince. After pouring the other man another cup of tea he settled back in his chair, studying the prince thoughtfully. The duke's letter had raised several questions about the other man and his politics, and Adam knew he might not have another opportunity to ask them. He took a moment to organize his thoughts, and then blurted out the first question that came to mind.

"How long have you known Miss Mattingale?" he asked, and then stopped, appalled that he had asked something so personal. It was no business of his how long the two might have been acquainted, or indeed how deep that acquaintance went.

Instead of taking offense, the prince fixed him with a measuring gaze. "Many years," he answered, blue eyes watchful. "And you, my lord? How long have you known her?"

"A few days only," Adam said, remembering how he'd first thought her meek and self-effacing. He didn't usually misjudge people and was annoyed he'd allowed himself to be so misled. The thought that the erroneous impression might be deliberate occurred, and considering her line of employment, he supposed he could not fault her. Meekness was, after all, a prerequisite of her position. Then he remembered her stormy defiance of him earlier that afternoon and flashed the prince an interested glance.

"Has she always been so headstrong?"

It was precisely the right thing to say. Bronyeskin threw back his head and roared with laughter.

"You may not know my little queen long," he said, chuckling, "but you know her well. Yes, she has always possessed the pride of a Cossack, and the temper of one as well. When she and her papa were staying with the Prezyskoffs, one of their oafish sons struck a small dog with his whip. Elizabeth was on him like a fury. I tried pulling her off, and she bloodied my lip. When I scolded her for it, she said it was no less than I deserved for getting in her way. That is when I started calling her little queen." His smile faded, and a hard expression settled on his features.

"But who is this Lady Derring, and why does she presume to treat my Elizabeth so?" he demanded of Adam. "This is an English custom, to order guests about as if they are no more than servants? If so, it is not one of which I can approve."

Adam was uncertain how to respond. "I will leave it to Miss Mattingale to explain," he said after a moment's consideration. "In the meanwhile, be assured I hold her in the highest regard. She is an exceptional lady."

"*Da,*" Prince Bronyeskin agreed, his gaze sharpening. "She is. You will let me know, my lord, the name of any man who does not share our opinion, that I might deal with him?"

"Certainly, your highness," Adam agreed, his mouth curving in a feral smile. "After *I* have dealt with him first."

The prince gave him a look of renewed respect. "*Ya saglasyen,*" he said, lifting his cup in a toast. "I agree. Only mind, sir, that you leave something of him for me. Now, Lord Falconer, tell me more of your country. I am most anxious to learn of your ways."

Three

"A *companion*, little queen?" Alexi's brows met in a puzzled frown. "I do not know this word. You will tell me its meaning."

Elizabeth gave a frustrated sigh. She had risked everything by coming to Alexi's rooms, and she really hadn't the time for a lesson in linguistics. If the angry scold her employer had read her for "presuming above her station" was any indication, then any contact she had with Alexi would be limited at best. It was imperative that she make him understand the delicacy of her situation while there was still time.

"Elizabeth?" He gave her a gentle shake. "What is companion?"

Elizabeth cast about in her vocabulary for a similar word in Russian but could think of nothing. *"Padrooga,"* she said at last, deciding the word for friend was as close as she was likely to come. "But in English it has another connotation. Simply put, Alexi, I am Lady Derring's servant, and you must treat me as such."

"Shto eta tako-ye!" he exclaimed in disbelief, and then shook his head. "What is this?" he repeated, this time in English, his blue eyes flashing with temper. "Your papa would never allow such a thing!"

For some reason his indignant outburst reminded her of her earlier confrontation with the marquess. A female could become heartily weary of having the men about her "allowing" her to do as she wished, she thought with a flash of resentment. She shook off the thought and concentrated on the matter at hand.

"Papa," she reminded Alexi sternly, "is in America, and in no position to 'allow' me anything. In any case the decision to become a companion was mine, and I must ask that you respect it."

Her adamant tones had the frown on Alexi's face deepening. "You cannot mean this, *dyevooshka*," he told her, this time in Russian. "You are too proud, too noble a lady to bow and scrape to such as that old crone. Why should you wish to do so? It makes no sense."

Elizabeth cast a frantic glance at the clock on the mantel. It was almost eight of the clock, and by her calculations she had less than a quarter hour before the countess would ring for her. As she'd yet to change into her evening gown, time was of the essence, and she reached out to lay her hand over Alexi's.

"Alexi," she implored, holding his gaze with her own, "I know this must seem strange, but I must insist you do as I ask. Please?" she added, when his expression remained adamant. "For me? You know I wouldn't ask unless I had a very good reason for doing so."

At first she thought he would refuse, but then he tipped his head in a way that was strongly reminiscent of another autocratic man she had recently encountered.

"Very well, little queen," he said, with visible reluctance. "I promise not to treat you so familiarly. But," he added, lifting a finger in warning, "I will not treat you as a servant." And he folded his arms across his chest, his mind clearly set.

Elizabeth regarded him in fond exasperation. "I might be a queen, Alexi Victoravitch," she said, shaking her head at him, "but you are every inch the prince. Prince Zaramoff would be amazed, I am sure."

Alexi's expression darkened with murderous intensity. "Do not mention that *svohluch*'s name to me!" he spat out, his lips tightening in fury. "He is a traitor to Mother Russia!"

"What?" Elizabeth gasped in disbelief.

"Da," Alexi gave a curt nod. "When that monster, Napoleon, came to rape and murder our country, Zaramoff acted as his whore. He sold his own serfs into the French Army, and acted as Napoleon's ears and eyes in St. Petersburg. He even betrayed his own father, allowing him to be slaughtered when the old prince refused to swear allegiance to that French devil."

"Are you speaking of the prince's son?" Elizabeth asked, horrified to hear the old man who had been so kind to her and her father had died at the hands of his traitorous son.

"Dimitri Constanovitch." Alexi sneered the name with obvious hatred. "He murdered his people with one hand and lined his pockets with the other. And now that Napoleon has been defeated, he dares to act the brave and noble patriot. I would kill him, gladly, but for the fact I dare not. He is the Czar's great good friend, and travels with him now to this country."

"Is that why you are here?" Elizabeth guessed.

Alexi's lips curved in a grim smile. "The Grand Duchess is not so easily deceived as her brother. He is a good man, but too much the dreamer to see what he does not wish to see. He chooses to believe whatever lies Zaramoff tells him, and the Grand Duchess fears he will betray her brother as he has betrayed everyone else."

"How?"

Alexi merely shrugged. "Who is to say?" he asked, with the Russian propensity for vagueness that had always driven Elizabeth mad. "In the meanwhile her highness has sent me here to make certain the preparations for the Czar's arrival go well. Both Lords Derring and Falconer are said to be close to the throne, and the Grand Duchess does not trust that fat fool of a prince.

"Not that you are to tell anyone," he ordered with an imperious look. "Especially not that *Breetanskee* lord who watches you closer than he should. He is sharp, that one."

Elizabeth didn't pretend not to take his meaning. Another glance at the clock showed her that she now had less than ten minutes left before dinner, but she knew she couldn't leave without telling Alexi about her father. He had trusted her with the truth behind his visit to Derring Hall; she could be no less honest with him.

"Alexi, there is something I must tell you," she said, shame pinking her cheeks. "I am writing to my father."

Alexi's blue eyes widened in shock. "No, little queen," he gasped, laying his hand on his chest. "Say it is not so!"

Her faint blush darkened in embarrassed fury. "Beast!" she accused, doubling up her fist and hitting his arm. "And to think I was feeling guilty for deceiving you!"

He gave a hearty laugh and flicked a teasing finger down her cheek. "A little sister can never deceive a big brother," he said smugly. "Especially a big brother as clever as me."

The temptation to strike him again was strong, but unfortunately there wasn't enough time. Sending him a look rife with the promise of revenge, she turned to take her leave. He caught up with her at the door, opening it before she had the chance to do so herself.

"Do not worry, little queen," he said, carrying her hand to his lips and lavishly kissing her fingers. "I will keep your secrets. Just mind you keep mine, hmm?"

Elizabeth's flare of temper vanished at the seriousness she sensed behind the teasing words. "Of course, Alexi," she said, her gaze softening as she smiled up at him. "You may rely on me."

"I know I can, *dyevuchka,*" he said, giving her fingers another kiss. "As you may rely upon me. *Dus veedanya,* Elizabeth. I shall see you at dinner."

"I will keep your secrets. Just mind you keep mine."
Adam glared into his glass of wine, the conversation he'd overheard between Miss Mattingale and Prince

Bronyeskin echoing in his head. He'd been returning to his rooms, located in the same wing as the prince's, when he'd seen Miss Mattingale emerging from the prince's private chambers. His first thought was that she was coming from an assignation, and the unexpected flash of fury he'd felt had him stepping into the shadows before they could see him.

When he saw the prince kissing her hand, he was certain they were old lovers renewing a liaison, but the words he'd offered in parting were not in the least loverlike. What secrets could a companion have? he wondered, his fingers clenching around the stem of his glass. And, more importantly, what secrets did a member of the Russian nobility expect her to keep for him?

"If you hold your glass any tighter, my lord, I fear you will break it."

The drawling voice to his right had Adam glancing up to find his dinner partner regarding him with a knowing smile. He stared at the luscious blonde for a moment before carefully setting his glass to one side.

"I beg pardon, Lady Barrington," he said, giving the notorious widow a brief smile. "I fear my thoughts were elsewhere."

The woman's lips formed a perfect moue. "That is hardly complimentary, Lord Falconer," she complained, fluttering her lashes at him. "You must know I expect more from a gentleman than that."

Recognizing an overture when it was offered, Adam didn't know whether to be horrified or flattered. The stunning duchess was notorious for her affairs and was said to be most particular in her requirements for a lover. The man had to be rich, high-born, and accomplished in the boudoir. He acknowledged that it was patently obvious he met the first two criteria, but he was puzzled as to how she knew of his ability to meet the third. His mistresses were well paid not to gossip about him, even when they were no longer his mistresses.

"Come, sir, you cannot be such a slowtop as that." Lady

Barrington leaned forward, offering him a glimpse of her creamy white breasts. "I was offering you the perfect opportunity to ask exactly what it is I require of a man."

Such boldness offended Adam's fastidious nature, but he was too astute a politician to let his distaste show. Despite the fact that her reputation was more than a trifle tarnished, the duchess was a force to be reckoned with in the *ton,* and her legion of lovers included some of the most powerful men in London. He could not afford to snub her, but neither did he wish to encourage her.

"I would, my lady," he replied, his smile filled with polite regret, "but I am terrified you would tell me, and I'd find I was sadly lacking. My pride should never recover from such a blow."

She studied him for a few moments, and then leaned back to pick up her glass of wine. "Somehow I doubt that would be a problem, Lord Falconer," she said, accepting his unspoken refusal with a delicate shrug. "Ah, well. Tell me more of that delicious Prince Bronyeskin. I vow I find him most intriguing."

Adam shot a speculative glance to the head of the table, where the prince was flirting with a pretty brunette who was seated to his left. The lady was the daughter of the Duke of Hadley, and was rumored to be one of the greatest heiresses in the country. It appeared the prince was even more clever than he suspected, Adam thought, his lips thinning in cold anger.

"He is an attaché to the Russian court," he said shortly, reaching once more for his wine. "A nice enough fellow."

"Mmm," the duchess purred, her eyes gleaming with sensual intent. "I see he is making up to the Hadley chit; how nice. I admire a man with ambition and the wit to make use of his opportunities. I must make an effort to become better acquainted with his highness." She took a languid sip of wine before turning to the older man seated on her other side.

Left alone with his dark thoughts, Adam cast a quick glance to the farthest end of the table, where Miss Mat-

tingale was sitting beside an ancient cousin of the Derrings. The elderly woman was as deaf as a post, and she
kept asking Miss Mattingale to repeat the conversations
going on about them. From the flush on the younger
woman's cheeks it was obviously not a task she relished,
and for a moment Adam felt a brief flash of pity. Then
he remembered the conversation he'd overheard, and his
scowl descended once more.

Following dinner there was to be dancing, and because
of it the gentlemen had magnanimously decided against
the customary decanter of port. Since the crowd was still
small, only thirty or so persons, the dancing was to be
held in the Derrings' music room rather than their ballroom. Miss Mattingale was already at the pianoforte, and
another young woman with a flute was standing beside
her, turning the pages of the music book.

"Something gay, Miss Mattingale, if you will," Lady
Derring instructed. "Unless there is something you would
most particularly like to hear, your highness?" She turned
a diffident smile upon the Russian.

"Whatever is your pleasure is fine, *babushka*," the
Prince said suavely, bowing over the delighted countess's
hand. "You choose."

The older woman preened at the lavish words. "Your
highness is too kind," she said, and then frowned. "But
what does *babushka* mean? I don't believe I've heard it
before."

The prince lifted his shoulders and smiled apologeti-
cally. "I am afraid my English is not so good, my lady. I
do not know how to explain. Miss Mattingale"—he
turned to Miss Mattingale, who was sitting as if frozen
in place—"you will translate, please."

Miss Mattingale's eyes remained fixed on the pages in
front of her. "I am not certain there is an English equiva-
lent, your highness," she said, her voice sounding suspiciously strained to Adam. "But it is a term of great
affection and respect in Russia."

"Indeed?" The countess looked pleased. *"Babushka,"* she repeated, smiling. "I must remember that."

The rest of the evening passed tediously for Adam. As the party was small and the gentlemen in great demand, he spent far more time than he would have preferred on the dance floor. With his innate good manners, he also made certain to do his duty by the wallflowers and dowagers, taking care to dance with each lady present. He was returning one painfully shy young lady to her grateful mama when he saw Miss Mattingale making her way to the countess's side, a cup of punch cradled in her hand. It occurred to him that there was one lady with whom he'd yet to dance, and with that thought in mind he hurried over to where the countess was sitting.

"Lady Derring, Miss Mattingale." He bowed to each lady in turn. "I've been enjoying the music, ma'am," he told Miss Mattingale with a warm smile, "but I note you've yet to have the opportunity to do likewise. I should be pleased if you would honor me with the next dance." And he held out his hand commandingly.

To his amusement her soft cheeks were instantly warmed with color. She cast a hesitant glance at the countess before replying.

"That is very good of you, Lord Falconer," she said in the diffident tone he'd come to suspect, "but I fear I must decline. Lady Derring may have need of my assistance."

As he was expecting just such a refusal, Adam had his response at the ready. "I am certain her ladyship possesses far too kind a heart to deny you one dance," he said, turning his gaze next on the countess, who was looking decidedly sour-faced. "Is that not so, my lady?" he added, lifting an eyebrow in polite inquiry.

"Indeed, my lord, I must insist she does just that," she said, her lips thinning in a grim smile. "Dance, Miss Mattingale, do; no reason why you shouldn't have a bit of fun as well."

Outmaneuvered and clearly knowing it, Miss Mattingale accepted her defeat with suitable gratitude. After murmuring her thanks to the countess, she gave an elegant curtsy and then turned to accept Adam's hand. A light and airy reel was beginning as they took their place on the dance floor, making conversation difficult, if not impossible. He was not surprised to learn Miss Mattingale was both graceful and talented, her slender body swaying as she performed the intricate steps.

All too soon the last notes faded, but Adam was not yet ready to relinquish his reluctant partner. Since he couldn't demand a second dance without risking scandal, he decided to do the next best thing. Taking Miss Mattingale's hand once more and carrying it to his arm, he deliberately led her to the far side of the room, where a table had been set up with a variety of cold meats and other treats for weary guests who wished to refresh themselves.

"Sir, what are you doing?" Miss Mattingale demanded in an indignant whisper. "Lady Derring is expecting me. I must insist you return me to her at once."

"You may insist as you wish, Miss Mattingale," he said, spying a pair of chairs set somewhat apart from the others. "And as for Lady Derring, I daresay she can do without your company for another five minutes without suffering irreparable damage."

He led her to the chairs, leaving her only long enough to secure each of them a glass of the chilled fruit punch being offered. After serving her, he took his seat beside her.

"You and Prince Bronyeskin seem to be on the best of terms," he noted, sipping the punch and glancing about himself with apparent indifference. "How long have you known one another, if I may ask?"

"Several years, although I've not seen him since we left Russia," she replied, not seeming unduly discomfited by his question. "We met when my family and I were visiting an estate near his family's *dvaryets*. Palace," she added, by way of explanation.

"You speak Russian exceedingly well," he observed,

still taking care to betray no more than polite interest. He slanted her a knowing look. "I don't suppose you'd care to tell me what *babushka* really means, would you?" he drawled, grinning when her cheeks grew even rosier.

"It is as I explained, my lord," she replied, her full lips curving in a smile. "A term of great respect and affection for ladies of . . . a certain age, shall we say?" Her silver-blue eyes danced as she cast him a roguish look beneath her thick lashes.

Adam smiled back. "I can see where speaking a foreign tongue would be of great use to a companion," he noted wryly. "One can say what one truly feels in some obscure dialect, and no one is ever the wiser. How many languages do you speak, by the by?"

"Did I say what I truly feel in plain English, sir, it is doubtful I should retain my position above a fortnight. And I speak four languages: French, Italian, Russian, and English."

"Four?" He was suitably impressed. "You are a lady of many accomplishments, Miss Mattingale."

She shrugged aside his praise. "More like I am a lady who detests having nation after nation of shopkeepers and servants swindle her," she said calmly. "Papa is a gifted linguist, but he was so often gone, and Mama could never manage above a word or two in any language save English. Circumstances dictated I become fluent in several tongues, else I doubt we should have survived; especially when we were in France."

"France?" he repeated, his senses stirring in alarm. "Were you there during the internments?"

She nodded. "Indeed," she said, her expression somber. "Fortunately we were in the country at the estate of Comte Dulane, who'd managed to keep both his head and his title during the Terror. He gave us shelter and kept us safe until we were able to leave the country."

Adam digested what he'd heard before answering. "Yet you say it was doubtful you should have survived," he said, studying her curiously. "May I ask what you meant?"

She cast him another glance, this one rueful. "I was being dramatic; a severe failing of mine, or so my father is always telling me. As it happens, I was referring not to France's soldiers, but rather her shopkeepers; a far more terrifying opponent, I can tell you."

Adam smiled, even as he was wondering how much of what she was letting slip should be passed on to the duke. "I notice you mention your father, but not your mother," he said, choosing his words with meticulous care. "Is she with him in America?"

"No," Miss Mattingale said, her fingers tightening about her cup. "She died shortly before we left Russia. Father was disconsolate. That's the reason he went to America, I think," she added, then bit her lip, as if worried she'd said too much.

Adam's interest sharpened, although he was careful to keep it hidden. An embittered, well-traveled Englishman with ties to France bore watching, especially as that Englishman was now deep in what must be considered enemy territory. Determined to learn more, he offered Miss Mattingale a sympathetic smile.

"I'm sorry," he said, covering her hand with his. "I didn't mean to make you sad."

She pulled her hand free of his. "You didn't," she said, setting her cup to one side and rising gracefully to her feet. "If you will excuse me, I must return to the countess. I have been neglecting my duties, and I fear she will be quite cross with me."

Accepting that he'd learned all he was going to for the moment, Adam also rose. "And if she should read you a scold, what then, Miss Mattingale?" he teased, driven by some desire he could not name to bring a smile back to her lips. "What name might you call her in a language she cannot hope to understand?"

At first he feared his ploy had failed. Then her misty blue eyes began sparkling, and her mouth curved in an enchanting smile even as she was lowering her gaze with a demure sweep of her lashes.

"That, my lord," she murmured, "would be telling. Now kindly return me to her ladyship. You have done quite enough damage to my reputation for one evening."

"I say, don't know about this," William muttered, casting a furtive glance over his shoulder. "It's one thing to wag our tongues about Miss Mattingale, but it's another to deliberately incriminate her like this. Don't seem gentlemanly, if you want my opinion of it."

"Will you hush, Wills!" Derwent snapped, his own nerves frayed to the breaking point. "And no one has asked for your opinion of anything. Just hold the candle steady so Charles can see what he's doing and we can get the devil out of here. I've no desire to be caught pilfering an earl's papers."

"We're not pilfering them, we're borrowing them," Charles corrected, his brows wrinkling as he quickly sorted through the papers he and the others had just removed from the earl's private box. None of it made the slightest bit of sense to him, and for the first time he cursed himself for not paying more mind to his tutors and his father when they lectured him on the importance of king and country. Still, he had some idea of what to look for, and he patted himself on the back for having the good sense to confide their plans to another. It wasn't really breaking his promise to the others, he assured himself, not when the other person had promised most solemnly to keep his secret.

"Bad enough when we only had the marquess to worry about," William continued in his morose fashion. "Did you see that Russian prince she is so thick with? Wears a sword as big as a claymore and knows how to use it, if the size of his arms are any indication. He'll cleave us in half if he tumbles to what we're doing."

"Then we'll have to make certain he doesn't tumble to

it, won't we?" Derwent snapped, his uneasiness mounting. "Besides, Charles assures me the prince will be suitably diverted. It's Falconer we need to concern ourselves with, and he won't be so easily diverted, I can tell you."

"Will the pair of you be quiet!" Charles snapped, his breath easing out as he picked up a particular piece of paper and held it to the flickering candlelight. He'd been told what to look for and was fairly certain this was it.

"Perfect," he said, smiling in anticipation of a sweet reward. "We shall just tuck this away for a bit, and no one need be the wiser, eh?" He stood up, slipping the paper between his tightly cut jacket and fine lawn shirt. "Now put the box back, Wills, and we'll return to the drawing room before we are missed."

William hesitated, glancing at the portrait of his grand-father hanging above the fireplace. The old boy had got himself slaughtered on some battlefield when his own fa-ther was scarce out of leading strings, he remembered, recalling how his grandmama had wept when she'd told him the story. The man was a dashed hero. How would he feel about his grandson taking the crown's most secret papers, even for an innocent lark?

"You'll put the papers back, won't you, Charles?" he asked, squirming beneath the relentless blue stare of his ancestor. "You'll put them back the moment we've had our fun?"

"Of course I will!" Charles snapped, eager to be gone. "We'll put them on the top of a shelf or some such place, and let them be discovered once a big enough dust has been raised. Your papa will doubtlessly think he left them there and feel foolish for all the havoc he has caused. You're always saying he's an absentminded old hum, so no one is likely to be surprised, are they?"

William shifted again, deciding he didn't care for his good friend calling his papa an old hum. "Just remember your word," he said, a note of surprising strength creeping into his voice. "You will return the papers the moment we are done, and if things begin looking serious for Miss Mattingale, we confess everything at once."

"Never say you are developing a conscience, Wills!" Derwent sneered. "How very tiresome of you. It is all Falconer's fault, I am certain. You have been too long exposed to his stultifying air of duty and honor, and it has quite ruined you. Did your mama never warn you of the danger of falling in with bad companions? It will be the death of you, dear fellow, mark me." And he laughed at what he clearly considered to be a rare good joke.

But William did not laugh. Even after he'd returned his father's dispatch box to its hidden location and led the others back to the drawing room, he could not help but brood upon the matter. Derwent might think his words a jest, but to him they held a far more sinister import. He thought once more of the painting of his grandfather staring down at him from the study wall, and the prickle of uncertainty he'd been doing his best to ignore became a shiver of apprehension.

Four

Over the next three days Elizabeth had cause to regret her decision to become a companion. Lady Derring remained hipped with her, and took great delight in keeping her running from cock's crow to the smallest hours of the morning. When she exhausted her store of menial tasks for Elizabeth to perform, the countess lent her out to her many guests, who made eager use of Elizabeth's services. Subsequently she often found herself in the unenviable position of attempting to please not one demanding mistress but several, and usually all at the same time.

A lesser woman would have tossed up her hands and given notice, but Elizabeth was made of sterner stuff. She didn't mind the extra work, and if truth were told, she welcomed the staggering list of duties expected of her. It kept her from brooding over the last letter from her papa, and the astonishing request he'd made of her.

"You are in a position to do your father a great service," he'd written. *"You wrote your employer is on the Privy Council, which means he has access to information that would prove most helpful to my new friends. I have told them how very clever you are, and they are hoping you will agree to be of assistance. It need not be much; any bit of intelligence you have to offer would be welcome."*

A spy, she thought, frowning as she shifted her burden

from one arm to another. Her father expected her to become a spy, and what was worse, he expected her to spy against England. She supposed she should be shocked, but upon reflection, she was not. Her father loved her mother with the same ferocity with which he now hated the country he held responsible for her death, and it was plain he meant to take his revenge.

She loved her father dearly, and even though it had been almost two years since her death, she grieved still for her mother. But there was no way she could do as he asked. It would be treason, and even if it meant driving a wedge between her papa and herself, she would not betray her country. Now all that remained was telling him of her decision. It would, Elizabeth admitted with a heavy sigh, be the most difficult letter of her life to write.

"Miss Mattingale! Miss Mattingale!"

The shrill voice of one of the guests penetrated Elizabeth's reverie, and she turned to see a well-dressed lady in a pink gown and a cream spenser hurrying toward her. At the lady's side was a familiar figure, and Elizabeth bit back a disgruntled sigh. Wonderful, she thought, keeping her face expressionless. She needed only this to make her day complete.

"Good morning, Lady Barrington, Lord Falconer," she said, dropping as graceful a curtsy as she could muster, considering both arms were full. "Is there something I might do for you?"

"We were about to ask the same of you," Lady Barrington said, smiling as they reached her. "We saw you setting out burdened down like one of Hannibal's elephants and thought to offer you a ride. Didn't you hear us calling?"

The kind offer left Elizabeth momentarily nonplussed. "No, your grace, I did not. I fear my mind was elsewhere," she apologized, not certain what to say. While the scandalous beauty hadn't been as smug and condescending as had many of the other guests, neither had she been welcoming. She'd assumed the widow was one of those ladies with little interest or use for her own sex, but now it seemed she had done the duchess a disservice.

"Considering we've been chasing after you for the past five minutes, I don't doubt that," Lady Barrington continued, still smiling. "Wherever your mind took you, I trust the journey was a pleasant one?"

Elizabeth smiled at the other woman's patent friendliness. "Pleasant enough, your grace," she said, thinking the other lady was a great deal nicer than the gossips had credited her.

"Let me take those from you, Miss Mattingale." Lord Falconer stepped forward to lift the pile of shawls, pillows, and other necessities from her arms. He gauged their weight and then fixed her with a reproving frown. "These are too heavy for a lady to carry," he said, making it sound as if it were somehow her fault. "Why haven't you a footman with you?"

"There are none to spare, your lordship. Most of the servants have been pressed into helping prepare for the ball tomorrow night," Elizabeth replied, both annoyed and touched by his insistence upon treating her as he would any other lady in the house party. She appreciated his concern, but there was no denying it didn't make things difficult for her. The other ladies had noted his behavior and were not behindhand in remarking upon it.

"Ah, yes, the costume ball," Lady Barrington said, stroking a gloved finger down the marquess's arm and sending him an intimate smile. "What will you be wearing, my lord? Or do you mean to appear in some mysterious costume and surprise us all?"

The marquess's handsome face was set in even colder lines than usual. "I haven't decided if I will attend, your grace," he informed the duchess in his precise tones. "I am not the sort to be comfortable in a costume."

The duchess gave a pretty laugh. "Don't be foolish, sir," she teased, dimples flashing in her cheeks. "No gentleman is ever comfortable in costume; not that it matters. These balls are really for us ladies, aren't they, Miss Mattingale?" she appealed to Elizabeth for support. "They provide us with the perfect excuse to dress in panniers and powdered wigs and be mysterious. There is not a woman alive who can resist the challenge of being thought of as mysterious." She struck a pose, as if lifting an imaginary mask to her face.

"Indeed?" The marquess's topaz eyes flicked to Elizabeth. "And what of you, Miss Mattingale?" he asked coolly. "Do you enjoy being thought mysterious?"

Elizabeth thought of the letter her father had written her and nearly blanched. "I am a companion, Lord Falconer," she reminded him in what she hoped was a suitably prim tone. "It is our lot to appear dull and ordinary, for that is what we are."

"But you would look delightful in the costume you described, your grace," she added, turning to the duchess who was watching them with interest. "Rather like Madame de Pompadour."

Lady Barrington's provocative smile froze. "A king's mistress?" she said, and then shook her head. "No, I've another costume in mind. But I hope you'll at least wear a mask and a domino, Miss Mattingale. Lady Derring says she intends providing them for guests who neglected to bring a costume with them."

Elizabeth said nothing, deciding this wasn't the time to remind her grace she was at Derring Hall not as a guest but as a servant. It was doubtful she'd be allowed to attend the masquerade at all, and if she did, it was a certainty she would not be in costume.

They returned to the courtyard, where the marquess's phaeton and high-stepping pair of matched grays was waiting for them. After lifting the duchess up onto the seat, Lord Falconer turned next to Elizabeth, his light gold eyes studying her from beneath the curved brim of his beaver hat. His handsome face was set in its usual mask of icy propriety, and yet there was something in his powerful gaze that sent Elizabeth's pulses scrambling. His hands closed about her waist, lifting her off her feet with astonishing ease. Her own hands grasped his shoulders, and she could feel the iron strength in his arms as he raised her up onto the seat of the phaeton.

Her heart had scarce settled when he leapt gracefully up onto the driving box. He took the reins from the groom, but before he could whistle to the team Lady Barrington gave a sharp cry.

"My bonnet!"

Elizabeth turned her head to see the duchess's pretty bonnet of rose chipstraw dangling from a broken ribbon.

"Oh, will you only look at this!" her grace exclaimed, removing her bonnet and frowning over the frayed end of blue satin. "And it is the first time I have worn it!"

"I should be more than happy to repair it, your grace," Elizabeth volunteered, knowing what was expected of her. "I am quite good with a needle and thread."

"I shouldn't dream of imposing," the duchess assured her. "My maid can see to it for me. But I am afraid I shall have to cry off, my lord," she said, turning to Lord Falconer with a charming pout. "I refuse to risk my complexion to the ravages of the sun."

"We can wait while you fetch another bonnet," Lord Falconer offered, also clearly aware of his responsibilities as a gentleman.

"No, there's no reason to do that." The duchess was already signaling to the groom to help her alight. "I would have to change my gown as well, and the others would be back and taking their tea by then. Please, the two of you go on, else I shall feel guilty for having spoiled the day."

Faced with so pretty an appeal, there was little either Elizabeth or Lord Falconer could do but comply with her wishes. A few minutes later they were rolling down the road toward the ruined chapel, where the others were awaiting them.

"Lady Barrington seems most kind," Elizabeth said, anxious to break the silence stretching between them. "Not at all as I thought a duchess would be." She slid a curious glance at him. "Are you well acquainted with her, my lord?"

"Not well," he replied, easily controlling the spirited team. "We move in different circles." He let several seconds pass before sending her a glance of his own. "She's after your friend, you know."

Elizabeth didn't pretend not to take his meaning. "He will be delighted to hear it," she said, smiling as she pictured Alexi's probable response to the lady's overtures.

"It doesn't bother you?"

She frowned at the question. "Heavens no! Why should it?" Her frown deepened as realization dawned. "If you're hinting there is anything untoward in my friendship with Alexi, you are very much mistaken!" she informed him, her eyes flashing in indignation. "Alexi is but a friend, as dear to me as a brother, and you wrong us both by implying otherwise!"

"Peace, Miss Mattingale," he said, tearing his gaze from the road long enough to send her a reproving frown. "I was implying nothing of the sort. I merely meant that if the prince is indeed your friend, you might wish to put a flea in his ear about her grace. I've no wish to appear ungentlemanly, but the lady's not as careful with her reputation as one would think a duchess would be."

Considering the gossip she'd heard both above and below stair, Elizabeth couldn't pretend to be shocked by his lordship's observation. "Alexi is hardly a callow youth, sir," she said, remembering the wild youth Alexi had been. "He cut his teeth on ladies like her grace many years ago. And as I said, Lady Barrington has been quite kind to me. That is all there is to be said on the matter as far as I am concerned."

Another silence stretched between them. Elizabeth supposed she had offended him and was wondering if she should apologize when the marquess spoke.

"You can be quite haughty when you've a wish to be," he observed, his cool tones giving no hint as to his feelings. "I can see why his highness calls you little queen. What is the Russian word for that, if I may ask?"

The question took Elizabeth aback. *"Karalyevak"* she replied, puzzled he should ask. "You seem rather interested in the Russian language, my lord," she observed, wondering if his question was spurred by mere politeness, or if there might be some other reason behind the remark. "Is it your intention to study it?"

His answer was another enigmatic smile. "Perhaps," he said coolly. "It would seem to have its advantages."

He said no more, and this time Elizabeth saw no reason to break the silence. With her chin held high and her lips firmly sealed she sat beside the marquess, her troubling secrets and anguished doubts pulled tightly about her like a woolen cloak.

Adam spent a miserable afternoon avoiding the obvious machinations of the matchmaking mamas and listening to Viscount Camborne prattling on about sheep dip. Usually he suffered such tortures in noble silence, regarding them as another aspect of the duty he owed to his title. Yet for reasons he could not explain, he was finding it increasingly difficult to retain the aura of cool civility for which he was known.

It little helped his black mood to see Miss Mattingale being run ragged by Lady Derring and her crowd. As he watched in seething silence, the pert companion was kept busy fluffing pillows, fetching glasses of lemonade, and, in the case of one sharp-tongued young beauty, fanning the creature while she lolled on her blankets looking smugly pleased with herself. He was considering going over and putting a stop to the nonsense when Prince Bronyeskin suddenly appeared at his side.

"I am sent by the ladies to collect you, Lord Falconer," he said, his accent lightly musical. "You will come now, yes?"

In answer Adam turned his head, his lips pressed together in cold disapproval. "And you call yourself her friend," he said, his voice tight with leashed fury.

A dark blond eyebrow raised in princely irritation as Bronyeskin glanced toward the languorous brunette. "That one?" he asked, his mouth curling in disgust. "That one I do not know, nor do I wish to. She is . . . common."

Although Adam shared the prince's estimation of the young lady, he wasn't about to let him off the hook so easily. "You know perfectly well I was referring to Miss Mattingale," he said, swinging around to confront the younger man, his eyes blazing. "How can you stand by and do nothing when she is treated like a blasted lackey!"

Ice-blue eyes regarded him challengingly. "How can you stand by and do nothing, my lord, if you are so offended?"

Adam flinched, furious because, curse it all, the man was right. He dipped his head in curt acknowledgment. "Point taken, your highness."

"Da." The Russian gave a cool nod. "I can see that it is. Why you do nothing, I cannot say. For me, I must bite my tongue and act the proper guest, or my little queen will box my ears. But never fear, my lord," he added, his voice soft with menace, as he studied the young woman, "I will have my revenge upon the oh-so-lovely Miss Clarvale, that I do promise you."

Again Adam was struck by the prince's resemblance to his friend, Lord St. Jerome; warriors, the pair of them, and neither to be trusted when they had that particular tone in their voices. Hoping to relieve the tension of the moment, he flashed Bronyeskin a look of polite inquiry.

"And how do you mean to do that?" he asked, regarding the other teasingly. "Without getting your ears boxed, that is?"

In answer, the prince gave a slow smile. "We Russians are not so big the fools as you *angleechankas* like to think," he said coolly. "We do two things very well: We fight like demons from hell for what is ours, and we know when and where to take our revenge. A little something you might wish to share with your prince and his circle. Good day to you, Lord Falconer."

The odd conversation was much on Adam's mind later that evening as he sat in the library, staring into the flames dancing in the fireplace. The soft summer afternoon had given way to a sudden storm, and wind and rain lashed against the leaded glass windows as fierce thunder boomed across the valley. The others were in one of the drawing rooms, playing whist and chatting, but he'd slipped away, seeking solitude to brood over what Bronyeskin had told him.

The prince's remark haunted him, and he wondered if it had aught to do with the coming congress in Vienna. He knew the Russians were fiercely determined to get back Poland and other lands lost to them, and knew as well the Austrians were equally determined to keep those same lands out of the Czar's sphere of influence. A break in the alliance at such a crucial juncture would play directly into Napoleon's hands, and that—

"I say, a word with you, Falconer, if I may."

The diffident voice shattered Adam's concentration, and he glanced up to find his host hovering before him. Biting back a sharp retort, Adam managed the semblance of a smile.

"Of course, my lord," he said, hiding his annoyance as he set the book he'd been pretending to read to one side. "What is it?"

"Don't wish to accuse, you understand," the earl muttered, looking every day his age as he eased himself onto the club chair facing Adam. "Daresay you must have had a good reason for doing so, but I might have wished you'd asked permission first before taking them. It would have been dashed awkward if I sounded the alarm needlessly, eh?"

Adam leaned back, trying to make sense of the earl's rambling conversation. "And what is it I am suspected of having taken?" he asked at last, his voice carefully neutral.

"The papers from my dispatch box, of course," Lord

Derring replied, then paled at Adam's lack of expression. "Never say you don't have them?" he said, trembling.

Adam snapped to attention. "Which papers?" he demanded, his preoccupation with Bronyeskin forgotten in light of this alarming development.

"Not quite sure, to be honest," the earl admitted, shrugging his shoulders and tugging at his cravat. "Hadn't had a chance to study them in any great detail. Arrived the same time as his highness, so I had but a moment to peek at them. They were from the Secretary, or at least they carried his seal. Mentioned Blücher, though, as I recall." He sent Adam an apologetic look. "You'd know more about that sort of thing than I."

Adam remained silent for several seconds, digesting the enormity of what he had heard. "Are you saying these papers are missing?" he asked, his voice carefully controlled.

In light of his response the earl abandoned all pretense and slumped in his chair like a broken puppet. "If you don't have them, then aye, I would have to say that," he said, rubbing a hand across his ruddy face. "When I went into my study this morning to catch up on my correspondence, they were nowhere to be found. They weren't in my dispatch box, which is where I am certain I left 'em. Even checked the shelves, just to be certain, but they weren't there. Suppose this means I shall have to write the Secretary after all. Not looking forward to it, I can tell you," he added glumly.

Envisioning Viscount Castlereigh's probable reaction to discovering one of his dispatches had gone missing, Adam could well imagine the trepidation the earl was experiencing, but at the moment he had far greater concerns. "Who has access to these papers?" he demanded, deciding to send off a letter to the duke without delay. His grace had several highly placed friends in Whitehall, and they would know better what ought to be done.

"No one. I keep them locked in my dispatch box,"

Derring answered, frowning at Adam. "Weren't you listening?"

"*Where?*"

"Eh?" The earl blinked at Adam's snarled demand. "Oh, in my study. Locked in my desk, to be exact."

"Then why the devil did you think I had them?"

In answer the earl drew himself upright. "Well, stands to reason, doesn't it?" he replied with a sniff. "The world knows the Regent and the Secretary don't get on, and are always keeping secrets from one another. You're the Prince's man; thought perhaps you wanted a look at the papers so you could see what was what. Besides, who else but you would be interested?"

Adam didn't bother cursing the earl for his appalling stupidity, any more than he bothered answering the accusation that he was the Regent's man. He was England's man, pure and simple, and he could think of several groups who'd do murder and more for a glimpse of the Foreign Secretary's correspondence.

"Have you told anyone the papers are missing?" he asked, shifting his mind to the matter at hand.

"Of course not!" the earl retorted indignantly. "Ain't a dashed loose screw, you know! I told no one other than my wife and Leeds, my valet. And I suppose I may have mentioned it in passing to my idiot of a son," he added, scowling. "Not that that dolt knows anything of value, mind."

In other words, Adam thought, bitterly, he had told the whole bloody world. He was about to make a caustic remark when he remembered the conversation he'd had with William the day he'd encountered Miss Mattingale in town. The young dandy had taken him to one side, asking if his father had seemed distracted to him. He recalled thinking at the time that the action had seemed deliberate, but he'd never pursued the matter. Now he could kick himself for his carelessness.

"When did you have this conversation with your son?" he asked, taking care to keep suspicion out of his voice.

"Not long ago, after the lot of you returned from the trip to the meadow," the earl provided. "Why?"

"No reason," Adam answered. So, the son mentioned his father's unease before the papers had been discovered missing, he brooded, tapping his fingers on the arms of the chair. It might be a coincidence, or perhaps something a trifle less innocent. In any case it might be worth his time to have a word with the younger man, and with his malicious friends as well. As near as he could tell they traveled about like a pack of jackals, one seeming incapable of acting without the goading of the other.

"What's to be done, do you think?" The earl's plaintive question interrupted Adam's reverie.

Adam took a few minutes to plan. The storm was still raging, but with luck it would have moved on by morning. A messenger traveling by coach could be in London late tomorrow evening, if he left at first light, but a good rider supplied with fresh horses along the way could make the same trip several hours faster.

"First we must get immediate word to Lord Castlereigh," he said, meeting the earl's gaze with stern authority. "If the missing papers contained sensitive information, the sooner it is known, the better. Send your most trusted servant to London with word tomorrow morning, and since speed is of the essence, send him by your fastest coach."

Derring nodded, clearly relieved to have someone other than himself in command of the situation. "Yes, my lord. What else?"

"Speak with your wife, valet, and son. Threaten to divorce the first, dismiss the second, and murder the third if they so much as breathe a word of this to a single soul. Our best hope is that our thief thinks his crime to be undetected; that will give us time to plan and then time to move."

"Eh?" The earl gave a disapproving frown. "Are you quite certain, Falconer? I think we ought to do the opposite. Sound a hue and cry, by heaven, and drive the devil out into the open, and then hand him over to the gallows."

"And if we drive him to ground instead? What then, my lord?" Adam inquired, taking cold satisfaction in the distressed look that flashed across the older man's face.

"Just so," he said softly. "We say nothing. We appear to do nothing. We let our friend think us as ignorant as babes, and then when he thinks himself safe enough, we spring our trap."

"What trap?"

Adam's smile took on a decidedly wolfish quality. "I will let you know."

Exhausted, Elizabeth trudged up the stairs to her room. She'd just come from Lady Cossinley's room, where she'd spent the past two hours rubbing the elderly lady's temples with eau de cologne. The poor woman was afflicted with the megrims, and she was so pathetically grateful for Elizabeth's assistance, she couldn't find it in her heart to be angry. But as strong scents gave *her* a headache, her own head was now pounding like a native's drum, and she much doubted anyone would offer to rub it for her. She pushed open the door to her room, coming to a startled halt at the sight of Alexi lounging uncomfortably on her chair.

"Alexi!" she exclaimed, quickly closing the door behind her and casting him a furious glare. "What on earth are you doing here?"

"Waiting for you, little queen," he replied, rising coolly to his feet. "You did not come to dinner and no one would tell me where you were, so I came to find you myself.

"And look at you," he added accusingly, striding across the small room to gently cup her face in his large hands. "So tired, so pale. What have you done to yourself, little *rebyonuk?*"

The tender endearment was almost Elizabeth's undoing. It annoyed and frightened her to feel her eyes filling with tears, and she hastily blinked them back.

"I am not a child, Alexi," she said, turning away from his obvious concern. "I was attending the dowager Countess of Cossinley, who had taken ill. Now you really must leave my room," she added, casting him a stern look over her shoulder. "You must know this will not do."

As she feared, Alexi remained where he was standing, his arms folded across his chest and a resolute expression upon his face. "You . . . what is phrase . . . ah"—he nodded—"you refine upon nothing, my Elizabeth. I was but assuring myself a friend was all right. Who but your fierce lord could find fault in this? And if anyone else should find fault, what do I care? I am a prince. It is for me to say where I will go."

His imperiousness had her longing to bash a bed warmer over his skull. "And I am a companion, your highness," she reminded him, rubbing her head and wishing desperately for the dinner she had missed. "I care very much what people may think. I've no desire to lose this position, and my reputation along with it, if you do not mind." She stopped rubbing her head as the middle part of what he had said penetrated the pain in her temples.

"Which fierce lord are you talking about?" she demanded, her hand dropping to her side as a terrible suspicion dawned.

"Falconer, but of course," came Alexi's easy reply as he beamed at her. "He was as displeased as I to see these parasites treat you like the lowliest of serfs. I know I promised you to behave, *karalyevak,* but I will not see you worked to death."

"Alexi . . ." she warned, refusing to be diverted even as he reached out to capture her hand in his.

"Elizabeth." To her surprise, he carried her hand to his lips for a tender kiss, his expression abruptly solemn. "When my sweet sister died, you took her place in my heart. I love you. I will not see you hurt, even if it means I must displease you. Now come, say you will do the sensible thing and marry this marquess and make me uncle to your children."

"Alexi!"

"What?" Alexi's pale blue eyes widened in innocent surprise at her strangled shriek. "It is the best answer, yes? He must have a care for you to be so angry with the others. It means he wishes to marry you, for if he wishes anything else, I will have to kill him. Honorably in a duel, of course." He added this last part with an aristocratic lift of his chin.

"His lordship is a peer of England, you dolt." Elizabeth was so tired as to forget herself. "You cannot kill him without risking an international scandal. And he might kill you, you know," she reminded him, remembering several conversations she'd overheard regarding the hard-faced marquess. "I've heard talk, and he is said to be the deadliest shot in England."

"In a shooting gallery, killing little birds in the meadows." Alexi dismissed the danger with an arrogant wave of his hand. "I have hunted wolves in the snows of Russia, *syestra,* and survived in the thick of battle. Who should fear whom, hmm?"

Elizabeth opened her lips to protest, and then closed them in feminine frustration. "This is foolish beyond all bearing," she told him, planting her hands on her hips and glaring at him in reproach. "No one is killing anyone, do you hear me? I am pleased his lordship is concerned, but you must understand it implies nothing; it is simply his way. He told me that he considers it his duty to protect those weaker than himself. Rather like another thick-headed male I could name." She gave a meaningful sniff should he fail to take her meaning.

Instead of taking offense, Alexi looked thoughtful. "This is so," he said, rubbing his jaw with his hand. "A man's duty, a prince's duty, must always be to the people who have need of his strength. I had not the thought *angleechankas* would feel as this. I find this interesting."

He gazed off into space for a few moments, and then sent Elizabeth a disapproving frown.

"But why are you standing there arguing with me, *kooreestachka?*" he demanded, hurrying forward to drape a protective arm about her shoulder. "You should be in bed!"

Elizabeth didn't know if she should laugh or scream. "And so I should be, sir, if you'd be so good as to leave!" she said as he guided her toward the narrow bed shoved against the room's sloping walls. "Go away, do, Alexi, and don't call me a little chicken!"

"As you wish," he agreed, shoving her gently onto the sagging mattress. "But perhaps it is a little chicken I shall have the servants fetch you, hmm? And some bread and cheese as well?"

The thought of food had her mouth watering. "That would be wonderful, Alexi, thank you," she said, hoping she could stay awake long enough to eat it. It was past midnight, and she'd been up and about her duties since early that morning.

"It is my pleasure, little queen," he assured her, brushing a brotherly kiss over her curls. "Into bed with you, now. I will send one of the servants up to have a care for you."

After he'd gone Elizabeth got up and wearily saw to her night's ablutions. She'd donned her nightgown and robe by the time the maid arrived with her food. Too exhausted to care what damage might have been done to her reputation by Alexi's stubbornly protective nature, she devoured every morsel of food on the tray before climbing back into bed.

She was about to blow out the candle when she remembered her father's letter. The milliner had sent word through one of the footmen that her brother would be making another run at high tide, which meant she had two days' time in which to draft her response. With the masked ball tomorrow night the house would be in utter chaos, and it was unlikely she'd have a moment to herself.

If she wanted the letter to reach her papa within the month, she'd have to write it now. She thought about closing her eyes and saying to the devil with it all, but her sense of duty was too strong. Muttering heartfelt imprecations beneath her breath, she tossed back the heavy covers and scrambled out of bed.

She kept her writing desk in the bottom of the wardrobe, and after dragging it out she retrieved her father's letter from the hidden compartment. She was about to unfold it when she noticed something amiss; something so small and insignificant, it took her a moment to understand what she was seeing. When she'd tucked the letter away she'd carefully pressed the small circle of wax back into place, sealing it closed. The letter was still closed, but the circle of wax was no longer quite as it had been. A small red stain showed the wax had been disturbed, and she could think of only one way such a thing might have happened. Someone had opened the letter.

Five

Elizabeth stared at the wax seal in horror, her heart pounding and the breath lodged painfully in her throat. She tried to think, but her mind refused to function, and for a mortifying moment she feared she would disgrace herself by succumbing to the vapors. In the next moment her usual sense of logic asserted itself, and she breathed a shaky sigh of relief.

Idiot! She scolded herself silently, her hands shaking as she returned the letter to the case. Of course no one had read her letter. Why should they? The only person in the household aware she was writing to her father was Alexi, and she knew he would sooner die than betray her trust. Still, the thought of the letter and its contents being revealed didn't bear contemplating, and she resolved to find a safer hiding place at the first opportunity. In the meanwhile, she had a letter of her own to write.

The next day was a repeat of the previous one, and once more Elizabeth was kept running from cock's crow to sunset. But if the day's labors were arduous, they also contained an unexpected benefit. A guest had demanded a book, and while she was searching for the wretched thing, it occurred to Elizabeth how little used the library was. The books at the very top, coated as they were with a discreet layer of dust, were apparently used even less, and it occurred to Elizabeth that they were the perfect place in which to hide her illicit correspondence. Who would think to look for such a thing in the earl's own library? All she needed was a few free moments to secret them away, and she would be safe.

After assisting several of the ladies into their costumes, Elizabeth dashed up to her room with less than a quarter of an hour to dress for the festivities. She quickly donned her best gown of rose-colored silk, and was debating whether or not to wear the pearls her mother had left her when there was a knock at the door. Muttering at the thought of another interruption, she opened the door to find a maid standing there with a folded cloak draped over her arms.

"For you, miss," she said, offering the cape to Elizabeth with a pert curtsy. " 'Tis from Lady Barrington. She asks that you accept it with her compliments."

Stunned at such largesse, Elizabeth accepted the cape and carefully opened it. "Oh, it is a domino!" she exclaimed, understanding dawning as she examined the cape with its deep hood.

"And this is to wear with it," the maid replied, handing Elizabeth a black velvet mask trimmed with black lace. "She brought her own and thought you could use this one," she added, pushing her way into Elizabeth's room and glancing about her with ill-disguised curiosity.

"Indeed? How very kind of her grace," Elizabeth replied, touched and more than a little surprised by the duchess's generosity.

"Oh, she's kind enough in her way," the maid answered with a shrug. "But she has a sharp tongue, and she'll use it quick enough when she's of a mind. She's almighty particular about what's hers, although you'd never believe it, the way she mistreats her things. Why, t'other day she deliberately broke a ribbon on her new bonnet and then demanded I fix it. Quality"—she shook her head in obvious disgust—"there's no understanding them."

Elizabeth remembered the incident. "Are you quite certain it was deliberate?" she asked, frowning. "I was there when it happened, and as I recall, her grace was most distressed."

"It was deliberate, all right." The other girl gave a knowing sniff. "I was apprenticed once to a milliner, and I learned a thing or two about bonnets, I can tell you. That ribbon was ripped a'purpose; you could tell the way the threads was dangling. But she did give me an extra shilling and tell me thank you pretty enough when I was finished." This last was added as if in apology for gossiping about her employer.

She took her leave soon after, and after donning the domino and mask, Elizabeth slipped downstairs to mingle with the other guests. Several were in costumes of one kind or another, and others were dressed as she was, in a black domino and mask. Still others wore their usual evening dress, and she wasn't surprised to see Lord Falconer among those who had eschewed the use of a costume. She smiled slightly, recalling his icy disdain when Lady Barrington had dared to tease him on the matter. It would seem the coolly controlled marquess had little patience for such artifice.

Without warning he turned his head, his topaz eyes narrowing in recognition. He was at her side seconds later.

"Miss Mattingale." He favored her with one of his low bows. "I was hoping we might be honored with your presence this evening."

Elizabeth tried to be put out, but it was hard to feign indignation when her heart was racing with delight. "So much for the effectiveness of disguises," she drawled, favoring him with another smile. "It would seem I am suffering all this discomfort for naught if you recognized me so quickly."

His response was an elegant lift of his jet-black eyebrows. "I would hope I am not so easily misled, ma'am," he replied. "My eyes are sharper than that, I assure you."

Deciding discretion would be the wisest course, Elizabeth took refuge in socially acceptable pleasantries. "And how are you enjoying your stay at Derring, my lord? I trust you are being kept suitably entertained?" she asked, wishing she had brought a fan to unfurl. It was the one feminine ploy of which she approved, and she would have enjoyed having something to occupy hands that seemed suddenly restive.

"It has been interesting," came the reply, and Elizabeth wondered what he meant. The words were innocuous enough, and yet they seemed to portend something. She was tempted to demand an explanation, but Alexi was already joining them. Like the marquess, he was not in costume.

"A prince dress up like a fool?" he demanded when Elizabeth chided him on the matter. "Never, little queen. It would be too lowering to my pride."

"Your pride could stand a blow or two, your highness," Elizabeth returned in kind, noting the way the marquess was watching them. His expression remained as rigidly indifferent as always, and yet she could sense a sharp sense of awareness emanating from him.

Naturally, with two such eligible men clustered about her, it wasn't long until the other ladies began making their way to their corner. The detestable Miss Clarvale was among them, and as she had done the day of the picnic, she took unholy delight in ordering Elizabeth to do her bidding.

"Miss Mattingale, I am thirsty; kindly fetch me some punch," she ordered, smirking at what she clearly saw as her power over a weak and inferior woman.

Elizabeth bit her tongue and turned to do her bidding, only to find her way blocked by Alexi. He was smiling at Miss Clarvale, and the wolfish gleam in his eyes had Elizabeth bracing herself for what came next.

"Your costume is most attractive, Miss Clarvale," he told her suavely. "It makes you look"—his voice trailed off and he gave a beguiling grin—"forgive," he added, "I do not know how to say in English. Like a *sveenya*. You will agree, Miss Mattingale?" Blue eyes danced with innocence as he glanced at Elizabeth.

Elizabeth glanced at the other woman's sheer pink concoction that was, she assumed, supposed to resemble a fairy's attire but instead made her look like the barnyard animal Alexi had called her. Choking back a laugh, she schooled her face to politeness before replying.

"I would say, as do you, your highness, that that shade of pink is particularly becoming to Miss Clarvale," she said, offering a strained smile. "It makes her look precisely like a—rose."

"A rose?" The petulant beauty looked smugly delighted at such a fine compliment.

"An English *sveenya, da,*" Alexi assured her, bowing gracefully. "But you must allow me to fetch your punch for you, Miss Clarvale. It would be an honor." And he led her away, her giggling and desperately jealous friends following in their wake.

Lord Falconer remained with Elizabeth, a thoughtful expression on his face. "His highness has a great deal of charm," he observed coolly, glancing back at Elizabeth as if to measure her response.

Too vexed with Alexi to be cautious, she said the first thing to pop into her head. "And a great deal more cheek," she retorted, glaring after him. "That beast; I vow one day I shall have to throttle him."

There was a moment of silence, and then the marquess's lips were curving in one of his rare smiles. "I am the first to admit my grasp of Russian is poor at best," he murmured, "but why is it I sincerely doubt *sveenya* means rose?"

"Indeed, sir, it does not," Elizabeth retorted, still annoyed with Alexi. "And no," she added, anticipating his response, "I'm not telling you what it *does* mean."

His clear golden gaze sharpened as it rested on her face. "You have piqued my interest, ma'am," he murmured, his cool voice tinged with an enticing hint of laughter. "Unfortunately, as a gentleman I cannot demand a lady reveal her secrets to me. Should you choose to share them, however, I promise to be the soul of discretion."

Even though she knew his lordship's words to be spoken in jest, a guilty flush stole across Elizabeth's cheeks. Fortunately her mask covered most of her face, else she doubted her discomfiture would have escaped his sharp-eyed notice. One of the first things she had remarked about the marquess, aside from his autocratic propensities, was his cutting intellect. She had no doubt but that he would be merciless in ferreting out the truth if he even suspected her of dissembling. Realizing she had to say something, she threw Alexi to the wolf without so much as a backward glance.

"As you wish," she said, feigning a sweet air of submissiveness. *"Sveenya* is one of the few Russian words to bear some semblance to its English counterpart. If one were to think in terms of common livestock and change the *v* to a *w,* one would come closer to the word's true meaning."

There was a moment of silence as the marquess considered the matter. His eyebrows shot up as comprehension dawned.

"Then *sveenya* means—?"

She nodded, trying her best to keep from smirking. "Indeed it does, my lord," she assured him. "I fear his highness was behaving quite poorly. It was very unkind of him."

"But not altogether untrue, I think," he replied, glaring across the room at Miss Clarvale. "I found her behavior most objectionable, and decidedly piglike at times. Although I do not suppose I should say as much," he added, surprising her with a self-effacing shrug.

Sensing the perfect means of escape, Elizabeth was quick to make use of it. "Do not concern yourself, my lord," she told him, her lips curving in a teasing smile. "Like you, I promise to be the soul of discretion. Now, if you will excuse me, Mary Queen of Scots has been signaling me for the past few minutes, and it is never wise to keep royalty waiting. Good evening." And she took her leave with what good grace she could muster.

What was the little minx about? Adam's hooded gaze followed Miss Mattingale's progress, his jaw clenched in silent frustration. Since the earl had taken him into his confidence he'd given the matter a great deal of consideration, and he'd come to the reluctant conclusion that out of the entire household there were only two people who had reason to take the missing papers. The first was Prince Bronyeskin, and the second was the enigmatic woman who already commanded far more of his attention than was either proper or wise.

The prince's reasons for taking the papers were obvious. They might be allies now, but Russia had no more reason to trust England than did England to trust Russia. It was an open secret that both sides employed spies, just as it was an open secret that there was a discreet struggle for power being waged between the Czar and his imperious sister. Given such facts, it made perfect sense that the prince would avail himself of his host's private papers. All that remained was for Adam to recover the papers in such a way as not to endanger the already fragile coalition. Provided, he thought grimly, that it was Bronyeskin who had nabbed the papers. If it was Miss Mattingale who had taken them, matters were far more serious.

The idea that the pretty companion could betray her country was anathema to Adam. Everything in him rebelled at the thought, and it was because of this that he clung even more tenaciously to the notion. He'd never allowed his emotions to govern his actions in the past, and he couldn't allow them to do so now when the safety of his country was at stake. However painful it might be, he couldn't ignore the facts, and the facts as he saw them were decidedly grim.

From what Miss Mattingale had let slip, she'd lived abroad for a number of years and was obviously close friends with the only other suspect. But how close friends were they? She insisted there was nothing intimate between them, and he believed her—to a point. The absence of intimacy didn't necessarily mean an absence of emotion, and if she loved Bronyeskin, what would she be willing to risk for him? Love, or so he had heard, was the most powerful of motivators, and it was entirely possible Miss Mattingale would commit treason to aid the handsome and personable prince.

Then there was her father to consider. He lived in America, with which his country was now at war. Derring might be fool enough to think his edict would keep her from writing to her father, but Adam wasn't so easily gulled. He'd seen beneath the diffident façade she presented to the rest of the world and knew the companion was as proud as a duchess. He saw how ill she was treated; if it rankled him, how much more must it infuriate her? But how deep did that fury burn? Was her anger and resentment enough to goad her into risking the hangman's noose?

"Are the festivities not to your liking, my lord? You are looking properly fierce."

A low, feminine voice, flavored with mocking amusement sounded on Adam's right, and he turned his head to find a lady standing at his side. Like Miss Mattingale she was masked, her riper body draped from head to foot in one of the enveloping dominoes being sported by many of the other guests not in costume. Were it not for the slight differences in their height and physical attributes, he would have been hard-pressed to tell them apart. Fortunately his ears were as sharp as his eyes, and he had no trouble identifying his mysterious companion.

"Your grace," he inclined his head politely. "How are you this evening?"

"Bored, if the truth be told," the duchess told him with an affected sigh. "Country parties are so unutterably dull, and country masquerades are even duller still. One might have known Catherine would plan something so predictable.

"Of course," she added, sending him a languid smile, "there are ways of relieving one's ennui. Have you seen the conservatory? It is said to be quite—inspiring."

The bold offer had Adam holding back a shudder of well-bred distaste. He'd thought the duchess had accepted his unspoken refusal of her charms, but evidently she had not.

"I am afraid I have little interest in conservatories, your grace," he said, deciding bluntness was his only recourse. "Although I thank you for your offer."

The duchess remained silent for several seconds, her eyes flashing behind her mask. "That, my lord, was rather bad of you," she said, opening her fan with a snap. "However, to show there are no hard feelings, I shall allow you to partner me once the dancing begins. You do have an interest in dancing, do you not?" she added, with an arch of her eyebrows.

Adam unbent enough to smile. However forward Lady Barrington might be, there was no denying she could be diverting. "I have been known to engage in the occasional quadrille," he told her with a low bow. "And I should be honored to dance with you."

After the duchess had taken her leave, Adam spent the next hour mingling with the other guests and keeping a wary eye on the prince and Miss Mattingale. The prince, with his height and wearing the glittering white and gold uniform of the Romanoff court, was easy to spot, while Miss Mattingale, dressed in the ubiquitous domino, proved harder to track. Still he always managed to find her, learning to pick out her slender and graceful form from amongst the black-clad horde.

Dinner was as dull as ever, and it was with some eagerness that he waited for the dancing to begin. With so many of the ladies wearing dominoes, he knew he could dance with Miss Mattingale without risking tattle, but when the time to form sets came he discovered to his chagrin that she was nowhere to be found. He searched the ballroom twice, just to be certain, but there was no trace of his quarry.

His first thought was that she and Bronyeskin had slipped away for an assignation, but the prince was standing against the wall flirting with the usual court of ladies who surrounded him. Much as he hated appealing to a potential enemy for assistance, Adam didn't feel he had a choice and made his way through the crowd to the Russian's side.

"I beg your pardon, your highness," he said when he'd managed to separate the other man from his giggling harem. "Have you seen Miss Mattingale since dinner?"

"No, I have not," the prince replied, a frown knitting his dark gold eyebrows as he searched the ballroom. "Are you certain she is not here? With so many crows about, it is hard to tell if one of the flock is missing."

The telling phrase had Adam hiding an appreciative smile. "I am certain," he said. He also found it intriguing that while he could easily find Miss Mattingale in the crowd, the prince could not. He spotted Lady Derring, dressed as Queen Elizabeth, sitting across the ballroom, and decided to next approach her.

"Perhaps Lady Derring has sent her on some mission," he said, thinking that the most likely explanation for Miss Mattingale's absence. "If you will excuse me, Prince Bronyeskin."

He wasn't surprised when the prince followed him.

"I will go with you," Bronyeskin said, his expression stern. "It is not like my Elizabeth to desert her post."

"Miss Mattingale? She is somewhere about, I am sure," Lady Derring said when Adam questioned her.

"Might I ask why you seem so eager for her company?" she added, an expression of arch speculation on her painted countenance. "I ask because she is my companion, and as her employer I must take care to safeguard her reputation. We wouldn't wish people to remark unkindly on your—attentions to her."

A sharp and extremely impolite sentiment burned on Adam's tongue, but before he could utter it Prince Bronyeskin began speaking smoothly.

"We have need of her to act as interpreter, *babushka*," he said, favoring the older woman with a dazzling smile. "His lordship and I have matters of great import to discuss, and as my English is as poor as his Russian, this does not make things so easy."

The prince's explanation had the countess beaming. "Of course, your highness!" she exclaimed, simpering up at him like a schoolgirl. "Naturally Miss Mattingale will be happy to be of service. If you can find her, that is." And she began glancing about the crowded ballroom with a scowl.

"We will find her," Bronyeskin said, kissing her hand lavishly. "As you say, she is somewhere here about. Thank you again, *babushka*. Your kindness to a poor stranger is a credit to you."

"Poor stranger?" Adam drawled as he and the prince walked away.

Bronyeskin gave an elegant shrug. "A prince may be humble when it suits him."

"Evidently," Adam agreed, "and this time I must insist you tell me what *babushka* means. I asked Miss Mattingale, but she refused."

The prince's lips twitched in a half smile. "It is a scarf to cover the head," he said, shooting Adam a look of shared camaraderie. "But since it is often older peasant women who wear such things, the word has another meaning. Grandmother," he clarified, blue eyes dancing in mischief.

Adam was unable to prevent the snort of laughter that escaped him. "God help you if her ladyship ever learns that," he said, imaging the older woman's likely response. "Just as He should help you if Lady Derring remembers the language of diplomacy is French, not English."

"That one sees only her own reflection." Bronyeskin dismissed such a possibility with a regal shrug. He spent the next several minutes at Adam's side, searching the crowds for Miss Mattingale.

"Pah!" he exclaimed, his hands fisted on his hips as he glared about him. "Where is my little queen? I see no sign of her."

"Nor do I," Adam returned, suspicion giving way to genuine alarm. By his reckoning it had been over fifteen minutes since he had first noticed her absence, and who knew how long she had been missing before then? He began searching the ballroom to see if he could discern who else was missing, and it was then he noted that there was no sign of either Derwent, Colburt, or Derring's half-witted son. The trio was easy enough to recognize; they'd come dressed as Roman senators.

"Those bastards!" he growled, his temper slipping its leash as a killing rage filled his head. "If they have dared hurt her, this time by God I shall call them out!"

In a flash Bronyeskin was transformed from indolent prince to the deadly warrior Adam knew him to be. "Who?" he demanded, his eyes growing hot with murderous intent. "Who are you speaking of? If someone has threatened my Elizabeth, they will die!"

"Our host's idiot son and his repellent friends," Adam answered, striding purposefully toward the hallway leading to the rest of the house. "They've not harmed Elizabeth that I know of, but that's not to say they've not thought of it. And if there is any killing to be done, your highness, I shall be the one to do it."

"By what right?" Bronyeskin easily kept pace with Adam. "I claim Elizabeth as my sister. If she has been hurt, it is my honor to take the life of those responsible. Do not think to interfere, Falconer, I warn you."

Adam remained silent. Who would kill whom would be something they would resolve later; at the moment finding Elizabeth was all that mattered. With Bronyeskin at his side, they searched the conservatory, the music room, and were walking toward the morning parlor when they heard a burst of raucous male laughter from the room to the prince's left. Moving as one, they threw open the door and dashed inside, both of them battle-ready and spoiling for a brawl. Charles Colburt glanced up from the billiard table, where he was about to take his shot.

"Good evening, Falconer, your highness," he drawled, his pale blue eyes bright with mocking laughter. "Come for a game, have you? Pick up a cue and join us."

Without being aware of moving, Adam was on him. He grabbed him roughly by the front of his toga, throwing him against the wall and holding him there with one hand. "Where is Miss Mattingale?" he demanded furiously. "Tell me, or I'll break your damned neck!"

"What?" Charles plucked ineffectually at Adam's iron grip. "Have you run mad? Let go of me! Why would I care where that icy bitch has gone? I—" His protest ended in a gurgle as Adam's hand released his costume and closed instead about his throat.

"One word," he warned, shoving his face closer to Charles. "Just one, and I'll kill you. Again, where is Miss Mattingale?"

"I don't know!" Charles choked out, terror obvious in his bulging eyes. "None of us do! We've been in here for the past half-hour! Upon my word we have!"

"I—I saw her leaving the ballroom, my lord," Geoffrey Derwent volunteered hesitantly, his attention divided between Adam and Bronyeskin, who had drawn his sword from its scabbard and was looking eager for an excuse to make use of it. "She was making for the hallway leading to the north wing."

"What is there?" Bronyeskin asked, his voice silky even as he brought the point of his sword up and rested it against the dandy's trembling chin.

"The library and Mama's drawing room." William had stumbled to his feet. "Perhaps she's gone there?"

Recalling how Elizabeth was dressed, Adam sent him a cold look. "How do you know it was she and not some other lady?" he demanded, keeping his hold tight about Charles's throat.

The younger man looked puzzled. "I don't, I suppose," he admitted. "But it was a lady wearing a domino. If none of the other ladies have gone missing, who else could it be?"

However much he might have wished to do otherwise, Adam was forced to concede William's point. With almost painful reluctance he released his grip from about Charles, dusting off his hands as he stepped back.

"If I find out you have lied, any of you," he warned, glancing at each man in turn, "you will regret it."

Bronyeskin appeared even less willing than Adam to quit the field. Resheathing his sword, he turned to Charles, his eyes as cold as death. "We will talk later, you and I," he said, his voice rife with the promise of violence. "If you are fortunate, I will only cut out your tongue. If not, I will take instead your heart."

"You might at least have let me kill that one," he complained to Adam after they were back in the hallway. "The world would thank me for it, I assure you."

Despite the seriousness of the situation, an appreciative smile touched Adam's lips. "Undoubtedly," he agreed, "but in the meanwhile what of Elizabeth? We will make better time if we divide the search. Which do you prefer, the library or the drawing room?"

"The drawing room," the prince decided. "Elizabeth may have fled there for a few minutes' rest."

"It's the library for me, then," Adam said. "Whichever of us finds her first, we shall bring her back here."

"And if we do not find her?" The other man studied him grimly.

Adam didn't have to think before responding. "Then we tear this damned place apart until we do."

Six

"Blast!"

The unladylike epithet burst from Elizabeth's lips as she set down her flickering taper and pulled off her mask and enveloping domino. Both might serve their purposes as an effective disguise, but their very effectiveness rendered them all but useless when it came to moving about with any degree of stealth. Considering the amount of Horrid novels she'd devoured featuring similarly attired villains and heroines creeping about any number of crumbling castles and palazzos, Elizabeth thought the authors of the Minervian Press had rather a great deal to answer for. Such dexterity of movement was clearly a work of fiction, and they were doing their readers no favors by perpetuating so obvious a fraud.

Still grumbling, she extracted her letter from the bodice of her gown and turned to eye the ceiling-to-floor shelves of books. The shelves were tucked in the corner of the room farthest from the fireplace, well hidden in the shadows of the room. It took her a few minutes to locate the folding step chair and drag it into place, and another few moments to locate the book she'd selected as her temporary safe. The book was a treatise on horticulture, and if the layer of dust coating it was any indication, it hadn't been opened in the fifty years since it had been printed.

She climbed up on the top step, teetering slightly on

tiptoe as she reached for the book. Her fingers closed around the spine and she began tugging it cautiously toward her.

"There you are!"

The sound of the outraged male voice behind her had Elizabeth jerking in alarm, and her balance was instantly lost. With a cry, she went tumbling back.

"Elizabeth!"

In the next moment a strong pair of arms was closing about her, and a hard male body was cushioning her fall as she landed on the floor in an ignominious heap. The book struck her shoulder, but even as she was gasping in pain, she found herself on her back and gazing up at the marquess. She blinked up at him, fear giving way to wild fury. She forgot about the letter, the disparity of their ranks, even their current scandalous position, and reacted purely out of instinct.

"You idiot!" she cried, doubling up her fist and punching his velvet-clad arm as hard as she could. "What do you think you are doing? You might have killed me!"

"What am I doing?" Hot, gold eyes glared down at her out of a face that was surprisingly pale. "What are *you* doing?"

"Dying of fright, you beast," she retorted, her heart pounding as she fought to draw in sufficient breath. With the return of sanity came an uncomfortable awareness of the proprieties, and of the letter still clutched in her hand.

"I meant, what are you doing in here?" Falconer demanded, his jaw setting in a way that was becoming far too familiar. "We have been searching for you for the past half-hour!"

By *we* she assumed he meant he and Alexi, and wondered how best to turn the knowledge to her advantage. "Mrs. Tremaine thought she recalled a book from her last visit," she said at last, striving for what dignity she could muster. "She was certain it was here, and I promised her that I would try to find it for her."

"And so you decided to look for it in the middle of a

ball." He continued to glare down at her in apparent disapproval, not seeming any more aware than she of the impropriety of their situation.

"Can you think of a better time?" she demanded. "I thought the room would be deserted, and I wouldn't have to worry about any unfortunate interruptions." Her chin thrust out in a deliberate show of pride. "It would seem I was mistaken."

As she expected, his lean cheeks suffused with hectic color, and she saw the moment he became aware they were lying on the floor, her limbs tangled with his. He levered himself up at once and reached for her.

"A moment, sir, if you please," she said, playing the part of innocence outraged for all she was worth. "I need to adjust my gown. If you would be so good as to turn your back?"

He was on his feet at once, presenting his rigid back to her as he turned to face the opposite wall. It took Elizabeth less than a second to slip the letter into the book and close it again.

"Thank you," she said, making the silk of her gown and petticoats rustle as she flipped them down over her ankles. "Now, if you would be so good as to assist me to my feet, I shall return to the ballroom." And she held out her hand imperiously.

He turned back to her, his expression shuttered. His strong fingers closed about hers, their touch gentle as he tugged her effortlessly to her feet. He next bent down to retrieve the book, his brows lifting as he glanced at the title.

"What book were you looking for?" he asked, raising his head to study her.

"A book on the older families in Yorkshire," Elizabeth replied, recalling the title of the book next to the one she had grabbed. It had been her first selection, but the dust on it wasn't nearly so thick as it had been on the other one. She didn't want to risk her safety on some guest developing a sudden interest in a long-dead relation.

Falconer silently held up the book, and she pretended to study the title for the first time.

"The Scientific Gentleman's Guide to Soils and Crops in Derby," she read, and gave an impatient exclamation. "All that, and I chose the wrong book?" She picked up her skirts and moved toward the chair. Her way was blocked almost at once.

"What are you doing?"

She didn't have to feign the annoyance brimming inside her. "Getting the book, of course," she said, tilting back her head to meet his stony gaze. "After nearly dying, I am not about to return to Mrs. Tremaine empty-handed."

His lips compressed in a thin line. "You didn't almost die," he retorted. "And you're mad if you think I will allow you to climb up on that thing a second time. Stay here."

He climbed on the chair, scarcely straining as he reached up to return the first book and retrieve the second. "Here," he said, thrusting it at her with obvious ill grace. "And the next time you need something on the very top shelf, have a servant fetch it for you, for heaven's sake."

As much to remind herself as him, Elizabeth sent him a frosty glare. "A servant did fetch it, my lord," she informed him aloofly. *"I* fetched it."

The reminder had its desired effect, and he remained silent as she redonned her mask and domino. A few moments later they were hurrying toward the main staircase, and Elizabeth took the opportunity to begin fretting about Alexi.

"I hope his highness isn't overly upset," she said, worrying at the thought of the havoc a concerned Alexi could cause. "He is even more protective than you are."

She sensed more than saw the heated glare he sliced her way. "I will leave it to Prince Bronyeskin to make his feelings known," he told her in icy accents. "But if I may be so bold, his highness wasn't the only one to be *upset* when it appeared you had vanished without a trace."

There wasn't time for Elizabeth to puzzle over the stiff words, as Alexi was upon them.

"Elizabeth! *Duragoy!*" She was scooped up in his arms and subjected to a hug that would have had a bear gasping for air. "Where have you been?" he demanded, blue eyes stormy as he set her on her feet again. "How dare you worry your Alexi so!"

Alexi's powerful hug jarred Elizabeth's injured shoulder, but she managed not to cry out. Covering her involuntary wince, she subjected both men to her sternest look of disapprobation.

"I vow," she lectured, shaking her head at them, "was there ever such a pair? One would think this was the wilds of Africa, to hear the two of you ranting on! I couldn't have been gone above half an hour! What do you think could happen in so short a time?"

Alexi gave one of his shrugs. "Half an hour can be a lifetime, little queen," he told her coolly. "And if you wish that *sabaka,* Colburt, to continue breathing, you will not remind me of the things that can befall a beautiful woman.

"But," he added, as Elizabeth opened her mouth in automatic protest, "it is grown late, and we must return you to the others before your absence is noted. Come." And he placed a hand on her shoulder, turning her toward the stairs.

This time she was unable to suppress a gasp, and both men instantly surrounded her.

"Elizabeth! What is it?" Alexi demanded, his touch gentle as his worried gaze swept over her.

"It is all right, Alexi," she soothed, unable as always to resist his genuine concern. "A simple bruise, nothing more. A book fell from the shelf and struck my shoulder. I shall rub it with mint and chamomile before retiring and it will be fine."

"If you are certain . . ." he began, and then broke off, frowning. "But I do not understand. How could a book fall from a shelf?"

"Not now, Alexi," Elizabeth said, twining her arm through his and leading him away. "As you said, it is best I return to the ballroom before my absence causes tattle."

She was halfway down the hall before realizing the marquess wasn't with them. She paused and cast a confused look over her shoulder.

"Aren't you coming with us, sir?" she asked, thinking how grim and alone he looked standing there in the flickering candlelight from the wall sconces.

"I will be along shortly," he replied, remaining in the center of the shadow-filled hall. "Good evening, Miss Mattingale. Mind you take proper care of that shoulder."

Deciding there was no understanding the masculine mind, she allowed a still scolding Alexi to guide her back to the ballroom. They parted at the door, and Elizabeth made for the small figure of a lady draped from head to foot in a colorful mound of shawls.

"Here you are, Mrs. Tremaine," she said, smiling as she carefully set the book in the older woman's lap. "I found the book you were asking about."

The elderly lady started, peering down at the book through faded blue eyes. "Oh, thank you, Miss Mattingale, thank you indeed," she said, her thin voice warm with gratitude. She used a gnarled finger to trace the gold letters stamped deep in the maroon leather. "Er—did I request a book?"

"Yes, Mrs. Tremaine, you did," Elizabeth replied, praying she wouldn't go to eternal perdition for lying to such a sweet lady. "Just before dinner, if you will but recall."

"Oh. Oh, of course," Mrs. Tremaine responded with a vague nod. "Then I am sure I must have wanted it. Thank you again, my dear," she added, flashing Elizabeth a shy smile. "You are very kind."

Elizabeth gave a weak smile in response before settling back to listen to the music, her conscience paining her along with her throbbing shoulder.

Idiot! Ham-fisted fool! Adam cursed himself furiously, his hands clenched at his sides as he stormed up and down the flagstone balcony overlooking the Derrings' gardens.

Every time he pictured Elizabeth jerking back and falling, he felt physically ill. If he hadn't been quick enough to catch her, she could have been seriously injured, a fact he was certain would haunt his dreams for some time to come. As it was, she'd been hurt anyway, and he knew it was entirely his doing. If he hadn't come bursting into the room like a jealous husband in search of a wayward wife, she would never have lost her balance. He was strongly tempted to confess his sin to Bronyeskin, figuring the thrashing the prince would give him was no less than he deserved.

When he'd done cursing himself for his appalling stupidity, Adam decided it was time to return to the ballroom. There was still the matter of the missing papers to consider, and after observing his two chief suspects together, he was more convinced than ever that they couldn't be involved. Miss Mattingale, he was certain, was far too proud to do such a thing, while Prince Bronyeskin was too much the aristocrat to sully his honor with something so sordid as espionage. That meant the thief had to be someone whose motive for taking the papers were less obvious. He had only to deduce what that motive might be, and then he'd have his thief.

Feeling better now that he'd come to a decision, he turned back toward the French doors leading back to the ballroom. He hadn't taken but a few steps when the sound of soft, feminine laughter, echoed by an answering masculine chuckle came from the shadows. Lovers, he thought with a sigh, and since they were between him and the doors he could either risk causing yet another scandal or find some other way back to the ballroom. It took less than a second for him to choose, and he slipped quietly down the balcony's wide stone steps and out into the moonlit garden.

To his chagrin he almost stumbled across several other pairs of lovers, before making his way toward the conservatory. He'd achieved his objective and was making his way toward the door when he saw yet another pair of lovers slipping inside. For heaven's sake, he thought sourly, was he the only man in the house party not to have made an assignation? It was too lowering by half.

"There, darling," a familiar voice cooed from the shadows. "Didn't I promise I would come? Stop pouting and make love to me."

The duchess, he realized, his lips thinning in fastidious disdain. It was as well he'd rejected her invitation; it was one that had evidently been extended to most of the household. Not in the least interested in learning the identity of her grace's *inamorato,* he ducked behind the potted plants, keeping carefully in the shadows until he was able to affect his escape.

Back in the ballroom, the dancing and merrymaking continued unabated. Not wishing to rouse suspicions, he was careful to dance with several of the ladies, but his attention was never far from the corner where Elizabeth sat with Mrs. Tremaine and several older ladies. That he now thought of her as Elizabeth as easily as he thought of her as Miss Mattingale was another thing that troubled him, for it indicated he had crossed one of the lines of intimacy he seldom allowed himself to cross.

It was better—safer, he amended with a brutal flash of honesty—to keep that barrier of propriety between them. As she was forever pointing out, she was but a companion and he a marquess. Any hint of anything untoward between them was certain to end in disaster for her, and he was too fond of her to allow that to happen. He had always possessed the ability to bend his more impulsive nature to the iron control of his will; he would simply have to do so now.

Still clinging to his resolve, Adam rose early the next morning and set out for his daily ride. Most of the household was still abed, recovering from the night's festivities, and he was looking forward to a bruising ride and an entire hour of blissful solitude. He accomplished the first easily enough and was well on his way to enjoying the second when he charged over the crest of the hill and glimpsed a hooded figure trudging through the fields paralleling the road. His eyes narrowed in instant recognition, and he set off down the hill in angry pursuit.

The figure turned at the sound of his approach, and for a moment he thought she looked as if she might bolt. Instead she squared her slender shoulders, standing her ground as he thundered to a halt a few feet from where she stood.

"I thought it was understood you would be taking your ease today," he said, scowling as he dismounted.

"Understood by you, perhaps, my lord," Elizabeth replied in those precise tones he knew meant she was highly displeased. "For myself, I can recall no such conversation."

"I told you to have a care for your shoulder," he reminded her, lips twitching as he approached her. Annoyed as he was, he still couldn't help but be amused by her recalcitrant nature. He also couldn't help but admire the pride that was as much a part of her as her soft blue eyes and delightfully pointed chin.

Up came that delightful chin. "And so I have every intention of doing," she told him with a sniff. "But since I do not walk upon my shoulders, I am sure I shall be fine. Good day, sir; you won't wish your horse to grow restive, I am sure." And she turned and stalked away, the conversation clearly finished as far as she was concerned.

He grabbed the reins of his horse before falling easily into step beside her. "You are bound for the milliner's again, I see," he observed, gesturing at the familiar hatbox swinging from her arm. "How many bonnets does her ladyship possess, if I may ask? Every time I come upon you, you seem to be carrying a hatbox."

She jerked as if shocked by his observation. "No more than any other lady, I am sure," she said, keeping her eyes firmly fixed in front of her. "But as it happens, this is a bonnet Lady Derring purchased a few weeks past. She wishes to have the ribbon changed to another color, and asked if I would see to the matter for her."

"And naturally you said you would." The bitter words slipped from between Adam's clenched teeth before he could stop them.

She turned her head long enough to cast him a puzzled look. "Naturally. I *am* in her employ, after all."

"So you are constantly reminding me, but what you haven't said is why it must be so," he said, a burning curiosity to learn more of the secretive woman walking beside him tearing at him. Yesterday he would have excused such interest as no more than his duty, but today he could find no such comfort. His interest in Elizabeth was entirely and deeply personal.

"Didn't your father make arrangements for you prior to emigrating to America?" he asked, aware of how far over that invisible line he now trod.

"No," Elizabeth said quietly, "he did not. When I refused to remain with him in America, he made it plain I could expect no further assistance from him. My mother's mother is set well enough and would have been happy to have me remain with her, but I've no wish to batten myself on an old woman. We agreed this position with Lady Derring would serve as a sort of test, and if I do well, Grandmother promised not to oppose me when I sought a more permanent position."

Adam couldn't say why, but he was greatly relieved. "Then this is only a temporary position for you?"

She nodded. "For six months. If I manage to survive that long without being given the boot or resigning, I shall be free." She clapped a hand over her lips and cast him a look of such horror that this time there was no holding back the chuckle that seemed to come from deep inside him.

"Six months isn't so great a time," he said, smiling. "And who is to say, perhaps this ruinous war will have ended by then, and you and your father will have reconciled."

A look of profound sadness flashed across Elizabeth's

face. "Perhaps," she agreed, tightening her hold on the hatbox.

Adam said nothing, a lifetime of reticence making it impossible for him to speak. He wanted to demand that she explain herself, but he felt hampered as much by the conventions as by his own wary nature. The loss of his parents within months of each other, followed by the mad scramble to gain control over his staggering inheritance had left him wary, and he'd learned to survive by holding himself aloof from everyone and everything. But he was finding he couldn't hold himself aloof from Elizabeth, and it troubled him that she could so effortlessly hold herself away from him.

Keeping such thoughts private, he escorted her the rest of the way to the milliner's shop. His desire for her company was almost enough to overcome his masculine aversion to such places, but in the end he decided it wouldn't suit. Halting, he laid a staying hand on her arm and gazed down into her face.

"I'll wait for you there," he said, indicating the inn across the narrow street. "Come and fetch me when you have finished. Do not," he added with a stern look, "even think of returning to Derring Hall without me."

Her response was a raised eyebrow, followed by a mocking curtsy. "Yes, my lord," she murmured, a lively sparkle in her aquamarine eyes as she tilted back her head to meet his gaze. "Very well, my lord."

He grinned. "Imp," he accused, flicking his finger down her pert nose. "Just mind you do as I say, else I shall be most displeased."

Relatively certain she would do as he ordered, Adam led his ever-patient mount over to the inn. He turned him over to the waiting linkboy and was about to leave the stables when he caught sight of an elegant traveling coach. Recognizing the heraldic device painted on the side, he turned and hurried into the inn.

He hadn't taken but a few steps inside when he heard his name called out.

"Falconer! Ho there!"

"Your grace," he said, hurrying forward to greet the older man with the magnificent mane of white hair flowing about his ruddy face who was striding toward him. "What are you doing here? You can't have received my letter already!"

"Indeed, I have," Arthur, Duke of Creshton, exclaimed, clapping his hand on Adam's shoulder and adroitly guiding him toward the private parlor. "Came tearing down the moment I read it. But let's have a glass of wine, shall we? We've much to discuss, and precious little time."

Adam took his meaning and fell silent, holding his tongue until the door had closed behind him.

"What do you think?" he asked, studying the man he regarded as both a mentor and a friend. For all his bluff ways and hearty manner, the duke was possessed of one of the most brilliant political minds Adam had ever encountered, and he was relieved to have the older man in his corner once again. His grace would know precisely what was to be done and the best way to do it.

"What I think is that dashed fool Derring ought to be shot," the duke grumbled, his magnificent brows meeting in a scowl as he settled into his chair. "Why the Foreign Secretary saw fit to entrust so much as a piece of foolscap to him, I am sure I shall never know. Fellow has the brains of a flea.

"Ah, well." He gave a philosophical shrug. "No use wringing our hands now. What's to be done, that's what's important. We discussed it on our way down, and I believe we've come up with just the thing."

"We?" Adam brightened in relief. "Is Lord St. Jerome with you?"

"I should say not!" the duke thundered, looking properly shocked. "You must know his viscountess is expecting his heir any day now, and it would take a brace of cannons to dislodge him from his estate. I've Elinore with me."

"What?"

"Stands to reason, don't it?" If the duke was offended by Adam's strangled gasp, he gave no indication. "Girl's accepted everywhere, and her being in the house gives us the perfect excuse to slip an agent into place. Daresay no one is likely to notice an extra footman or two about, eh?" He winked at Adam.

Put like that, Adam had no choice but to agree. "No, I suppose not," he conceded, albeit with a frown. "But still—an agent? You think matters that serious, then?"

The duke gave a grim nod. "Deadly serious. You must know the Austrians dislike the Russians even more than we hate the bloody Frogs, and it's likely they'll square off over the Polish Issue. Prince Bronyeskin is in to it up to his neck, and because of his closeness to the Grand Duchess we dare not touch him."

"Are you certain Bronyeskin is involved?" Adam asked, having already given the matter considerable thought. "I've come to know the man, and I can't see him skulking about stealing papers."

"Perhaps not," the duke said with another shrug. "But he bears watching, regardless."

"What is your agent's name?" Adam asked, deciding to let the matter drop for the moment. "I should like to meet with him so I can give him the information I have already gathered."

To his surprise the duke shook his head. "Not the way it's done, I am afraid. Marquesses don't meet with footmen, and if you was to seek him out, people would wonder. You tell me what you have, and I'll see it's passed on."

The answer was not at all to Adam's liking, but before he could demand a more satisfactory explanation the door opened and a tall woman with her dark chestnut hair pinned back in an elegant chignon stepped into the room. When she saw Adam she gave him a cool nod, her gray eyes indifferent as they swept over him.

"Lord Falconer," she said, her voice as precise and

emotionless as if she were greeting a stranger. "How nice to see you again."

Adam rose to his feet, his manner equally stiff as he offered her a bow. "Lady Elinore," he said, pride and a lingering hurt he refused to acknowledge making him wary. "You are well, I trust?"

"There, you see?" The duke chuckled before his daughter could reply. "The two of you can pass a polite conversation without coming to blows. Sure you won't offer for her again, Falconer?" he added, giving Adam a roguish wink. "She might even say yes this time."

"Papa!" Lady Elinore's pose as a haughty lady dissolved into mortification as she cast her father a horrified look.

"Don't take on so, m'dear," he responded with a smug chuckle. "I was just having a bit of fun. A blind man can see the pair of you would not suit. And you needn't poker up like a dashed suit of armor, either, my lord," he said, shaking his finger at Adam. "You always were too serious by half."

Adam could think of no reply. His offer for Elinore and the way she had flung it back in his teeth was still something of a sore point with him. However grateful he might now be that she'd had the good sense to refuse him, it would be some time before he could look upon the incident with anything approaching levity.

"How is Mary, dearest?" the duke asked after a moment, covering the awkward silence with his usual ease. "Has she recovered?"

"Yes, Papa. The tea seems to be settling her stomach. We should be able to resume our journey whenever you are ready.

"Mary is my maid," she added by way of explanation to Adam. "Traveling upsets her stomach."

"I see," he replied politely, although in truth he did not. Derring Hall was but a mile distant, and it made far more sense to him to press on rather than stopping. But that was Elinore for you, he decided; the woman never did what you expected. Rather like another lady he had recently come to know, he thought, biting back a smile as he thought of Elizabeth. Then he frowned.

"Have you room in your traveling coach for one more?" he asked, a sudden thought occurring to him.

"Certainly, dear fellow, certainly," his grace assured him affably. "In need of a ride, are you?"

Adam shook his head. "Not me, no. I rode in. But Lady Derring's companion walked into town, and I believe she would welcome a ride home. She injured her shoulder yesterday, and I fear she may have overestimated her strength."

"Then we should be delighted to oblige her," the duke said with a gracious nod. "Where is she?"

"In the milliner's shop across the way," Adam said, rising to his feet. "If you'll excuse me, I'll just go fetch her."

It was the perfect solution, he decided, making his way out of the crowded inn. Not only would it provide Elizabeth with a ride back to the manor, but it would also give his grace the opportunity to take her measure. However convinced he might be of her innocence, the fact remained that until the real culprit was apprehended, he couldn't completely dismiss her from suspicion. His own feelings for her were so tangled, he feared he'd long since lost his objectivity, and that he knew would not do. For Elizabeth's sake, if she was to be truly exonerated, it was best if that exoneration came from a neutral party. It was the only way she could be completely safe, and her safety was rapidly becoming a matter of paramount importance to him.

"Consider it done, me darling." Mrs. Treckler gave Elizabeth a saucy wink as she slipped Elizabeth's letter inside the bodice of her gown. "Tom sails tonight, and this will be in America a'fore ye know it. Will there be an answer?"

Elizabeth thought of the letter she'd written her father

and shook her head. "No, Mrs. Treckler, there will be no answer."

"All right, then," the milliner answered brightly, opening up the box and taking out the bonnet. "And what's to be done with this one, then? Not more fruit? The thing already looks like a bleeding orchard."

Elizabeth bit her lip, her sadness giving way to amusement at the other woman's good-natured humor.

"Her ladyship would like a different-colored ribbon, Mrs. Treckler. Something in peach, perhaps?" she said, giving thanks as she often did that her employer was so devoted to her hats. It was because of her devotion that she'd met the milliner and learned of her brother's interesting business; and, of course, carrying Lady Derring's bonnets to and from the manor had provided her with the perfect means of covering her true purpose for the meetings.

"Peach?" Mrs. Treckler turned the bonnet this way and that, studying it with a knowing eye. "Aye, I reckon that would serve, although I've a lovely shade of pink that would be even better. I'll send a length of it along as well, shall I? That way you'll not need to make another trip. I trust we'll not be seeing as much of you as before?" And she gave Elizabeth a knowing look.

"That would depend upon her ladyship," Elizabeth answered pedantically, although she thought it unlikely she would be spending quite as much time in the tiny shop. Most of her visits on Lady Derring's behalf had been the result of some gentle hint on her part that there was some problem with one of the countess's many bonnets.

The door opened behind her, and when she glanced over her shoulder she wasn't surprised to see Lord Falconer entering the shop. She'd been there for almost half an hour, and he'd never struck her as being the overly patient sort.

"Have you finished?" he asked, walking up to join her.

"Almost," she replied, more amused than vexed. "Mrs. Treckler and I were just discussing ribbon colors. Which do you think would look best on Lady Derring, peach or a soft pink?" she asked, unable to resist the urge to tweak him. He was behaving in his usual autocratic manner, and in her estimation such high-handedness deserved retribution.

He refused to rise to the bait. "I am afraid I have little experience in such matters," he replied, taking her arm and guiding her toward the door. He sent a glance back to Mrs. Treckler, who was watching them with obvious interest.

"Have the bonnet sent to the house when you are done, Mrs. Treckler, if you would be so kind," he said, and then pulled Elizabeth out the door before she could so much as protest.

"Sir, that was very presumptuous of you!" Elizabeth protested, hurrying to keep up with his longer stride. "Lady Derring will have my head if I return without her bonnet. She plans to wear it this afternoon."

"Her ladyship can make other arrangements," he replied, his jaw hardening. "I encountered the Duke of Creshton and his daughter, Lady Elinore, at the inn. They're on their way to the Hall; you may ride back with them."

"What?" Elizabeth skittered to a halt, her eyes wide with horror. "But his grace sent word refusing the invitation!" she cried, imagining the fit of vapors her employer would have upon hearing the news. "He can't come now; it will upset the numbers!"

He took possession of her arm again and began pulling her along with him. "You're not well-acquainted with his grace, else you'd know he is prone to changing his mind at the last moment," he said coolly. "As for Elinore, there's nothing she likes better than upsetting things."

Elizabeth wasn't certain she cared for the sound of that. She already had a house filled with demanding ladies tugging at her skirts like a pack of unruly children. A duke's daughter with a penchant for mayhem didn't sound like a particularly welcome addition to her.

"Be that as it may," she replied truculently, her low-heeled shoes slipping on the cobblestones as she struggled for purchase, "I can hardly invite myself into their coach; it would be too forward by half. Adam!" She skittered to a halt and jerked her arm free, her face set in a furious scowl. "Let go of me!"

He sent her a stunned look. "You called me Adam," he said, sounding faintly shocked.

"And I suppose you think I am going to beg your pardon," she retorted, too defiant to be cautious, "but you may think again. When you behave like a marquess, I shall address you as such! If you persist in behaving like an ill-mannered schoolboy, then that is how I shall address you!" She folded her arms across her chest and glared at him, daring him to protest.

To her surprise he merely shrugged and availed himself of her arm once more. "You mistake me, ma'am," he said, shouldering open the inn's door and pulling her inside. "I've no objection to your using my Christian name. It will give me leave to call you by yours.

"But," he admonished, topaz eyes dancing as he grinned down at her, "I am sure you'll understand if I insist you only do so when we are in private. I have my reputation to think of."

She was still sputtering in indignation when he introduced her to the duke and his stunning daughter. Less than five minutes later she found herself being bundled into the coach, a warm lap robe draped across her knees.

"And mind you stay there," he told her, his expression stern. He tipped his hat to the duke and Lady Elinore, and then slammed the carriage door closed.

The carriage started with a jerk a few seconds later, and an embarrassed Elizabeth turned her head to study the other occupants of the coach. To her surprise, Lady Elinore was smiling at her, with a decided sparkle in her eyes.

"Overbearing, isn't he?" she asked, her cultured voice rich with laughter.

Too taken aback to prevaricate, Elizabeth said the first words to pop into her head. "Yes, my lady, he most assuredly is."

"He means well, one may suppose," Lady Elinore observed, looking bored, "but I find it quite tiresome. Lord Falconer has always presumed far too much, if you want my opinion."

"You are too hard on his lordship, Elinore," the duke said, sending his daughter a censorious frown. "I still say it's because the two of you are so alike. That is why I want you to rethink his offer of marriage; he is just the man to tame you. Do you not agree, Miss Mattingale?" He glanced at Elizabeth, his steely expression making it plain what he expected her answer to be.

For a moment Elizabeth couldn't breathe; her breath lodged in her throat along with her heart. Despite the many years she'd spent away from England and the *ton,* she was well aware most marriages were contracted for reasons that had little to do with anything so tiresome as love. Lady Elinore was of the highest birth, a consideration certain to be a matter of great importance to a man like the marquess. In addition she was beautiful, unquestionably elegant, and possessed of a cool sangfroid that more than matched his own. To Society, it would be a match as brilliant as a diamond, and every bit as cold.

"I am sure it would be a most advantageous marriage, your grace," she managed, ignoring the heart that now plummeted to the toes of her half boots.

"Yes, if I were in want of taming, which I am not," Lady Elinore responded to her father's observation with a haughty sniff. "You don't hint *I* should tame his lordship, I note."

"Of course not, m'dear." The duke gave his daughter's hand an indulgent pat. "A tame husband would bore you to tears within a sennight. Just remember your promise to me and consider the matter. That is all I ask."

To Elizabeth's great relief the conversation turned general after that, and she spent the rest of the brief ride acquainting Lady Elinore and her father with the Hall's inhabitants. She wasn't surprised her ladyship was acquainted with most of them.

"The Derrings must indeed be hard-pressed to fill their numbers to have allowed that lack-wit Derwent to put up there," she said, unfurling her fan with easy grace. "And if he is there, I suppose that worm Charles Colburt is not very far away."

"He is also there, my lady," Elizabeth volunteered, relieved she wasn't the only woman to find the men's company objectionable. "I believe the two are good friends of Lord Derring's younger son, Mr. William Carling."

It was the duke who responded. "Dashed loose screw, that one," he muttered, his blue eyes flashing with contempt. "Lad's been given free rein for too long, and it's been the ruin of him. He'll come to a bad end, mark me."

Since she could not in all good conscience defend William, Elizabeth decided a change of topic was clearly in order and began describing last night's masquerade with a great deal more enthusiasm than she'd felt for the actual event. She was describing the various costumes worn by the guests as the carriage rolled up to the front doors.

Judging from the army of footmen who swarmed out of the house to meet them, Elizabeth assumed Lord Falconer must have arrived ahead of them with news of their unexpected guests. Her assumption proved correct a few moments later when Lady Derring came scurrying forward to greet them.

"Dear Lord Creshton, how wonderful to see you!" she exclaimed, holding out her hand for his kiss. "And Lady Elinore. I vow we are honored; one hears you so seldom leave the country these days!"

Lady Elinore offered her cheek for a quick buzz. "How could I possibly resist the lure of one of your parties, my lady?" she asked, her smile as sweetly insincere as the countess's own. "And I hear you have been making quite merry without me. Last night's masquerade sounds most delightful."

"You have heard of that?" Lady Derring preened with delight.

"Miss Mattingale was kind enough to describe it to me," Lady Elinore said, including Elizabeth in the conversation. "She is full of praise for you, my lady, and says you worked like a Trojan to get everything done just so."

As it happened Elizabeth had said nothing of the kind, and she was deeply grateful for the other woman's tact. It would seem Lady Elinore was as kind as she was beautiful, and she could understand why Falconer had offered for her. Perhaps there was more to the cool, self-possessed young beauty than she had first supposed.

"I did work rather hard," Lady Derring allowed with a simper. "Indeed, I have been resting all day from my labors. I—" She broke off suddenly and frowned at Elizabeth.

"Miss Mattingale, I quite forgot, but my husband has been asking for you all morning. He said you were to go directly to his study the very moment you returned."

Sensing an escape, Elizabeth dropped a curtsy and hurried up the stairs to where the earl's private study was located. It had been pointed out to her shortly after her arrival, and she'd been admonished never to venture inside. This would be her first glimpse of the room, and she was more than a little curious to see if it resembled the rest of the house.

"Enter." The earl's curt greeting made Elizabeth jump, and she stepped cautiously into the room.

"I am sorry for disturbing you, my lord," she began, swallowing nervously at the harsh expression on the earl's face. "Is there something you wish?"

In answer he rose from his chair behind the desk and placed his hands on the lapels of his dark jacket. "Come in, Miss Mattingale, if you would," he said, his voice as cold as his expression. "And close the door behind you."

More alarmed than ever, Elizabeth did as instructed, crossing the room to stand nervously before the desk. The letter, she thought, her heart beating a frantic tattoo within her breast. *He knows about the letter.*

The earl continued glowering at her. "Well?" he snapped out, his face reddening with temper.

Elizabeth moistened her lips. "Well what, my lord?" she asked, genuinely puzzled by the clipped demand.

"Well, what is this about you being a demmed Frenchie spy?"

Seven

"Who says Miss Mattingale is a spy?"

Adam bit off the low command furiously, his jaw
clenched as he struggled to gain control over his errant
emotions. He'd only just reached his rooms, and learning
that the earl's missing papers and Elizabeth's part in their
disappearance was a matter of open speculation for the
other guests had set fire to his temper.

"Everyone, my lord," his valet replied, wringing his
hands in his agitation. " 'Tis all the talk above- and be-
lowstairs. Lord Trewby's valet says he overheard Mr. Colburt talking to his master, and he said he was going to
suggest Lord Derring have the magistrate in to search her
room."

Adam's eyes flashed with deadly fury. "Did he, by
gad?" he growled, and swung toward the door.

"My lord!" His valet leapt in front of him, his arms
spread out as he blocked Adam's path. "Where are you
going?"

Adam glared at him. "To speak with Lord Derring, of
course. The sooner this nonsense is nipped in the bud, the
better."

"But you are still in your riding togs!" his valet wailed,
indicating Adam's elegant attire with a wave of his hand.
"You must know this will not do." He straightened with
pride. "We have standards."

Adam's lips thinned in a dangerous line. "Our standards be damned," he snarled, and stormed out of the room.

He reached the top of the stairs when the door to one of the bedchambers opened and Lord Creshton stepped out into the hall.

"Ah, there you are," he said, blue eyes bright with pleasure. "I was hoping someone would come along to show me the way to the drawing room. Place is a dashed rabbit warren." His smile faded when he noted the dark expression on Adam's face. "What is it?"

Adam was in too much of a hurry for protracted explanations. "The word is out about the missing papers," he said, starting down the stairs. "And that devil Colburt is doing his best to lay the blame for it at Elizabeth's doorstep."

To his surprise the duke laid a detaining hand on his arm. "A moment, Falconer, if you would," he said, his expression stern. "Before you go tearing off to defend your lady fair, might I suggest you at least consider the possibility he could be right?"

Adam couldn't have been more stunned had the duke kicked him down the stairs. He wanted to shout curses at the older man for daring to cast aspersions on Elizabeth's name, and yet how could he, he wondered bitterly, when he had done the very same thing?

"I have considered it," he said in a tight voice, hating himself for the fact. "And I rejected it. Elizabeth is no thief."

"And if you are wrong?" the duke pressed, holding Adam's gaze with his own. "What then?"

Adam stiffened in awareness. The duke had contacts everywhere, including the Home Office. What did he know? Adam wondered rawly. And what did it portend for Elizabeth?

"What are you saying?" he asked, his fingers tightening on the rail until he feared the wood would splinter beneath his hand.

"I am saying Miss Mattingale is a most interesting lady with some most interesting associates. As you yourself pointed out in your missive, she has only recently returned to England from an extended stay abroad, and she has a close relative living in a country hostile to our own. In my mind, she bears watching."

Adam felt suddenly ill. He lowered his head, his eyes squeezing shut as he ground out, "Elizabeth would not betray her country. She could not. She doesn't have it in her to do something so vile."

"I am sure she does not," the duke agreed. "But it is a possibility that cannot be discounted merely because we find it not to our liking."

Adam's head snapped up in disbelief. "Then you're saying I should say nothing and let an innocent woman be taken up on charges I know to be false?" he demanded furiously.

"Indeed not," Creshton assured him, his lips curving in a crafty smile. "Defend her by all means, if that is your wish. If she is innocent, it will do no harm, and should she be guilty, having her believe she has gulled us can only work to our advantage."

Adam was appalled, both by the duke's icy pragmatism and by the realization he'd once been as coldly calculating. *Emotionless as a block of stone.* The words Elinore had flung at him along with his offer of marriage came back to taunt him, and he shuddered at the memories they invoked. The man he'd been had no room in his life for emotion, and so he'd shut it out, blockading his heart from any possible hurt. The realization that he was no longer that man occurred, but he brushed it ruthlessly aside. At the moment Elizabeth was all that mattered, and with that thought in mind he started back down the stairs again. But first—

"Elizabeth is not a spy," he stated coldly, shooting the duke a warning glance over his shoulder. "And anyone who says otherwise had best be prepared for a fight."

* * *

"Well, miss?" The earl glowered down at Elizabeth. "What is your answer? Or do you mean to stand there and tell me you have no idea what I am talking about?"

Elizabeth fought the urge to swoon, her nails digging into the palms of her hands. The pain helped her concentrate, and she used it to beat off the waves of darkness swirling about her. This is a nightmare, she thought, clenching her hands tighter, and what made it more horrific was the knowledge that this was a nightmare from which there was no awakening.

"But I don't know, my lord," she insisted, scrambling to organize her thoughts into some semblance of order. Clearly the letter from her father had been discovered and read, and the worst possible connotation put upon it. But who had found the letter? And more importantly, why had they been looking for it?

Lord Derring's unprepossessing features twisted themselves into a sneer. "You will forgive me if I fail to be moved by your protestations of innocence," he said, the lash of the words as sharp and cruel as a whip. "Of course you took the papers."

Now there was no need for Elizabeth to feign her confusion. "What papers?" she demanded, frowning. "Lord Derring, I truly have no notion what you are talking about!"

"The papers from my dispatch box that have gone missing," he replied, smirking at her stunned expression. "And kindly spare me the look of wide-eyed horror, madam. You know full well what I mean. Those papers are vital to England's security, and if you do not surrender them at once I'll hand you over to the magistrate for the king's justice. We'll see how pert you are when you are dangling from the end of the rope," he added, gloating when she turned pale in horror.

Despite her terror and confusion, Elizabeth's pride stirred to life. It was one thing to allow herself to be sneered at and accused of an unspeakable crime, she decided, but it was another to allow herself to be browbeaten by a pompous, self-important prig like the earl. She drew herself up, meeting his malevolent stare with what equanimity she could gather.

"I know nothing of your missing papers, my lord, and that is the truth," she said coolly. "If you have proof otherwise, then let me see it. I will not allow you to slander me."

The earl's jaw dropped, and his eyes flew so wide, Elizabeth expected them to pop. "You won't allow—" he began, sputtering in indignation. "By heavens, gel, do you know to whom you are speaking? I can have you hanged!"

The door flew open behind Elizabeth and Adam strode in, his face set in a harsh mask of displeasure.

"What is going on?" he demanded, glaring at the earl as he took his place beside Elizabeth. He didn't touch her, but his presence was vastly comforting as he smiled at her. "Are you all right?" he asked, his voice gentle.

"Is she all right?" Lord Derring all but shrieked the words, his face red with indignation. "What the devil ails you, sir? She stole my papers!"

Adam glanced up, silencing the blustering earl with no more than a look. "Did she?" he asked coldly. "What proof have you?"

"Proof?" Derring repeated, his voice as high-pitched as a cat's. "Proof?"

"Proof," Adam repeated in accents of icy displeasure. "You may be an earl, but even an earl must have proof before having a person hanged. That is what you were threatening to do when I walked in, was it not?" he added, his eyes taking on a menacing sheen that had the earl turning pale in alarm.

"Who else could it be?" he protested, pointing an accusing finger at Elizabeth. "Speaks French, don't she? *And* is as close as you please to that Russian prince! Always chattering with him so no one understands a word of what is being said, and saying who knows what? I shouldn't be surprised if it was him who put her up to it!"

Elizabeth opened her lips to leap to Alexi's defense only to have Adam silence her with a warning nudge.

"His highness is a member of the Grand Duchess's retinue," he reminded Derring. "And as such he must be considered a foreign diplomat. If you accuse him without proof, it could cause a rift in the Alliance." His eyebrows arched in unmistakable challenge. "Are you accusing him, my lord?"

"Certainly not!" the older man denied, appalled.

"Then why do you mention him?" Adam was relentless.

"I—well, because, that is why!" Derring exclaimed, clearly outgunned and realizing the futility of his position.

" 'Because' is not good enough," Adam told him, his smile decidedly wolfish. "This is England, sir, not France, where one may be shut in prison upon another's whim. Show me your proof against Miss Mattingale or it is *you* I shall have brought up on charges of gross incompetence and neglect. The papers disappeared while in your possession, if I may remind you, and it is you who must account for their whereabouts. You muddy the waters by casting aspersions upon her, and one is left to wonder why."

"The papers!" the earl latched eagerly on to the words. "That is my proof! If we find the papers in her possession, that will prove she is a thief. And a traitor," he added, shooting her a gleeful smirk.

Adam turned to Elizabeth, touching her for the first time as he took her hand in his. "Miss Mattingale," he began, the warm look in his eyes belying the formality of his words, "will you consent to having your rooms searched? Understand we cannot compel you to do so at this time," he continued, ignoring the earl's muttered imprecations, "but it would help resolve this unpleasantness as quickly as possible."

Elizabeth nodded, accepting that she had no other choice. "Certainly, my lord," she said, praying whoever had read her letter hadn't left behind anything of an incriminating nature. "I should be delighted to be of assistance. Search my room, by all means."

A hasty council of war was held, with Adam quickly assuming command. It was decided that the earl, his wife, Adam, and the Duke of Creshton would search her room while Elizabeth waited for them in the countess's study. The arrangement was not at all to her liking, but she supposed it might have been worse. She could have spent her time locked in the cellar awaiting their pleasure.

They stepped out into the hall and were stunned to find several of the other guests clustered around the door. Elizabeth was painfully aware of their suspicious glances, and of the angry mutters of "Jezebel!" and "Traitor!" being aimed at her.

"*Syestra!*" Alexi pushed his way through the crowd, his handsome face set in furious lines. "What is this? Who dares accuse you of thievery?" He rounded on the earl, his hand closing around the sword fastened at his side. "You?" he demanded, taking a menacing step forward.

The earl swayed and stumbled back. "I—I—"

Adam stepped in front of him, placing himself between the terrified earl and the prince.

"There is no need for bloodshed, your highness," he said, fixing Alexi with a warning look. "His lordship is as anxious to clear up this small misunderstanding as are we. Aren't you, my lord?" And he glanced at the earl.

"Eh?" The earl's gaze flicked from Adam's hard face to Alexi's hand, still resting threateningly on the hilt of his battle sword. "Indeed, your highness," he stammered, bobbing his head in agreement. "Most anxious!"

Evidently assured that the earl wasn't about to be slaughtered where he stood, Adam addressed their fascinated audience.

"Miss Mattingale has consented to having her room searched to locate the missing papers," he informed them in the cool, imperious tones Elizabeth had once found so vexing. "She does so freely, with no coercion from anyone. I trust when they are not found, the rest of you shall prove equally as cooperative."

Even as the others began vociferously voicing their objections in loud, indignant voices, Alexi was nodding.

"*Da,* and you may begin first with my rooms. I insist." he said, blue eyes contemptuous as his glance flicked over the others. Without waiting to hear their response, he laid a gentle arm across Elizabeth's shoulders.

"Come, little queen," he murmured, his touch comforting. "You are looking tired. You will allow me to escort you."

Acting on her direction, he led her to the smaller drawing room, where the countess entertained her guests. The others followed them, and battle lines were soon drawn. Alexi and Elizabeth sat on one side of the room, the rest of the company on the other, the middle of the room lying between them like a wasteland.

Despite her attempts to send him away, Alexi remained at her side, pressing food and tea upon her and ignoring the others with regal disdain.

"You are only making matters worse, you know," she hissed, her face pinking with embarrassment at the daggers being cast at her. "Those who won't think me guilty of selling my country's secrets will now have me warming your bed."

Alexi's mouth thinned with anger. "Let them say such a thing to me and I will take much delight in correcting them," he said, making no attempt to lower his voice. "And the ladies need not think their sex will protect them. A word from me to her Imperial Majesty, and they will find they are not welcome in her presence."

The threat had the desired effect, and several of the ladies looked as if they might swoon. The fêtes and balls being planned around the visit of the Russian court were all anyone could speak of, and the thought of being excluded from the festivities was too terrifying to be borne. The mutters stopped and the glares lost much of their heat, but none of the ladies, Elizabeth noted, made a move toward them. She was trying to decide how she felt about that when Lady Barrington picked up her cup and crossed the room to join them. She had a catlike smile on her lips and a speculative look in her blue eyes that had Elizabeth stiffening in awareness. Alexi sensed her unease and bristled protectively at her side.

"Peace, your highness," Lady Barrington drawled with an amused laugh as Alexi rose to his feet to greet her. "I am only here to offer Miss Mattingale good day and my support, should she have need of it." She cast a cool glance over a creamy shoulder at the others, who were now clearly whispering about her.

"Gossip is such a tiresome thing, don't you agree?" she observed, turning back to Elizabeth. "All the more so when it is fueled by nothing more than boredom and idle speculation."

Elizabeth felt a sharp stab of guilt at the duchess's words. There'd been a great deal of gossip regarding her grace, and to her shame, she'd believed every word of it. Given the kindness the other lady had shown her, what did that make her? The words also made her realize that she'd been behaving like a coward, sitting in meek silence while her friends defended her. Well, no more, she vowed, her mouth firming in resolve. From now on she would defend herself, and heaven help those foolish enough to attack her.

"That is so, your grace," she said, offering the other woman a smile of kinship. "And the more bored the tattler, the more vicious the tattle, or so I have observed." The outraged gasp from across the room made it plain her little barb had struck home, and Elizabeth was human enough the savor the small victory.

At Alexi's insistence the duchess joined them, and the two shared an animated conversation on the coming festivities. Elizabeth was content to sit back in silence, sipping her tea and trying not to think about what was happening in her rooms. Over half an hour had passed; she brooded, doing her best not to take another peek at the clock on the mantelpiece. What had they found, she wondered, and what would happen to her if what they found were the earl's missing papers?

"But of course your grace must call upon the Grand Duchess!" Alexi's voice recalled her back to the present, and she glanced up to find him beaming at Lady Barrington. "It will be my pleasure to introduce you, *dama*. You will come to visit us in London, yes?"

The duchess murmured the proper words of gratitude, and Elizabeth fell back to brooding. Lady Elinore entered the drawing room, her sharp gaze noting the division between the two groups. Without hesitating, she walked over to join Elizabeth.

Since it was evident Lady Barrington and Lady Elinore were already acquainted, Elizabeth introduced her to Alexi, and wasn't in the least surprised when Alexi immediately began flirting with the haughty beauty.

"Lady Elinore, a pleasure, I am sure." Alexi was all charm as he kissed her hand. "Such beautiful women England has. No wonder that devil Bonaparte was so determined to conquer you. He wished to claim all you charming ladies as his own."

Elinore stiffened, her gray eyes chilling. "We charming ladies may have had something to say about that, your highness," she said, withdrawing her hand and turning a slender shoulder on him.

Elizabeth saw the shock and then the annoyance flare in Alexi's eyes. It was quickly followed by a sparkle of pure masculine determination, and she hid a quick smile. If Lady Elinore had taken Alexi into dislike, she would have to have a quiet word with her. Alexi was too much the autocrat to tolerate a snub, and he was also far too much the rake to allow a beautiful woman to treat him with such disdain. Whether or not it had been her intention, the other woman had just issued a challenge.

Elizabeth's smile faded as quickly as it had bloomed, and she stole another glance at the clock. Forty minutes, she thought, chewing her bottom lip. What was keeping them?

"Nothing." Adam didn't even attempt to mask the satisfaction in his voice as he met the earl's baffled stare. "Just as I told you there would be."

They were standing in the plain, almost bare room Elizabeth occupied, the contents of her drawers and trunks spread about them. Touching her things and watching the others rifle through her few belongings had struck Adam as the foulest sort of violation, and he was determined someone would pay dearly for causing Elizabeth a moment's pain.

"But I do not understand," Derring said, looking genuinely baffled as he gazed about him. "I was led to believe the papers would be here."

"Led to believe by whom?" Creshton demanded, before Adam could speak. "Think, man!" he barked when the earl remained silent. "It is of vital importance!"

"I don't know!" Derring exclaimed, looking ill. "A note was slipped under my study door this morning, suggesting the papers would be found here."

"Let me see it," Adam demanded, holding out his hand imperiously. Derring hesitated and then handed over the neatly folded piece of paper.

Adam unfolded it, his face impassive as he glanced at the note. The script was crabbed, almost illegible, making it impossible to tell if the writer had been a man or a woman. The words, however, were perfectly plain.

That which you seek is in the companion's room.

He re-read the letter a second time before handing it to the duke.

"Written with the left hand, I shouldn't doubt. A common practice when one wishes to disguise one's identity," Creshton said, handing it back to Adam. Without a qualm of guilt, he slipped it into his pocket.

"I—I beg pardon, my lord," Derring stammered, looking properly outraged, "but I believe that is mine."

Adam studied him with icy calm. "And your pardon, sir, if I should choose not to return it. Papers have a way of disappearing about you, I've noted."

"Lord Falconer! I must protest!" Lady Derring bristled in outrage. "You will not insult my husband in his own home."

"Why should I not?" Adam challenged, making no attempt to soften either his tone or his expression. "He didn't hesitate to insult Miss Mattingale."

The countess gave a loud snort. "That is hardly the same thing, my lord, and well you know it. My husband is a peer of England and a member of the Privy Council. Miss Mattingale is . . . or rather, *was,* my companion. Naturally"—her thin lips twisted in a self-satisfied smile—"I shall have no choice but to dismiss her."

"Good."

"I think not."

Adam and the duke spoke at the same time, and Creshton silenced Adam with a speaking look before turning to Derring. "We shall speak later, my lord," he told the earl. "But in the meanwhile, you will give me your word you will not allow anyone—guest or servant—to leave this house until the missing papers have been located. Is that understood?"

Derring opened his mouth and then apparently thought better of it. "Yes, your grace," he said, nodding stiffly. "As you wish."

"Why the devil did you do that?" Adam demanded the moment the door had closed behind the Derrings. "Surely you can see it is best for Elizabeth to be out from beneath that harpy's thumb!"

"And surely you can see allowing her to leave would tip our hand to the real thief," Creshton answered calmly. "He has gone to some risk to point us in Miss Mattingale's direction. If we let her go, he will know he has failed. It will better suit our purpose to leave things as they are, for the moment, at least."

Much as he would have liked to deny it, Adam was forced to admit the duke's objections made sense. "But if we don't have her taken up, won't that be obvious?" he asked after a moment, forcing himself to view things from a strictly pragmatic point of view.

"Perhaps," the duke said with an eloquent shrug. "But again, that is something we can only turn to our advantage. Since it will be impossible to keep secret the fact that our search turned up nothing of interest, we simply allow people to hear the tattle and think what they will."

Adam's lips thinned in a grim line as he considered the most likely response. "Most will think her guilty and make her life a sweet hell."

"That cannot be helped, I fear," the duke's reply was inflexible. "And who is to say she is not guilty?" he added, studying Adam with a lift of his brows. "She could simply be clever enough to have found another hiding place for the missing papers. Or she may even have managed to smuggle them out of the house. That is what I should have done."

Adam shifted uncomfortably, the need to defend Elizabeth warring with his duty to his title and his king. He *knew* she was innocent, and yet could he wager that knowledge against his country's safety? If there was even the smallest chance she could be involved, how could he let her go? And if she was innocent, how could he stand by silently and let her face her accusers alone?

"What is next to be done?" he asked, his head beginning to pound from the battle inside his head.

"Next I shall return to London," Creshton replied decisively. "I'll meet with the Home Secretary and apprise him of matters here. I'll also contact the Foreign Secretary and seek his advice. Prince Bronyeskin presents something of a complication, and I fear it may prove necessary to remove him."

Adam thought of the volatile Russian prince he'd come

to admire, despite his many doubts. "What do you mean 'remove'?" he asked, eyeing the duke suspiciously.

The duke gave a rich chuckle. "Nothing so grim as what you seem to think," he said, his eyes twinkling. "I merely meant I may have to arrange to have him recalled to London. It's dashed odd he should be here in the first place, if you want my opinion. But"—he waved his hand, dismissing the matter—"that is for another time. First things first, eh?"

"Yes, your grace," Adam agreed, thinking proving Elizabeth innocent was the first of his priorities. "But it is a pity I shan't have more time with you—and Lady Elinore, of course," he added, not wishing to appear less than a gentleman.

"Oh, Elinore remains here," the duke replied, studying Adam with an enigmatic expression. "The agent I spoke of, remember? He can hardly be here if she is not, what?"

Adam grimaced, recalling the footman Creshton had only just put into place. "I'd forgotten about that," he admitted, feeling sheepish. "But won't it be considered odd if she remains behind when you leave?"

"Shouldn't think so." Creshton led the way out into the hall, carefully closing the door behind them. "Gel's no green miss in the midst of her first Season, you know. She is more than of an age to make country visits without her papa trailing at her heels. Besides"—the smile he sent Adam could only be described as a smirk—"she already has the perfect reason for extending her stay."

Adam braced himself as if for a blow. "What reason is that?" he asked, already fearing he knew the answer.

"You, of course. She'll put it out, reluctantly of course, that she is here to consider if an agreement between the pair of you will suit."

Even though he'd been expecting it, Adam felt himself pale. "I beg your pardon?"

The duke gave a delighted chortle of laughter.

"You needn't look so horrified, old boy," he said, clapping a friendly hand on Adam's shoulder. "You had your

chance with the gel and you failed. No need to think Elinore would give you another. Besides, how else is she to
meet with you so that you may pass on what you have
learned?"

That was so, and Adam resisted the urge to heave a
relieved sigh. Then he thought of all that could happen
should the thief learn the truth behind Lady Elinore's presence.

"I'm not certain I approve of your making use of your
daughter in this fashion," he informed the duke as they
made their way down to the floor where the guests' rooms
were located. "What if something goes wrong?"

"I look to you to see that it does not," Creshton said,
shaking a thick finger at Adam. "Guard my little chick
well, Falconer, else I shall be most displeased."

It was past midnight before Charles was able to slip
away from the rest of the house party. The others were
already abed or engaged in some silly game or another,
and he was fairly confident his absence would not be
noted. And even if it was, what matter? He'd already seen
to it that the wagging tongues had more than enough to
keep them occupied.

The news that the earl had given orders that no one
was to leave the Hall until the papers were found caused
almost as much tattle as the fact Miss Mattingale had been
exonerated of all suspicions. It was obvious most of the
guests still believed otherwise, and Charles had done his
best to add to their suspicions, tossing out just enough
hints to make them wonder. Charles was also wondering,
and the sort of things he was wondering had the sweat
breaking on his forehead.

"I thought I made it plain you were not to contact me."

The soft voice sounded from the shadows, and Charles
whirled around as the hooded figure emerged from the
darkness.

"You lied to me!" he accused hotly, taking care to keep

his voice low-pitched. "You told me the papers would be found in that bitch's room, and they were not!"

"Of course they are there," the figured soothed, inching closer. "Those idiots just didn't look hard enough. Tell them to look again."

The memory of the chance he'd taken slipping the note under the earl's door had Charles sweating anew. *"You* tell them to look again!" he snapped. "Wills told me his father said they did everything but tear up the floorboards, and they didn't find anything, not even those damned letters you told me about!"

The figure jerked as if in shock. "They didn't find the letters?"

"No, they did not," Charles replied, temper and fear making him incautious. "If they even existed in the first place, which I am beginning to doubt."

There was a charged silence, and then the figure gave a wry chuckle. "Really, Charles, you're not questioning my honesty, are you?"

Charles thought of whom he was dealing with, and the suspicions he was beginning to have. "No, of course not!" he denied hastily. "It's just that Wills is beginning to make noises; saying we had ought to give the papers back before someone gets hurt. He says if I don't give them back by the end of the week, he'll tell his papa I am the one who took the damned things."

"Does he?" The figure sounded thoughtful. "That could make things awkward."

Charles thought of what could happen to him and tossed caution to the four winds. "Awkward?" he repeated with an ugly laugh. "They could hang me! And if they hang me, you had best be certain I shall make certain you are there beside me. Taking those papers was your idea, and so I shall tell them!"

There was another silence. "That sounds suspiciously like a threat," the figure observed coolly.

"And if it is?" he asked, deciding he'd had enough. He was the one who'd first thought of making Miss Mattingale the object of tattle, he reminded himself. Mayhap it was time he was taking charge of things, instead of playing the obedient lapdog.

"Then I take leave to tell you I do not take well to threats."

Now that he'd worked up his courage, Charles wasn't about to surrender his hard-won position. "I don't care if you take to them or not!" he sneered. "I'll tell, do you hear me? I'll tell them all about you."

"I hear you."

Charles turned his back at the quiet words, gazing out at the moonlit garden. "Then mind you believe me," he said, a feeling of raw power surging through him. To the devil with that damned prince and Falconer, he thought smugly. They'd just see who was the one to be reckoned with.

"Oh, I believe you, Charles," the figure purred, moving behind him. "I believe you." And slid the stiletto into Charles's back without a moment's hesitation.

Eight

"Will there be anything else, Miss Mattingale?" The footman hovered attentively at Elizabeth's elbow, the silver coffeepot clutched in his hand. "Some eggs, perhaps, or some ham?"

Despite her exhaustion, Elizabeth scraped up a smile for his benefit. "No, thank you, Thomas," she managed, her stomach rolling at the thought of food. "I fear I'm not very hungry this morning."

The footman's face flushed a dull red, and he ducked his head. "No, miss," he said, looking down. "I don't reckon you are." He stepped over to the sideboard, busying his hands for several moments before clearing his throat.

"Miss Mattingale?"

Elizabeth's fingers tightened about her cup. "Yes, Thomas?" she asked, steeling herself for his words of reproach. She'd spent most of last evening sitting in stoic silence while the other guests poked and jabbed at her. She supposed she would have to do the same while the servants let their opinion of her be known. Heaven knew it couldn't be any worse than what she'd already heard.

"I just wanted to say, miss, we—t'other servants n' me—we none of us think you done like they say," he said, his words tumbling over each other in a heartfelt rush. " 'Tis nonsense, and we know it. You're a lady."

The awkward words brought the sting of tears to Elizabeth's eyes. Dealing with kindness, she discovered, was much harder than dealing with animosity. With animosity one had but to construct barricades strong enough to keep out the pain, but there was no such defense against those who cared about you.

"Thank you, Thomas," she said, struggling not to cry. "That means a great deal to me. Please tell the others I am most grateful for their faith in me."

"Yes, miss," he said, and then, as if fearing he'd said more than was proper, he picked up the coffeepot and fled the room.

When she was certain she was alone Elizabeth indulged in a brief bout of tears, giving in to the fear and despair she'd refused to acknowledge, even to herself. Yesterday had been the most horrific day in her life, and she knew that had it not been for Adam and Alexi standing so solidly at her side, it would have been worse. Only their presence, she was certain, kept her from being clapped in gaol. As it was, she might as well be locked away, for all the freedom she would have.

"The fact that we failed to discover the missing papers in your possession changes nothing, Miss Mattingale," the earl had informed her during their private interview. "You are still suspect, and you may be very sure your every movement will be scrutinized.

"Naturally," he'd added, his eyes sparkling with malevolent glee, "you may not leave the grounds until this matter has been resolved. His grace's orders, you understand."

The idea of the powerful duke thinking her guilty was terrifying, and she wondered if even the support of her two knights-errant would be enough to protect her. *If* he thought she was guilty, that is, she brooded, dabbing at her cheeks. He'd been unfailingly kind to her last evening, and his daughter hadn't left her side for more than a few minutes. Surely he wouldn't allow Lady Elinore to consort with her if he suspected her of treason?

She was puzzling over the matter when she suddenly sensed she was no longer alone. Glancing up, she was annoyed to see the earl's younger son standing in the doorway. When he saw she'd finally noticed him, Mr. Carling nervously cleared his throat.

"Good morning, Miss Mattingale," he said, tugging at his cravat. "Might I join you? I'd like to speak with you, if I may."

Suspecting a trap, she inclined her head with wary graciousness. "Certainly, Mr. Carling. What is it?"

He shuffled into the room, his actions reminding her of a guilty pupil about to confess some heinous crime to his tutor.

"I—dashed awkward business, this," he muttered, taking his seat at the table and looking everywhere but at her.

"Awkward for me most certainly," she replied coolly, her eyes narrowing as she studied him. She'd noticed him watching her several times last evening, a look she couldn't describe on his unprepossessing features. He was up to something, she was certain, and her heart began hammering with a cautious sense of fury as she considered what that *something* might be.

He bobbed his head, his fleshy cheeks turning a bright pink. "To be sure," he agreed, picking up a knife, studying it, and setting it down carefully again. "I just wanted to apologize for my parents," he began, addressing his remarks to the table. "Mama's mama, don't you know, and the pater has always been a bit of a rasher of wind. Still, it will all turn out right in the end."

"Will it?" Elizabeth concentrated on keeping her voice from betraying her anger. Why hadn't she thought of this before? she wondered, annoyed she'd allowed her fear to block her reason. The missing papers smacked of nothing more than a schoolboy's prank, and the lout sitting across from her and his doltish friends were three of the biggest schoolboys in the vicinity.

"Bound to, eh?" Mr. Carling raised his eyes to hers

and quickly lowered them again. "Those papers are only mislaid; I am sure of it. Once they are found, all will be forgotten."

"One may only hope, Mr. Carling," she said, seeing no reason why she shouldn't make him experience a little of what she had endured. "Since I am like to hang if they should not be found."

He grew even redder, the tips of his ears fairly glowing. "Oh, they will be found," he said, the panicked edge in his voice confirming her suspicions. "In fact, I—I think we had ought to look for them. That ought to be fun, eh? Like a—a treasure hunt."

Elizabeth refrained from pointing out that there'd been no trace of the papers found last evening, despite the fact that more than half of the guests' rooms had been meticulously searched. Still, if the search revealed the missing papers, who was she to argue with the results?

"That might be just the thing," she agreed cautiously. "Where should we start the search, do you think?"

Mr. Carling's head came up, the expression of relief on his face obvious. "I'll just ask Charles!" he exclaimed, leaping to his feet. "He knows—that is," he corrected hastily, "he will know where to start looking. He's a dashed clever fellow, you know."

Elizabeth's lips thinned in a bitter smile. "Oh, yes, I know."

"I'll just go find him, then," he said, hurrying to the door. "You've not seen him this morning, have you? We was to ride out earlier this morning, but he never came."

Thinking it was just as well she hadn't seen the wretch, Elizabeth shook her head. "No, I have not."

Mr. Carling frowned. "Not like him to miss a gallop," he said, looking vaguely concerned. "Especially since he knew I was most anxious to speak with him."

"Perhaps he is merely still abed?" Elizabeth suggested. "He's prone to late hours, I take it."

"But his bed wasn't slept in," Mr. Carling said, and then blushed again as he realized the inappropriateness of his remark. "That is, I am sure that must be it. I'll just have his man take another look. Good morning, Miss Mattingale, and—and I am sorry for all this. I am truly sorry." And he bolted before she could think of the words to stop him.

Elizabeth scarce had time to draw a breath before a scowling Alexi stormed into the room.

"What was that *sabaka* doing in here?" he demanded, blue eyes stormy. "If he has upset you—"

"No, he hasn't upset me," Elizabeth retorted, gesturing at the chair opposite her. "Stop growling, Alexi, and sit down. I'm too tired to put up with your nonsense this morning."

Looking highly aggrieved, Alexi did as she ordered. "To protect a sister is not nonsense," he muttered. "And you would not be so tired if these English were not so thick in their heads. It is all the pudding they eat, yes? It makes them slow and stupid."

The return of Thomas and another of the footmen bearing fresh coffee and rolls prevented Elizabeth from responding. She waited until Alexi had been served his usual mountain of food before sending them away with a murmur of thanks.

"Now, little queen," Alexi began, before Elizabeth could speak, "enough of this dallying. You will tell me, then, why that dog was here. But I warn you," he added, pointing his fork at her, "if I learn he has made the bother, it will go very bad with him."

The confession she'd been about to make withered on Elizabeth's lips. "He wanted to apologize," she said, thinking it might make better sense to share her suspicions with the marquess first. He was much less volatile than Alexi, if no less dangerous.

"Oh," she added, as if in afterthought, "he also wanted to know if I'd seen Mr. Colburt. It seems he missed his riding appointment."

Alexi shrugged his shoulders and reached for another

roll. "Shake out the beds of the maids and the lady guests. He is bound to come tumbling out of one of them."

"Alexi!"

"What?" He glanced up indignantly. "Is truth, is it not? Colburt forever chases the ladies. I hear them laughing about it, when he is not there to hear. Or at least some of them laugh. Others make face. Like this." And he screwed up his face in a parody of feminine disgust.

Elizabeth enjoyed her first laugh in what seemed like days. She'd seen that very expression on the faces of several of the more discerning guests. "Well, wherever he may have spent the night, poor Mr. Carling seemed quite concerned," she said, and then paused as a sudden suspicion dawned.

"Alexi"—she fixed him with a stern look—"you didn't do anything to Mr. Colburt, did you?"

"Me?" Alexi was outraged, "What would I do to that one?"

"Any number of things," she retorted, her head reeling at the possibilities. "All of them unpleasant and certain to cause a scandal."

Another shrug. "What do I care for scandal?" he asked coolly, buttering his roll. "If I wanted to harm that pig I would do it, so"—he made a twisting gesture with the knife—"where everyone could see me. If you think he has come to harm, it is your *Breetanskee* lord you should be scolding, and not Alexi. He had Colburt by the throat the other evening and shook him like the rodent he is. But you do not lecture his lordship, I see. Only me do you treat so."

Elizabeth ignored the stab of guilt. "Lord Falconer has not appointed himself my brother," she informed Alexi coolly. "And speaking of his lordship, I want you to promise you'll stop insulting everyone in Russian and asking me to translate. He is already suspicious, and things are sticky enough as it is without your adding even more fuel to the fire."

He went on eating as if she hadn't spoken. "I will think

about it," he agreed in an off-handed manner that had her glaring.

"I mean it, Alexi," she scolded. "You take too many chances. Sooner or later you are going to be found out."

"And if I am? I am a prince; what can they do to me? Besides"—he sent her a wink—"it is the chance of discovery that makes the game worth the playing. But for your sake, I will do as you ask. I would not risk you for anything."

"Alexi—"

"Good morning, Miss Mattingale, your highness." Lord Falconer strode into the room, looking handsome and more remote than ever in his somber jacket of dove-gray Superfine, his black hair brushed back from the sharp bones of his lean face.

"Ah, Falconer, you are welcome to join us," Alexi greeted him with a wide smile and a grand sweep of his hand. "Come, be seated, and tell us how you are this fine morning."

"I am well, sir," came the clipped reply as the marquess took his seat. "And you, Miss Mattingale?" he asked coolly, his deep voice edged with frost as he studied her.

"I am also well," she replied, wondering what was ailing him. She wanted to believe his coolness was nothing more than ill temper, but a glance at his face put paid to that faint hope.

His jaw was clenched so tight, she marveled it didn't shatter, and the firm, sensual mouth she'd taken to studying was set in lines as hard and grim as a statue's. But it was his eyes that betrayed him most, their brilliant golden color as sharp and deadly as the blade of a knife. His lordship was coldly furious about something, and her instincts warned her that that something had to do with her.

"You just missed our host's foolish son," Alexi said, seemingly oblivious to the tension stretching like a taut line between she and Adam. "He was here looking for his friend. Did you see him?"

"Carling? I passed him in the hall," Adam returned,

keeping the full weight of his unblinking stare trained on Elizabeth.

"Not Carling." Alexi gave a genial chuckle, helping himself to more eggs. "The other; Colburt. He is missing, it would seem."

That caught Adam's notice, and his gaze cut to Alexi. "Missing? What do you mean?"

"I mean he is not where he should be," Alexi replied, his brows gathering in a frown. "Elizabeth said Carling told her that his bed had not been slept in, and he was worried."

Adam was on his feet. "He has been missing all night?" he demanded, his anger giving way to the keen awareness Elizabeth had seen in him before.

"Perhaps, but not so long as that, I think," Alexi replied, setting down his knife and fork and scowling up at Adam. "The man is like a stag in rut where women are concerned. Doubtless he found some woman foolish enough to welcome his advances and—"

"Murder! Murder!"

The high, keening scream erupted in the hall behind them, followed by raised voices and the sound of running feet. Adam and Alexi reached the door first, but when Elizabeth would have followed them into the hall, she found her way blocked by Adam.

"Where do you think you are going?" he demanded, his expression fierce as he glared down at her.

"With you, of course!" she snapped, too overset by the wails and screams echoing through the halls to care about the niceties. A pair of footmen went tearing past the door, one of them carrying what looked to be a battle-ax from the Hall's armory. She tried slipping under Adam's arm, only to have him deftly countering the move. He scooped her up in his arms and presented her to Alexi.

"Guard her," he ordered, meeting Alexi's gaze over the top of her head. "For God's sake, whatever you do, don't leave her alone!" And with that he was gone, ignoring her furious cries to come back and face her like a man.

* * *

Adam followed the screams to the conservatory, where a considerable crowd was already gathering. Shoving his way past the other guests, he saw an obviously shaken Lord Derring kneeling over Charles Colburt. Although he'd not seen as much death as his friend, Lord St. Jerome, Adam had seen enough to know Charles wouldn't be making any further mischief in this life.

"Murdered," Derring said, raising stunned eyes to Adam. "A guest. Murdered in my home."

Adam knelt beside the earl, ignoring the shrieks and oaths behind him as he studied Charles's body. He was laying on his back, staring up at them with wide, unseeing eyes, his features frozen in a look of shock and mild outrage. The black, sticky pool of blood spreading out from beneath him made it plain that the cries of "Murder!" had not been without some foundation.

"Who discovered the body?" he asked, his gaze never leaving the pathetic figure sprawled on the floor. Death had been kinder to Colburt than perhaps he deserved, and instead of seeing a malicious, self-satisfied dandy intent only upon his own shallow pleasures, Adam saw only a young man who had died much too soon and much too hard.

"William," Derring replied, rubbing a hand over his face and looking as ancient as the hall itself. "He—he has been looking for Charles all morning."

"It would seem he found him," Adam replied, appalled he could make a joke at such a time. He also wished he had a better idea of what was to be done. It was a pity Creshton had already left for London. He could have done with the older man's cagey intellect. Then he remembered the agent the duke had brought with him, and glanced up at the group of footmen huddled at the entrance to the conservatory.

"Which of you is in the Duke of Creshton's employ?"

he asked, his sharp gaze scanning them for a likely candidate.

"That would be Henry, my lord," one of the footmen Adam had seen several times took a hesitant step forward. "He went into the village with Lady Elinore."

Adam swallowed an impatient curse. He desperately wanted to speak with the other man, but he didn't want to do anything that might bring him to the attention of the thief who'd graphically demonstrated his willingness to kill. A glance at the earl showed he was in a state of shock, and Adam realized he'd just been handed the perfect excuse to take command of the situation.

"Take two footmen and fetch the magistrate and the militia," he said, getting to his feet and addressing his remarks to the footman who had spoken first. "Then ride into the village and bring Lady Elinore back to the Hall. Until we have more of an idea of what is going on, I don't want anyone wandering off by himself."

"Yes, my lord!"

Several of the footmen went tearing off, and those who remained glanced at Adam, clearly awaiting instructions. He didn't disappoint them.

"See this room is cleared," he ordered, his eyes hard. "Then set up a guard. No one is to enter unless I have given permission."

"Yes, Lord Falconer!" they said, and hurried over to where the subdued guests were gathered. They began shepherding everyone from the room, and although there were a few mutters of protest, most seemed content to do as ordered. When he was content his instructions were being carried out, Adam turned to Derring.

The earl had risen to his feet and was standing over Colburt's body, his expression dazed. Realizing he was as much in need of direction as his servants, Adam walked over to join him.

"My lord," he said, placing his hand on the earl's arm, "you need to see to your wife. She is certain to be overset."

Derring looked at him, his eyes dull with horror. "Yes," he said, making no attempt to move. "Daresay you are quite right."

When several seconds passed and he hadn't moved, Adam took matters into his own hands and gestured at one of the remaining footmen. "Your footman will take you to your rooms, your lordship," he told the other man in a gentle but firm voice. "I will see to matters here."

Lord Derring gave another vague nod. "I just can't seem to get past it, you know," he said to Adam, a bewildered note of apology in his voice. "Nothing like this has ever happened to me before. First the missing papers, and now this. It makes one wonder what will happen next."

After he'd gone, following after the attentive footman like a meek child, Adam took a few moments to steady his own nerves and then turned back to Colburt. He hadn't any real notion what he might be looking for, but a search of the dead man's pockets seemed the most likely place to start. He knelt once again and began carrying out his self-appointed task. He'd only just started when he glanced up and saw Prince Bronyeskin standing in the doorway.

"Elizabeth?" he asked, his concern shifting from Colburt to the one person who mattered most.

"With some of the other ladies," Bronyeskin assured him, walking over to join Adam. "She needed to do something, to be of help. It will take her mind off this." He glared down at Colburt's body.

"Stupid fool," he said, a note of cold disdain in his voice. "He might have chosen a better time to die."

"I have a feeling this wasn't his idea," Adam answered mildly.

The prince merely grunted, making it plain he still held the dead man to blame for his plight. He studied the body for several seconds before gesturing at the blood staining the gray flagstones of the conservatory. "He was shot, yes?"

"I don't know," Adam admitted, the same possibility

having already occurred to him. "And to be honest, I'm not certain how to check."

In answer, Bronyeskin joined him on the floor. "It is a small thing," he said, rolling Colburt onto his side and, with Adam's help, carefully pulling up the dead man's coat and waistcoat.

"Not shot," he said, peeling back the badly stained shirt and studying Colburt's back. "He was stabbed with a very thin, very sharp blade; a bayonet, perhaps, or a stiletto. The wound is small, do you see?" His finger indicated the deep cut.

Adam swallowed the bile rising in his throat. "Yes, I see," he said, forcing himself to be as cold and contained as the prince.

"An upper thrust, fast and sure," Bronyeskin concluded after examining the wound for several moments. "The amount of blood shows the heart was hit, and he likely died within seconds. It was well done." And with that he pulled the shirt and jacket back into place and rolled Colburt onto his back.

Adam gave him a considering look. "You seem to know a great deal of such things, your highness," he observed, rising to his feet and facing the other man.

The prince's blue eyes were as cold and empty as a winter's sky as he met Adam's gaze. "I was in battle. One becomes acquainted with death rather quickly. And no," he added, his lips lifting in a humorless smile, "I did not kill him."

Adam raised his eyebrows. "I don't believe I asked if you had, your highness."

"Your eyes asked," Bronyeskin said, his chin coming up with regal pride. "Make no mistake, my lord, had he hurt my Elizabeth, I would have killed Colburt with my bare hands and not cared who knew of it. But this"—he indicated the body and the conservatory with a wave of his hand—"this I did not do."

Adam's lips lifted in a half-smile. "Oddly enough, your highness, I believe you. Which begets the rather interesting question, if you didn't kill Colburt, who did? And why?"

Prince Bronyeskin gave a slow nod. "And you think the *why* more important, yes?"

Adam's respect for the prince's intelligence rose another notch. "I consider it of the greatest importance," he said coldly. "Because once I have the why, I'll have the *who.*"

"And when you have the who?" Bronyeskin's question was faintly challenging.

Adam's eyes took on a decided chill. "Then, your highness," he said softly, "I will have it all."

"Here you are, Miss Mattingale." Lady Elinore's gray eyes were soft with kindness as she handed Elizabeth a cup of tea. "You look as if you could do with a bit of nourishment."

"Thank you, my lady," Elizabeth replied, feeling a sharp stab of guilt at the other lady's thoughtfulness. With Lady Derring indisposed, it fell to her to look after the guests, not the other way around. Never mind that it was just the two of them in the small drawing room; duty was still duty, and Elizabeth vowed to do a better job at carrying out hers. It was the least she could do.

"How is Lady Derring?" Lady Elinore asked, her back ramrod straight as she studied Elizabeth over the edge of her teacup. "Have her nerves recovered as yet?"

Elizabeth thought of the near-hysterical woman she'd left tucked in her bed. "I am afraid not," she said, sighing. "Dr. Lambert had to be summoned, and he prescribed laudanum for her ladyship and some of the other guests."

Lady Elinore's lips curved in a half-smile. "That would explain the blessed silence, then. With all the wailing and howling going on, I'd begun thinking the Hall had been invaded by a tribe of dervishes."

Elizabeth choked on the mouthful of tea she'd just

sipped, her eyes wide as she gazed in amazement at the other woman.

"Now you think me quite dreadful," the pretty brunette murmured wryly, "and I would suppose you are right. But really, I hardly knew poor Mr. Colburt, and what I did know of the man was scarce flattering. I refuse to be a hypocrite and feign grief for a man I could not like. Have I offended you?"

"Not at all, my lady," Elizabeth replied, not certain how she felt about the other woman's shocking candor. "I—I wasn't all that well acquainted with Mr. Colburt either, and I fear I didn't care for him as well." She bit her lip and glanced down, shamed by her lack of compassion. "How awful that sounds."

"It is honest," Lady Elinore responded coolly. "The fact that he was murdered doesn't change the fact that Mr. Colburt was a thoroughly reprehensible fellow. Only saints are canonized after death, and from all accounts *saint* is hardly a word one would use in connection with Mr. Colburt."

"Perhaps not," Elizabeth said, thinking of her suspicions regarding the missing papers. "But that doesn't mean he deserved to be murdered."

"Are you speaking of poor Mr. Colburt?" Lady Barrington came into the room, her pale cheeks and red-rimmed eyes mute testimony to her overset nerves. "I vow, I cannot bear to think of it, and yet that is all I can think of."

Since her grace's feelings so closely approximated her own, Elizabeth felt another flash of kinship with the other woman.

"Please, your grace, will you not join us?" she asked, indicating one of the empty chairs. "Shall I pour you some tea?"

"That would be lovely, my dear, thank you," the duchess said, offering a wan smile as she sank onto the chair. "I tried laying down in my rooms, but I couldn't get comfortable. I kept seeing poor Mr. Colburt facedown in his own blood and—" She broke off, clearly unable to continue.

"It is all right, Lady Barrington," Lady Elinore soothed, albeit in a cool tone. "This has been hard on all of us."

"Do you know, this all seems so strange," her grace continued a few seconds later, after taking a sip of the tea Elizabeth had given her. "I know this is real, and yet it feels like part of some macabre dream. I keep thinking I will awaken, even though I know I am already awake. Odd."

"I would think anyone unused to violent death would feel that way, your grace," Lady Elinore said, her voice thoughtful as she studied the duchess. "Your sentiments do you credit. For myself, I must own to being more curious than anything else."

"Curious?" Elizabeth and Lady Barrington echoed the word in unison.

"Of course," Lady Elinore replied, her eyebrows arching. "Oh, come, you must be wondering who killed Mr. Colburt the same as I."

Lady Barrington looked more stricken than ever. "But surely that is a matter for the magistrate?" she protested, hands shaking as she set the teacup and saucer to one side.

"Indeed," Lady Elinore agreed, inclining her head, "but that doesn't mean we can't discuss it amongst ourselves. Have you a theory, Miss Mattingale?" Her sharp gaze cut to Elizabeth.

"I—I don't know," Elizabeth stammered, blushing and turning pale by turns. She wanted desperately to discuss her fears and suspicions with the others, but it didn't feel right discussing it with anyone other than Adam. For whatever reason, he was the only one she dared trust with what she feared was the truth.

"Well, I for one think it must have to do with the missing papers," Lady Elinore declared with a decisive nod.

"What?" Elizabeth gasped out the word, wondering

how many more shocks she could be expected to bear in one day.

"Yes," Lady Barrington said slowly, tilting her head to one side and looking thoughtful. "I must admit I wondered, but hearing you say the words convinces me you are right. It is the only theory that makes any possible sense."

"But how do you know—" Elizabeth broke off, drawing a shuddering breath to calm herself. "That is," she tried again, "what makes you think that?"

"Well, my dear, it stands to reason, does it not?" the duchess asked, smiling at her in her kindly way. "If you didn't take the papers, then someone else did. And that someone killed Mr. Colburt because of it. We've only to learn the gentleman's name, inform the magistrate, and you shall be free of any taint of suspicion."

"In taking the papers?" Elizabeth's head was beginning to reel. Too much had happened too quickly, and she felt like a piece of crystal that would shatter under the smallest amount of pressure.

"In killing Mr. Colburt," Lady Elinore corrected, her manner as imperturbable as always. "Because if we have connected the murder to the missing papers, you may be quite certain we won't be the only ones to do so. And since you already have been accused of the one, it is likely you will be accused of the other."

She gave a cool nod at Elizabeth's horrified gasp. "Yes, Miss Mattingale, I see you take my meaning. Someone is trying to put a noose about your neck, and unless we can think of some way to stop them, they are very likely to succeed."

Nine

"Then you agree with me," Adam said, his eyes narrowing as he studied the young man sitting across the desk from him. "Whoever took the papers killed Colburt."

"I beg pardon, my lord, but what I said was that it was possible," the young man, Henry, corrected. "But it's just as possible he was killed because he owed money to the wrong sort, or cast his eye upon the wrong lady." Pale green eyes challenged Adam with surprising coolness. "He had a habit of that, one hears."

Adam's lips thinned at the reference to his own confrontation with the late and unlamented Charles Colburt. When he'd first met the erstwhile footman he'd been less than impressed, thinking the lad too young and too diffident to be an effective agent. It seemed now he had misjudged the situation . . . and the man.

"Is that what you believe happened?" he asked, deciding the less said of his quarrel with Colburt, the better.

Henry was quiet for a long moment. "No," he admitted, leaning back in his chair. "But it's safer to consider all possibilities. I've learned the hard way that the surest way to miss a vital bit of information is not to be looking for it in the first place. If I start thinking Colburt died because of the papers and no other reason, the true cause could be staring me in the face and I'd not see it. If I want to learn what killed the man, I must first discover what did not."

It made sense in a convoluted sort of way, and Adam gave a slow nod. "And how does one go about discovering that?" he asked, intrigued by the machinations involved in uncovering a killer.

"Nosing about, asking questions, buying my mates a pint at the inn and letting them win from me at cards," Henry replied. "A man can learn a great deal that way. For example, I've learned from his man that Colburt was deep in Dun territory, and that he had a new conquest he was mad about."

It came as no surprise to Adam that Colburt had been in debt, but it did surprise that him he'd found himself a new mistress. He tried to think of any of the ladies who'd shown Colburt the slightest degree of partiality, but none came to mind.

"Did he say who she was?" he asked curiously.

Henry shook his head. "He didn't know the lady's name."

"But he was certain it was a lady?" Adam pressed, recalling the conversation he'd had with Colburt that day in the library. Perhaps he could enlist Elizabeth's assistance in questioning the maids, he thought, since it was more than likely Colburt's ladylove came from the lower orders.

"Aye, and a regular high flyer to hear his man tell it," Henry said, his lips curving in a sneer. " 'Not at all his gentleman's usual style' is I believe how he phrased it."

A sudden memory of Lady Barrington meeting her unknown lover in the conservatory flashed in Adam's mind, but he quickly brushed it aside as ludicrous. *His* pockets were scarce deep enough for her grace's exacting expectations, and he couldn't believe she would squander her talents on a penniless nobody like Colburt.

"What else have you learned?" he asked, turning his thoughts back to the matter at hand.

"The way Colburt was killed leads me to believe it's

unlikely he was murdered by a jealous husband. A man defending his lady would be in a wild fury, and I can't see he would limit himself to a single stab wound. A killing over money would be equally heated, and equally bloody. No, this was done coolly, efficiently; not in the heat of the moment, but thought out instead. The killer knew precisely what he was doing."

"Prince Bronyeskin said it was well done," Adam murmured, recalling his conversation with the prince.

"Did he?" Henry looked thoughtful. "He would know. As a soldier I am sure he has killed any number of men, and would best know how to go about it."

Adam didn't care for the direction the conversation was taking. "His highness has said he didn't kill Colburt, and I believe him."

"As do I," came the surprising reply. "But I still mean to investigate the matter further. Until the true villain is caught, no one in the household can be considered above suspicion. No one," he added, his gaze meeting Adam's.

Adam swallowed a flash of anger and a considerable portion of his pride. "I understand," he said tersely. "I don't like it, mind, but I understand."

"Do you?" Henry's smile was cool. "I hope so, for as it happens, sir, I wasn't referring to you."

Adam's stomach tightened in a sudden awareness of danger. "To whom were you referring?" he asked coldly.

"Miss Mattingale." It was obvious from the way he tensed, that Henry was aware of Adam's mounting anger. "And before you tear off my head, Lord Falconer, let me remind you that she is the one with the best cause to want Colburt dead. She is known to have disliked him immensely, and with good reason, I am sure. And more importantly, she is also the one most likely to have taken the papers."

"Why?" Adam demanded, furious at everyone's eagerness to see Elizabeth convicted of a crime he knew she could not possibly have committed. "Because she is well-traveled? Because she speaks French? For God's sake, man, the same can be said of *me!*"

"And of most other gentlemen and ladies of your station," Henry conceded the point with a cool nod. "But none of you have a father in America who has been bragging to his friends of his daughter and her highly placed friends."

Adam jerked back his head. "Mattingale has been doing that?"

"An agent we have in Richmond says it's all he ever talks of," Henry continued in a grim tone. "He says Mattingale even claims his daughter will be sending him important information 'soon.' "

Adam felt physically ill. My God, he thought, struggling to keep his emotions from overwhelming him. With such evidence weighed against her, it was no wonder the duke and the others were so convinced of her guilt.

"Perhaps Colburt learned she'd taken the papers and meant to blackmail her," Henry said, seeming unaware of Adam's anguish. "Perhaps he helped her with the theft and then had a change of heart; we may never know. But we can't discount the possibility that she may have done so merely because it is displeasing."

Creshton had said much the same thing, Adam remembered, and wondered if the duke had been trying to warn him. He could now admit his feelings for Elizabeth went far beyond anything so lukewarm as mere affection, and he could also admit that short of betraying his duty and his country, there was little he would not do to see her safe.

"Will you arrest her?"

"If I must," Henry said, "although I should prefer not to tip my hand unless I have no other choice. It was very foolish of Derring to have confronted her about it," he added, his thin lips making his displeasure plain. "If there was any evidence to be had, I shouldn't wonder it has all been destroyed by now."

"When?" Adam asked, a daring plan forming in his mind.

"I've orders to see the matter resolved by the time the Czar arrives," Henry admitted with visible reluctance. "If he arrives when he is scheduled, that gives me less than a fortnight."

"Give me that fortnight, then, to prove you are wrong. To prove you are all wrong," Adam said urgently, infusing every ounce of his considerable will into his voice. "I know Elizabeth could never kill anyone, and I damned well know she wouldn't betray her country, regardless of what her father might say!"

"My lord—"

"Two weeks, that is all I ask," he interrupted, feeling raw and desperate. "For God's sake!" he snapped at the other man's hesitation, "we are talking of a woman's life!"

Henry was quiet a long moment, his face a study in conflicting emotions. "Very well, Lord Falconer," he said at last. "Two weeks. But no more," he added, his expression harsh. "In two weeks' time I will have the traitor in custody. If not Miss Mattingale, then whoever else is to blame. I give you my word."

After Henry took his leave, Adam took a few minutes to compose his thoughts and then set out in search of Elizabeth. He didn't have to look very far. She was coming out of the dining room, a list in her hand.

"Elizabeth?" he stopped her, gazing down at her wan face in disapproval. "What are you doing here?" he asked, laying a gentle hand on her shoulder. "Why aren't you in your room resting?"

"There is too much to do," she replied, glancing at her list. "The guests still need to be fed and entertained, and I need to talk to her ladyship about the plans for the Birthday Ball. I hate the thought of canceling it, and yet I fear we must."

"Because of Colburt, do you mean?" he asked, studying her face.

"Of course," she replied, sounding surprised. "It would hardly be proper to make merry at such a time."

"And it would hardly make him any less dead," Adam pointed out firmly. "Besides, the guests will need something to distract them from all of this, and a ball sounds like the perfect diversion."

"There is that," she agreed, her soft blue eyes brightening. "I shall suggest it to Lady Derring. Thank you, my lord."

He cast a quick glance about him and, satisfied they were alone, he took her elbow and guided her into the small study located off the wide hall. Once the door had closed behind them, he carefully drew her into his arms.

"Adam," he reminded her, brushing the back of his fingers down the curve of her cheek and watching her through half-lowered lashes. "I would you call me Adam."

Her flesh grew warm beneath his touch, and her eyes darkened with emotion. "I—it's not proper," she stammered, her voice sounding slightly breathless.

The prim protest brought an amused smile to his lips. "A man is dead, you stand accused of theft, and the entire household is under house arrest," he reminded her, using his thumb to tip her face up to his. "I hardly think your calling me by my given name counts very much when compared to that. Do you?"

"No," her cheeks grew even rosier. "I would suppose not, but that still doesn't mean—"

"Elizabeth"—he watched her intently—"how do you think of me? As Lord Falconer or as Adam?"

To his horror her eyes began filling with tears. "Don't ask that," she implored, raising her hand to cover his. "Please don't."

Panic filled Adam, panic and an overwhelming sense of aching desire. As a gentleman he knew he should release her, let her walk away and never importune her again. He should, but he could not.

"Why?" he demanded, slipping his hands down to

gently cup her face. "I think of you as Elizabeth. My Elizabeth. My beautiful Elizabeth," and he covered her mouth with his own.

Her lips were soft and warm beneath his, and he was helpless to resist their sweetness. Fighting the desire exploding inside of him, he drew her closer, savoring the feel of her pressed to his hungry body. It took every ounce of will he possessed to keep from taking more, but he cared for her too much to risk frightening her. Reining in his passion, he slowly raised his head, his heart pounding as he gazed down into her flushed face.

"Adam." His name slipped breathlessly from her parted lips, and her eyes were slumberous as she lifted her heavy lashes.

"Ah, my sweet, the things you do to a man's resolve," he murmured, tracing a finger along the bow of her mouth.

Her cheeks grew rosy, but to his delight she made no move to end their embrace. "You also have a deleterious effect upon my good sense," she said, smiling sadly. "But this changes nothing."

"You are wrong," he disagreed. "It changes everything."

"Adam—"

He silenced her with another kiss. This time she responded at once, her arms stealing up to circle his neck while she rose on tiptoe to press her warm body against him. The breath caught in his throat, and a feeling of wild exultation surged through him at her active participation. He subtly increased the pressure of his mouth over hers until her lips parted, and he slipped the tip of his tongue in to gently tease hers. When he heard her soft gasp he ended the kiss, lifting his head to smile down at her.

"My apologies, my dear," he murmured, his arms remaining tight about her slender waist. "I know you will find this hard to believe, but I truly didn't drag you in here to steal a few kisses from you."

"You didn't?" An expression of skepticism mixed with feminine disappointment flashed across her features.

"No," he chuckled, lightly tapping her nose with his. "I did not. I wanted your promise that you would call me Adam. Will you?"

She studied his cravat for several seconds before shyly raising her gaze to his. "I suppose it would be all right," she murmured, "when we are private. You must know my reputation is already dangling by a thread; I'd as lief not lose it altogether."

The rueful words recalled him belatedly to the reason he'd sought her out. "That is why I wished to speak with you," he said gently, hating the knowledge he would cause her pain. "We need to talk about Mr. Colburt's death. I am afraid you are suspected."

"I know."

He blinked at the calm words. He'd braced himself for anything from tears to fury and wasn't certain what to make of her cool acceptance. "I beg your pardon?"

The look she gave him could best be described as pitying. "They've already branded me a thief and a traitor. Why shouldn't they brand me a murderer as well?"

Although Adam was grateful Elizabeth was taking things so well, he couldn't help but feel a trifle put out. It was hard to act the knight-errant, he thought, when the lady fair was already taking the dragon's measure. "And why should they think that?" he asked, choosing his words with studied care.

"Because of the papers," she replied in the same calm manner. "Which reminds me; I am convinced Mr. Colburt, Mr. Carling, and that wretch, Mr. Derwent, took them."

Adam's pique vanished in a flash of temper. "Explain that," he demanded, listening in mounting fury as she did just that.

"A schoolboy's prank," he repeated, when she'd done speaking. "We've been in a lather of fear over a traitor, and it was nothing more than a schoolboy's prank." His hands balled into fists. "By God, we'll see how funny they think it when I am done with them!" He whirled around to leave, only to have Elizabeth grab his arm.

"Adam, wait! You aren't thinking of confronting them?"

"I damned well am!" he retorted coldly, his eyes flashing with rage. "And they'll be lucky if I don't kill the pair of them!"

"A noble sentiment, and one I more than share," Elizabeth retorted, hanging on to his sleeve. "But we cannot permit it."

"We? You and Bronyeskin?" he demanded, deciding he'd had enough of the imperious Russian's interference in Elizabeth's life. His highness might consider himself her brother, but that didn't give him the right to make a nuisance of himself.

"Good heavens, no!" Elizabeth replied, her soft blue eyes wide in alarm. "I'd never tell Alexi what I suspect. He'd run them through in a heartbeat, and then where would we be?"

"Considerably better off," Adam retorted, and then scowled. "If you didn't mean his highness, then who do you mean?"

"Lady Elinore, Lady Barrington, and myself. We've discussed it, and decided not to say anything for the moment."

Adam couldn't think at first. "You've decided," he repeated, wanting to make sure he'd heard aright.

"Of course me," she replied, meeting his gaze with a sudden coolness. "As Lady Elinore pointed out, I am the one most likely to hang if the real villain isn't found. Do you expect me to sit meekly by and do nothing to defend myself?"

Adam stared at her in stunned amazement, the conversation he'd meant to have with her regarding her father forgotten in a flash.

"I expect you to leave it to me!" he snapped, appalled at the thought of her putting herself in any sort of danger. "This isn't a game for three silly chits to play at! Whoever killed Colburt has made that plain. You will stay out of this."

Temper set her eyes to pure blue flame. "I will not stay out of this!" she said furiously. "This is my life, Adam, and I will do what I think is proper to save it. Good day to you, *my lord!*" She hurled his title at him like an epithet before storming out, leaving Adam feeling almost as frustrated as he was terrified.

"This isn't a game for three silly chits to play at."

The indignity of those imperious words rang in Elizabeth's ears as she slammed the door to her room. Of all the top-lofty, arrogant, *male* things to say! she fumed, pacing up and down the room. Leave it to him, indeed! Just who the devil did he think he was? He had no power over her. She'd told him that practically from the first moment she'd clapped eyes on him, and repeated it countless times since. She might have let him kiss her, but that didn't give him the right to dictate what she could and could not do. And if he thought it did, she would be more than happy to dissuade him of the notion.

The memory of that kiss burst in her mind, and a dreamy smile replaced her scowl. The kiss; kisses, she amended, sighing as she relived the moments lost in his arms and the feel of his lips taking hers. It wasn't the first time a man had kissed her, but those boyish pecks faded in comparison to the burning sensuality of Adam's mouth pressing urgently against hers. It had been everything she dreamed a kiss could be, and she was aware of the shameless hope that she'd soon know its magic again.

In the next moment she was angrily shaking her head. Of course she didn't want that insolent beast kissing her, she told herself, resuming her pacing. Her life was in utter chaos and she couldn't afford the luxury of foolishness. Even if she managed to clear her name, anything approaching an intimate relationship between her and Adam was impossible. It was certain to end in heartbreak and ruin, and she had no intention of escaping one disaster only to rush headlong into another.

Once she'd composed herself, she changed into her evening dress of gray sarcenet and went down for dinner. Lady Derring was still keeping to her rooms, and it fell to her to care for the rest of the guests as best she could. Lord Derring was keeping at his wife's side, passing word through Adam that by order of the Magistrate, the guests would regrettably be further detained until the investigation into Mr. Colburt's death was concluded. The idea one of them was possibly a killer occupied most of the guests' conversations, and the antipathy she'd encountered yesterday was much subdued. She was considering the change when Lady Elinore sat beside her.

"Being thought a murderess would seem to have its advantages," she observed, her eyes dancing as she smiled at Elizabeth. "They might still suspect you of treason, but they are too frightened to show it lest you take offense and kill them."

Elizabeth's lips twitched, although she was careful to keep her amusement hidden. "A tempting thought," she drawled, her gaze going to Miss Clarvale, who was watching her with a wary eye.

Lady Elinore gave an appreciative chuckle. "You show excellent taste, my dear. Constance has always been singularly unpleasant, but one cannot kill a person for that, I suppose."

"Indeed, my lady," Elizabeth replied, thinking she could come to like the cool beauty.

"Speaking of *unpleasant*," Lady Elinore continued, "have you had a chance to tell Lord Falconer of your suspicions?"

The question had Elizabeth hiding another smile. "Yes, my lady," she murmured. "I did."

"And?" Lady Elinore arched a golden eyebrow inquiringly.

"And he said it wasn't a game for three silly chits to play at, and I was to leave it to him."

"He said *what?*" Lady Elinore's response was precisely what Elizabeth thought it would be. "Oh, of all the arrogance!" she fumed, snapping open her fan and fanning herself furiously. "The man is an impossible tyrant! I cannot tell you how relieved I am to have had the good sense to refuse him. I shouldn't have him now if he were the last man left in England!"

The incautious remark jolted Elizabeth. She'd forgotten that Adam had once offered for the duke's daughter; an offer he must have reissued if the lady was now reconsidering it.

"Your forgiveness, my lady," she said, studying the other woman cautiously, "but I thought your father said you'd come to Derring Hall to reconsider his lordship's offer?"

Lady Elinore gave a guilty start, her cheeks pinking with embarrassed color. "I have reconsidered," she said, her slender fingers toying with her fan. "And I've decided I was right to refuse him from the start. Falconer would make the worst possible sort of husband for any lady with an ounce of intelligence, and I pity the poor female he marries.

"Although," she added, casting Elizabeth a worried look, "that is something I should prefer you keep private. Papa wanted me to give the matter all due consideration, and he'd be quite displeased if he thought I hadn't at least made the effort."

"Of course, my lady," Elizabeth assured her, ignoring the undeniable sense of relief washing through her. She genuinely liked the other woman, and her feelings for Adam were too tangled to examine closely. The thought that she might have betrayed one with the other was too painful to bear.

The conversation turned awkwardly to other matters, and while they were discussing whether to allow card playing after dinner, Adam and Alexi walked into the drawing room.

"Speak of the devil," Lady Elinore muttered, her eyes narrowing. "And he has that impossible Russian with him.

I know he is your dear friend, Miss Mattingale, but I find him wearying. That much charm is not to be trusted."

Alexi had spied them and was making his way toward them, a grim-faced Adam following in his wake.

"Lady Elinore, Elizabeth," he greeted them with a low bow, kissing each of their hands in turn. "How it pleases me to see you. You are recovered, yes, from this morning's unpleasantness?"

Lady Elinore's eyes grew frosty. "I believe a murder qualifies as something more than *unpleasantness,* your highness."

Alexi regarded her with regal hauteur. "And so it is, *dama,*" he agreed coolly. "Which makes it an unsuitable topic for ladies to discuss. We will not speak of this again."

Lady Elinore's lips thinned in temper, but before they came to blows dinner was announced. Lady Galbraith, one of the countess's oldest friends, held sway at the head of the table, doing her best to maintain some semblance of normalcy. Conversation was sporadic and subdued, with the other guests concentrating mostly on their food. Lady Barrington made some attempts to enliven the evening with an amusing description of a party she had attended at Carlton House, but when her witty remarks met with uncomfortable silence she soon abandoned her efforts. Elizabeth wasn't in the least surprised when most of the guests announced their intention to retire to their rooms once dinner was finished.

One thing that did surprise her was Mr. Carling and Mr. Derwent putting in an appearance toward the end of the meal. They both looked decidedly the worse for wear, their faces pale and haggard. There was also a decided strain between them, and they scarce spoke to one another after taking their places at the table. Mr. Derwent seemed especially brittle, drinking more than was customary, even for him. Mr. Carling was also imbibing rather freely, although without the defiant abandon Mr. Derwent was exhibiting.

She wasn't the only one to notice their behavior, and more than once she caught Adam studying them with narrow-eyed speculation. Finally the meal was ended, and the guests rose to their feet.

"Going off to sleep, eh?" Mr. Derwent sneered, wine sloshing over the rim of his glass as he raised it in a mocking salute. " 'And in that sleep of death what dreams may come when we have shuffled off this mortal coil.' I wonder what Charles dreams of, poor, stupid sot." And he downed the dregs of his glass.

Lady Galbraith gave him a look of icy disdain. "I think you have had rather too much to drink, sir," she announced in her loftiest accents. "You will oblige me by retiring to your rooms before you make an even bigger fool of yourself."

He blinked up at the older woman in drunken indignation. "What? Didn't I get the quotation right? Dashed odd. I've always had a bit of a hand with the old boy's words." He tipped his head back, blond curls spilling over his collar as he smiled spitefully at the scandalized guests.

" 'Treachery, seek it out,' an excellent bit of advice, eh?" He gave another drunken laugh. "Perhaps that's what got poor Charles killed. 'Virtue is its own punishment.' " He frowned thoughtfully. "Who said that, I wonder?"

Mr. Carling rose hastily to his feet, a look of horror on his face. "Come, Geoffrey, that ain't the way," he implored, taking the empty glass from his friend's hand and helping him to his feet. "Up to bed with you, now. You mustn't say anything else."

Mr. Derwent staggered as he freed himself. "Why shouldn't I?" he demanded belligerently. "Charles kept quiet, and look where it got him! And you know, Wills, don't you? You know!"

Mr. Carling looked as if he would swoon. He cast a terrified glance about the room and turned back to his friend.

"Geoffrey, please," he said, getting a better hold on the

other man's arm. "You're jug-bit. You don't know what you're saying!"

Mr. Derwent's face twisted in bitter fury, but before he could say anything else, Adam rose to confront him.

"Derwent, you are upsetting the ladies," he informed the other man coldly. "Leave the room. Now."

Oddly, the words had a sobering effect on the younger man. He straightened, and his face, which had been mottled with fury, turned pale instead. Accepting Mr. Carling's assistance, he left the room without uttering another word.

"Fool." Adam glared after him, shaking his head. "Damned fool."

Ten

After some discussion it was decided Mr. Colburt would be laid to rest in the Derrings' family graveyard. He had no family, and as he'd met his fate while under their roof, the earl decided burying the fellow was the least they might do. The day after the discovery of the body Lady Derring emerged from her rooms, and she wasn't long in making Elizabeth's position clear.

"Until this matter is resolved in your favor and I can dismiss you, you will be expected to carry on as you have always done," she told Elizabeth coldly. "Is that understood?"

"Yes, my lady," Elizabeth replied, refraining from pointing out that if the matter was resolved in her favor, it would mean she was innocent. She had no desire to spend one moment longer at Derring Hall than she had to.

"Naturally you will refrain from associating with our guests above that which is absolutely necessary to perform your duties," the countess added, her dark eyes spiteful. "I am sure you take my meaning, Miss Mattingale."

Elizabeth clenched her jaw, holding on to her temper with a will. Even though she and Adam hadn't been alone once since that wondrous kiss, she was aware of the speculative glances cast her way by the ladies, who'd noted his preference for her company.

"Yes, Lady Derring," she said, resentment simmering inside her as she kept her gaze fixed on the wall over her ladyship's shoulder. "Your meaning is more than plain."

The countess frowned at Elizabeth's stiff tones, and she gave a disapproving frown. "The funeral will be held tomorrow," she continued coldly. "You will be allowed to attend services at the church, but I see no reason for you to remain while he is buried.

"Indeed," she added with a sniff, "I can think of nothing in more questionable taste. Following the church services you are to return here to make sure all will be ready for the funeral breakfast. I will not have it said we did not see poor Mr. Colburt on his way in the proper fashion."

She continued in this manner for several minutes, rattling on until Elizabeth's patience was frayed and her jaw was aching from having been clenched so tight. Finally her employer ran out of orders and insults, and Elizabeth was dismissed. Naturally she wasn't allowed to leave until the countess hurled one final word of warning at her.

"Just mind you watch yourself, Miss Mattingale," she said, her voice fairly dripping with malice as she smirked at Elizabeth. "For I assure you, *we* shall be watching *you*."

Holding her head high, Elizabeth walked out of the countess's drawing room and straight into Adam's arms. His hands closed around her shoulders and his worried amber gaze scurried over her tense features.

"Elizabeth, what is it?" he demanded, ducking his head to better study her face. "You're shaking."

"With temper, my lord, I do assure you," she replied, her heart racing in her chest. Being this close to him was both torment and pleasure, and she knew she had best put some distance between them. If she didn't, she feared she'd do something foolish. Something foolish like kissing him or, worse still, putting her head on his shoulder and accepting the comfort and safety his presence offered. Drawing a deep breath, she raised her eyes to his.

"If you'll excuse me, sir, I must be about my duties,"

she said, smiling stiffly. She tried moving away, only to have his fingers tighten their hold.

"The devil with your duties!" he snapped, his eyes flashing with temper. "I want to know what is wrong. Has someone upset you?"

Abruptly Elizabeth decided she'd had enough of arrogance and demands. The growing softness inside her hardened, and she placed both hands on his chest and shoved as hard as she could.

"I am not upset!" She enunciated each word slowly so they would penetrate the thickness of his skull. "I am angry."

He studied her for several seconds before replying. "I can see that," he said, his lips curving in a slow smile. "Dare I ask with whom?"

Elizabeth gave careful thought to kicking him as hard as she could but decided against it. Considering her shove hadn't moved him so much as an inch, she'd probably end up breaking her toe.

"If you must know, I was hipped with Lady Derring," she said, scowling up at him. "But if you don't release me at once, I warn you I shall be more than a little vexed with you."

His smile deepened. "Then I fear you'll have to be vexed," he said, his hands sliding down her arms to grasp her hands. "I need to speak with you, and I prefer to do so in private. Come." And he led her out into the gardens, ignoring her indignant efforts to win her freedom. When they reached the center of the garden, she managed to pull free and turned to face him.

"Well, we are here," she said, glowering up at him. "I hope you know Lady Derring will doubtlessly have me drawn and quartered for this. What is so important it could not wait?"

"Have you been writing to your father?"

The unexpectedness of the question was like a slap in the face. "I—I beg your pardon?" she asked, so shocked she couldn't think.

"You heard me." His expression, like his tone, was implacable. "Have you been writing to your father? Don't lie to me, Elizabeth. Your very life depends on your being completely honest with me."

"I had no intention of lying," she replied, knowing the words in themselves were a lie. "It is just that I don't see what my father has to do with all of this."

His expression hardened. "Don't be naive, or expect me to be," he advised in a soft tone. "You know full well he has a great deal to do with what has happened. Now, have you been writing to him, or have you not?"

Faced with such a naked demand for the truth, Elizabeth could not prevaricate. "A few times, yes," she said, refusing to hang her head in shame. "He is my father; I cannot be expected to cut him dead merely because Lord Derring commanded it."

"I'm not here to argue that with you," Adam said, waving that aside. "I want to know what you wrote him, and what he wrote you. Do you still have his letters?"

Elizabeth thought of the letters she'd tucked away in the band of the hatbox. She'd hidden all but his last letter there after the fright she'd had, which was why they'd escaped detection during the search of her room. She knew if she told Adam she'd destroyed the letters he'd believe her, and because of that she could be no less than honest.

"Yes, I do."

"Where are they? Why weren't they found when your room was searched?"

"Because I'd hidden them," she answered truthfully. "I knew his lordship disapproved of the correspondence, and so I always took care to put them away after I'd finished reading them." She met his watchful gaze. "Shall I get them for you?"

His eyes flickered, as if surprised by the offer. "If you would," he said, inclining his head gravely. "Thank you."

Elizabeth flinched. "If you'll wait here, then, I'll go fetch them," she said, and hurried away, praying she reached her room before the tears stinging her eyes began falling.

Hell and damnation! Adam cursed silently, watching in frustrated impotence as Elizabeth slipped into the house. He would have given all he possessed and more to spare her this, but he knew he could not. He'd long suspected she'd defied Derring's orders, and knew as well how that defiance could be used against her if the truth ever came out. The only way to save Elizabeth was to make her innocence plain to all, and for that he needed her father's letters. He only prayed the information they contained would not hang her rather than free her.

The thought had him sweating, and by the time Elizabeth returned he was hanging on to his control by a fraying thread.

"Here you are, my lord," she said, averting her eyes as she handed him the packet. "I would like them back, if I may. They are all I have left of my father."

The pain in her voice shredded his heart. "I will try," he said, glancing at the packet of letters. There were six in all, and he flipped through them before glancing at her again. "Is this the lot?"

She gave a jerky nod, her gaze still avoiding his.

"Which were written after Lord Derring's edict?"

"The last three," she said, raising her gaze to meet his. "Will there be anything else, my lord?"

Her use of his title hurt almost as much as the tears he could see drying on her face.

"Elizabeth," he said, raw with the need to touch her, "I am sorry. You must know I am doing this only to prove your innocence."

She studied him sadly for several moments. "Must I?" she asked quietly. "To whom are you trying to prove my innocence, Lord Falconer? To the others, or to yourself?"

Adam had no answer and could only stand silently as once more she walked away from him.

He spent the rest of the afternoon studying the letters. The invectives Elizabeth's father poured forth against England had his lips thinning several times, but he was certain they didn't constitute treason. Under the recently passed Combination Acts, he supposed they could be considered seditious, but sedition was a far cry from treason. If Mr. Mattingale ever returned to England, he would doubtlessly face arrest, but from what he had read, he could find nothing that implicated Elizabeth in his crimes. The realization had his shoulders slumping in relief.

Not wanting to trust the information to anyone, even his valet, he spent several more hours meticulously copying the letters and setting them aside to be sent to the duke in London. It was while he was franking the letters that he realized he hadn't asked Elizabeth how she had maintained the correspondence with her father. A visit to the local postmaster was clearly in order, he decided, tucking Elizabeth's letters inside his jacket. But first he wanted to find Henry and let him know that his spy had been misinformed. The worst thing Mr. Mattingale had asked of Elizabeth was that she move to America as soon as she could manage.

Realizing he couldn't seek out Henry on his own, he went in search of Lady Elinore. He found her in the morning parlor, sitting in a patch of watery sunlight quietly embroidering. The sight brought him up short, and he leaned against the door to watch her. Almost at once her head came up, and her clear gray eyes met his gaze inquiringly.

"Is there something you find amusing, my lord?" she asked in the coolly polished accents he'd once considered essential in his marchioness.

He pushed himself away from the door, embarrassed at having been caught watching her like a moonling. "Not at all," he said, advancing toward her. "I am merely surprised to see you so happily engaged in the womanly arts. I thought you a bluestocking who disdained such things."

"I am a duke's daughter, Lord Falconer," she replied,

setting her hoop and threads aside. "My mother made quite certain I was well-acquainted with the duties expected of that station. And odd as it may seem, I like to embroider; I find it helps me think. Was there anything else you wished, or have you come only to question my domestic abilities?"

Adam was annoyed to find himself coloring. "I need to see Henry," he said gruffly, aware once more of his gratitude that she'd had the sense to refuse his suit. "Can you arrange it for me?"

"I can," Lady Elinore said, her light brown brows puckering in a frown. "Although it might be best if you tell me what it is you wish him to know, and allow me to pass it on to him."

Adam hesitated; he'd seen her and Elizabeth sitting together several times, and she'd been as quick as himself and Lady Barrington in defending her. Still . . .

"I should prefer meeting with Henry, if you do not mind," he said. "In addition to speaking with him, there is something I wish to show him."

"I am afraid I cannot allow that," Lady Elinore replied, her voice surprisingly firm. "It is certain to cause comment, and that we cannot afford."

"I know it will cause comment!" Adam retorted, affronted that she would dare question his authority. "That is why I want you to act as our intermediary. How can anyone suspect anything untoward if you summon your own footman, for pity's sake?"

"Nevertheless, it is a risk I should prefer not to take," she said, her face taking on an expression of feminine stubbornness. "We don't know who the thief and killer is, and what he may or may not know. Father said he told you to filter any information you might have through him, and since he is not here, you must filter it through me.

"It's not only Miss Mattingale who is in danger, you know," she added when he hesitated. "What do you think will happen to Henry if the villain ever guesses the truth about him?"

Adam swore silently, reluctantly conceding that she was right. "Miss Mattingale has been writing to her father in America," he said, doing his best not to sound petulant. "She gave me his letters, and I've examined them at some length. While his sentiments are decidedly questionable, I could see no hint of his having asked her to do anything illicit."

Lady Elinore tapped a finger to her lips. "Indeed? Are you quite certain of that?"

His temper stirred, but he didn't allow it to slip its reins. Instead he withdrew the letters and handed them to her.

"Study them yourself," he offered coldly. "But other than demanding that she return to America, her father made no request of her that can be considered treasonous. I've copied them out to be sent to your father. Have you anything you wish to add?"

Lady Elinore tucked the letters in her sewing basket along with her hoop and threads before answering. "As a matter of fact, there is," she said, glancing up at him and smiling. "You might tell Papa that I expect to see him by next week's end, and that he owes me that copy of Wollstonecraft he confiscated from me last year."

Adam shook his head. "You read Wollstonecraft," he said. "Why am I not surprised?"

She gave a pretty shrug. "I am sure I do not know. Now, if you do not mind, sir, I've a question I should like to ask you."

Adam tensed in sudden awareness of danger. "What is it?" he asked cautiously.

"Why did you offer for me?"

Adam stared at her. "I beg your pardon?"

"Why did you offer for me?" she repeated, her lips curving in an amused smile at his stunned expression. "And you needn't look so horrified, sir. I've no desire that you repeat the event. I am merely curious, that is all."

Adam fought down the sudden urge to shuffle from one foot to the other. "I suppose I offered for you for the same reason any man of my station offers for a lady," he muttered. "Because I admired you, and thought we would suit."

"Indeed, and so you said at the time," she said, nodding her head. "But surely there had to be some reason other than that. You must admire any number of ladies."

What did she want from him? Adam wondered, beginning to feel desperate. "I also admire your father," he said, trying to recall whatever lunacy had prompted him into making such a thorough ass of himself. "I suppose I fancied the notion of our being related in some fashion or another."

"Did you desire me?"

"Elinore!" he exclaimed, feeling his face heat in embarrassment. "What the devil sort of question is that?"

"A reasonable one, or so it seems to me," she replied calmly. "When you were speaking of marrying me, you prattled on about bloodlines and heirs, so I assumed ours would be a normal marriage in every sense of the word. Did you desire me?"

Adam was beginning to feel like a victim of the Inquisition. "Of course I desired you," he said, praying for deliverance. "You're a beautiful woman, Elinore; you must know that."

"And it was never more than that? It was never my heart you wanted, my mind, my soul? You would have taken my body and been content with that?"

"Yes!" he exclaimed, and then thought about it for a moment. "No," he said, realizing now that such a cold and bloodless match would have been the death of him. "The devil take you, Elinore," he muttered, glaring at her. "What is it you're after?"

"The truth," she said, settling back in her chair and looking oddly satisfied. "Now, as to the letters, have you any idea how Elizabeth has been corresponding with her father?"

The abrupt change of topic came as a relief and a surprise to Adam. "That is something I mean to discover," he said, intrigued that Elinore had come to the same conclusion as he. "I was thinking of riding into the village tomorrow and speaking to the postmaster. He may have some information that would be of use."

"He may, but you'd be better advised to talk to the milliner."

"Mrs. Treckler?" he asked, his facility for remembering names standing him in good stead. "Why should I want to speak with her? I've no need of a new chapeau."

"Perhaps not, but her brother is the leader of the local group of Gentlemen, and has been known to carry letters for those wishing to avoid the more conventional methods of communication."

Adam's jaw dropped in astonishment. "How do you know that?" he demanded, recalling his teasing remark about Elizabeth's frequent trips to the milliner's and her prim reply. The little devil! he thought furiously. *Just wait until I get my hands on her!*

"From Lady Derring's abigail," Elinore supplied, watching him with no little amusement. "My maid told her I was in a fret because I didn't have any silk, and she told Mary not to worry because Tom Pender would be making another run at high tide."

"But how do you know about the letters?" he asked, putting his anger aside for the moment. "Just because a man runs a load of silk and brandy past the excise men, it doesn't necessarily mean he is willing to carry letters, especially to enemy countries."

"That came from Cook. She told Mary if she had any letters she wished sent to her family in Ireland, Tom would take them for half of what the mails charged."

Adam manfully swallowed an oath. "We are mad to outlaw smuggling," he observed with considerable feeling. "We ought to legalize the whole bloody thing and be done with it."

"Ah, but then only think of the sorry mess we would make of it," Elinore observed with a chuckle. "No, we are far better served letting them operate outside the law. They are far more useful that way."

It seemed an odd remark for a lady, even Elinore, to make, but Adam shrugged it aside. He had far weightier matters to occupy his mind.

"Perhaps I should ride into the village today," he said grimly. "I find I may have some need for a new bonnet after all."

Lady Elinore gave a demure smile. "I am sure you will look delightful in it. In the meanwhile, I shall see Henry gets these. Have you anything else you would like to pass on?"

"Only that I want him to keep a sharp eye on both Derwent and Carling," Adam answered, remembering the dandy's drunken exhibition with a frown. "They're like to be in considerable danger now."

"Because of what that lackwit let slip?" she asked. "I'm sure he's already heard of it from the other servants, but in case he hasn't, I will let him know."

Once more her quickness of mind struck Adam, and this time he decided not to let the incident pass unremarked. "You seem rather well-versed in this sort of thing, if you do not mind my saying so," he said, eyes suspicious as he studied her.

"Not at all," Lady Elinore returned smoothly in her cultured tones. "A lady can learn a great many things from her footman if she but pays the proper mind."

Not certain how to take that remark, Adam elected to beat a strategic retreat. "Then I'll just bid you good day," he said, and turned to leave the room.

"Falconer, wait; there is one more question I should like to ask you," Lady Elinore called out just as he reached the door.

He paused, casting her a wary glance over his shoulder. "What is it?"

An expression that in another female might have been counted hesitation flickered across her classical features and was gone. "It's been a few years since you made your offer to me," she said, glancing down at her clasped hands.

"Since you are still unwed, I assume you've not made the same offer to anyone else?"

"No, I have not," Adam replied with a grimace. "Being called an unfeeling stone and having my head handed back to me is not an experience I care to know a second time."

To his surprise a faint blush of embarrassment colored her cheeks, but when she raised her head, her eyes were as remote as they had ever been. "Then a word of advice, if I may, my lord," she said. "The next time you offer for a lady, rather than cold reason, try offering her your heart instead. Much to my amazement, it would seem you do possess such an organ after all."

"Four?" Adam repeated, glaring down at the hapless milliner he'd spent the better part of half an hour interrogating. "You're certain it was four letters and not three your brother delivered for Miss Mattingale?"

"Aye, me lord, 'twas four, to be sure," Mrs. Treckler said, sniffing and dabbing at her eyes with the corner of her apron.

Adam noted her distress in grim silence. He'd disliked terrorizing a helpless woman, but his need to learn the truth left him no other choice. Threatening to have her brother hanged and her transported for smuggling might not have been the most gentlemanly thing he'd ever done, but it was effective. The moment the milliner realized he was in earnest, she'd been more than happy to provide him with whatever information was required. That the information was not what he wanted was of little consequence; it was the truth. All that remained was for Adam to decide what was to be done with that truth.

"How many letters did she send in return?" he asked, keeping his mind fixed firmly on the matter before him.

"The same number, sir, the same," Mrs. Treckler answered, blowing her nose with great vigor. "Four."

"When was the last letter received?" Adam pressed,

thinking quickly. There was no way of knowing with any certainty when the papers were stolen, but he believed it was likely they were taken within a few days of their arrival. That meant at least ten days had passed since the possible theft. If the last letter arrived within the past few days, that would do much to lessen the suspicion against Elizabeth. If it arrived earlier, however, the implications didn't bear considering.

Mrs. Treckler's face screwed up in a thoughtful grimace as she searched her memory. "Oh, more'n a sennight, I would say," she said at last. "And she sent her answer not so many days later. The day you was here, in fact," she added diffidently.

Disappointment, bitterness, and a dash of fear boiled up inside Adam, creating a potent witch's brew. He believed in Elizabeth's innocence, yet each step he took, each fact he discovered, pointed more firmly to her guilt. If he shared what he'd learned with Henry or the duke, it was almost a certainty that Elizabeth would be taken up.

"You're to tell no one that we have spoken," he ordered, fixing Mrs. Treckler with his sternest look. "And when the answer to Miss Mattingale's letter arrives, it is to be delivered to me. Don't even think of betraying me, or it will go very badly with you and your brother. Is that understood?"

"Aye," she promised, bobbing her head eagerly. "And I'll not play you false, I swear! 'Tis just . . ." Her voice trailed off and she twisted her hands in her apron.

"It's just what?" he prompted gently when she didn't continue.

She bit her lip and met his gaze. " 'Tis just, me lord, what if there ain't no answer?"

Adam paused in the act of pulling on his riding gloves. "What makes you say that?" he asked curiously.

"Because when I asked when Tom should look for an answer, Miss Mattingale said there'd not be one," Mrs. Treckler said, looking uneasy. "She sounded near to tears when she said it, too, and I remember wondering if p'raps the old gent had died."

Adam thought for a moment. "Perhaps he has," he said, recalling his conversation with Elizabeth on the day they walked into the village. "Perhaps he has. Thank you, Mrs. Treckler. You have been of great help to me."

With the funeral set for the next morning, Elizabeth spent a frantic afternoon making the final arrangements. Because the service would be held in the Derrings' family chapel, only the house guests would be in attendance, much to the disappointment of the neighborhood. Several local ladies had dangled for invitations, but Lady Derring had stood firm. A guest might have had the poor breeding to be murdered under her roof, but she was determined he would not be allowed to turn the event into a seven days' wonder.

Elizabeth was returning to the kitchens for a final consultation with Cook when a grim-faced Alexi waylaid her in the hall.

"I have been recalled to London," he began without preamble. "Do you remember when I spoke of that traitor, Zaramoff?" he asked, his eyes as blue and cold as sapphires.

"Yes," she answered, sadly remembering learning of the old prince's death at the hands of his own son.

"I have been sent word he has been conspiring with the Austrians," Alexi continued, his mouth twisting in regal fury. "He means to advise the Czar to agree to Poland's independence."

Elizabeth gave a stunned gasp and covered her mouth with her hands. "But his Imperial Highness would never agree to such a thing!" she said, studying Alexi worriedly. "Would he?"

Alexi thrust a hand through his hair and swore feelingly in Russian before finally answering. "Alexander is not like the Grand Duchess," he said with visible reluctance.

"Nor even like the Grand Duke, Constantine, who for all his faults is a good man. Alexander is the dreamer; a child who sees the world not the way it is, but the way he wishes it to be. If Zaramoff, who he admires, tells him that giving away Poland is the path to greatness, I fear he will do it." He met Elizabeth's gaze with determination. "I cannot allow this, little queen."

Elizabeth's heart went out to her old friend and the anguish he was undoubtedly suffering. "Of course you can't, Alexi," she said, standing on tiptoe to brush a kiss across his cheek.

"When will you be leaving?" she asked, trying to hide her sadness from his sharp gaze.

"I leave now," he said, taking her hand in his and carrying it to his lips for another kiss. "I know Falconer has said we must all remain until the true killer of Colburt is caught, but I have no time for such things. I will speak with him before I go, but first there is one thing you must promise me."

"Anything, Alexi," she said, not wishing to add to the great burden of worry he was already carrying.

"If these foolish *Breetanskees* make to arrest you, you are to send word to the Grand Duchess," he said, his expression stern. "She will tell me, and I will come at once. Promise me, Elizabeth, on your dear mother's soul, that you will do this thing for me."

"I promise," she said, fighting back tears at his fierce determination to save her.

"Good." He kissed both her cheeks. "And I promise on the souls of my sister and beloved parents that I will marry you. The wife of a prince they dare not touch."

"Marry you!" Elizabeth leapt back, staring at him in horror. "Alexi, are you mad? You can't marry me!"

He folded his arms across his chest, his face set in hard, implacable lines. "To save you, Elizabeth, I can marry you, and I will. In fact," he said with a frown, "perhaps we should wed now. There is something called a Special License, yes? We will get one."

Sheer shock robbed Elizabeth of the ability to speak. Her mind was racing like a mad thing, but she couldn't seem to find any words. He looked so solemn, so sure of himself and his duty, and looking at him, she thought suddenly of Adam; another man of honor and duty who would do whatever it took to protect those about him.

"Alexi, listen to me," she implored, her gaze holding his even as her fingers clung to his. "I love you, but only as a brother, just as you love me as a sister. For us to marry would be wrong."

Alexi studied her, his distress obvious in his eyes. "But they could hang you, *syestra*," he said, his voice husky with pain. "Or send you to a prison where you would die. How can I allow this?"

"And how can I allow you to squander your life to save mine?" she asked, neatly turning his words around. "You are such a good man, Alexander, one of the finest I have ever known. You deserve to marry for love. Real love. And as your sister, I will not let you settle for less."

"Little sister," he whispered, tears in his eyes as he bent to press his cheek to hers. "How I love you. And how hard you make it for me to protect you." He drew back to scowl down at her with mock ferociousness.

"But I mean it, Elizabeth," he continued, glowering at her. "I will not let them harm you. If you will not marry me, then you must promise me you will go to Falconer."

"Alexi—"

"Promise me, *dyevuchka*," he interrupted, lifting his eyebrows imperiously. "Or I will wed you regardless of what you say."

Elizabeth glared at him, knowing he meant every word of what he was saying. "Now I know what is meant by being caught between the devil and the deep blue sea," she muttered feelingly.

"What?" He looked puzzled.

"It is an English expression," she said, trying to think of some way to mollify him without committing herself to a course of action she couldn't carry out. "It means to be trapped between two equally disagreeable choices."

"Ah, and I am the devil, yes?" Alexi asked, looking pleased. "Good. And the sea would be Falconer. It fits him, I think; stormy, wild, but constant in his way. He is a man of honor I would trust with my sister's life. No one would dare harm you with him at your side."

Elizabeth thought of the merciless way Adam had pressed her for her father's letters. It might have pained him to do so, and she believed that it had, but in the end he had done what his duty required of him. If that same duty required her arrest, even her life, what would he do?

"Elizabeth?" Alexi was eyeing her anxiously. "What is it? What sad thoughts do you have you do not share with your Alexi?"

She shook off her melancholy thoughts and tried to think of an answer that would placate him. "I suppose I was wondering what made you think my going to Adam, to Lord Falconer," she corrected, "would serve. He is more likely to hand me over to the hangman than to shelter me."

"Because I trust him," Alexi replied with almost child-like simplicity. "As you should trust him, little queen. He is a good man, and if you tell him the truth, he will do what is right. You will see."

His words lingered long after Alexi took his leave of her and she returned to her own room. She did trust Adam, Elizabeth realized, nervously pacing the confines of her small room. She trusted him more than she had ever trusted anyone, but she'd been far less than honest with him almost since the first time she'd clapped eyes on him. "Tell him the truth," Alexi had advised, and even though it meant risking her life and that of her father, she realized he was right. She realized something else as well. She was in love with Adam.

The thought had her dropping on her bed, dazed and terrified by turns. It couldn't be, she told herself. It mustn't be. And yet it was. She placed a trembling hand over her heart, feeling its wild thumping, and gazed off into nothing. Tears glistened in her eyes, and her lips parted on a soft sigh of wonderment as she accepted the truth she had so long denied. She loved Adam.

Like a child with a new toy, she examined that love, turning it over and over in her mind. She remembered his every expression, his every smile, and above all she remembered the shattering power of the kisses they had shared. No wonder his kiss had so affected her, she thought, smiling ruefully. A lover's kiss was certain to be far more potent than that of a mere beau.

But if her newly admitted love brought joy, it also brought sorrow, and a growing sense of shame. How could she say she loved Adam, she scolded herself, when she'd deliberately deceived him? He was risking his reputation and his honor to save her, and instead of doing everything she could to help him, she put him off with half-truths and lies. If that was love, then it was a very poor sort of love indeed.

There was no hope for it, she decided, her legs somewhat unsteady as she rose to her feet. If she loved Adam, if she trusted him, then she would have to give him the last of her father's letters. Without giving herself time to change her mind, she dashed out of the room, slipping quietly down the staircase to the ground floor. Most of the guests were in their rooms, and the servants were busy with their duties, so she was able to slip into the library unobserved.

It was early evening, and most of the room was in shadows. She contemplated lighting a candle but decided it was a waste of flint and time. She didn't need a candle to find what she'd come for. Retrieving the ladder chair from the corner, she dragged it over and climbed up on top, holding her skirts in one hand as she reached for the book with the other. In the end it required the use of both hands, but she was finally able to retrieve the heavy tome. Sighing in relief, she flipped the book open. The letter was gone.

Even as her shocked gaze was registering the letter's absence, she heard a sound behind her, and caught the sharp smell of flint as a candle flared to life. She turned her head, the book dropping from her hands as she stared into Adam's cold, furious eyes.

"Hello, my dear," he drawled, holding up her father's letter. "Is this what you are looking for?"

Eleven

Adam watched in taut silence as the blood drained from Elizabeth's face. Even in the flickering light offered by the candle's meager flame he could see her pale. Her cheeks were so white, they might have been carved from purest alabaster, and her eyes burned like silver-blue flames. She swayed for a moment, and he wondered cynically if she was going to swoon. If she thought it would soften him, she was sadly mistaken. He was done being deceived by her.

The idea to search for the missing letter in the library had come to him on the ride back from the village. He was fairly certain the letter wasn't in her room, and he was trying to imagine where it might be when he suddenly remembered the night of the masked ball. A vivid image of her perched unsteadily on the ladder chair, her fingers outstretched as she reached for a book, had flashed in his mind, and he knew where the letter would be found. The moment he arrived at the Hall he'd gone directly to the library to begin his search. The letter was in the second book he checked.

The memory of what the letter contained slashed into him like the blade of a saber, the shock and pain of it so great it felt as if he'd been gutted. He wanted to scream in fury and howl out his agony at his staggering sense of betrayal, and for the first time in more years than he could remember, he doubted his ability to control himself. The feeling of impotence only added to his turbulent emotions, and he hated himself for his weakness. He glared at Elizabeth, his temper and impatience mounting when he realized she'd yet to speak.

"Well?" he sneered, bitterness welling up inside him. "Have you nothing to say? No tears to shed, no protestations of innocence?"

Elizabeth remained alarmingly pale as she met his gaze. "No," she said, her soft voice devoid of its usual animation. "It's plain it would be a waste of time. You've read the letter, I see."

Adam was out of his chair and roughly grabbing Elizabeth by the shoulders before he was even aware of having moved. "The devil take you, Elizabeth!" he snapped, driven by pain and despair to give her an angry shake. "Don't you dare presume to act the injured victim! This letter implicates you in your father's treason!"

Her hair tumbled free from its chignon, spilling around her shoulders in a golden-brown fall as she gazed up at him. Her eyes were wide with shock, but she made no move to free herself.

"I know."

The quiet words made him angrier. "Is that all you can say?" he demanded, giving her another shake. "This isn't a game, Elizabeth. They're going to hang you!"

"I know that as well," she replied, her breath hitching as she showed her first sign of emotion. "Please let go of me, Lord Falconer. You're hurting me."

In response Adam's fingers tightened; not to punish, he realized furiously, but because he couldn't bear to let her go. Angry as he was, hurt as he was, his first and strongest instinct was to protect Elizabeth. Damning himself for a fool, he released her, turning his back and stalking over to scoop up the letter he'd dropped. He unfolded it, his jaw clenching as he began reading it aloud.

" 'It need not be much; any bit of intelligence you have to offer would be welcome,' " he read, and then lowered the letter to fix her in his coldest gaze. "What did you send him, Elizabeth?" he demanded. "It may go better for you if you tell me now."

"I sent him nothing," she replied, her voice so soft he had to strain to catch the words. "Not that I expect you'll believe me."

Adam's lips curled in a bitter sneer. "When Mrs. Treckler has already confirmed that her brother sailed with your last letter a few days ago?" he asked with a bitter laugh. "Not hardly, my dear. You'll have to do better than that if you wish to avoid swinging. I'll ask you again, what did you send your father?"

For the first time since he'd made his presence known, Elizabeth's temper and pride flared to life. "Why should I bother telling you anything?" she cried, her small hands clenched in fists at her side. "You've already made up your mind, haven't you? In your divine estimation I've already been tried and found guilty, and of course there's no chance you could be wrong. You're never wrong, are you, my lord?"

"Damn it, Elizabeth!" He roared out the words. "Answer the question!"

"I did answer the question!" she roared back, and then drew a deep breath. She lowered her head for a moment, visibly collecting herself. When she glanced back up tears had turned her eyes to shimmering silver, and her face was a mask of raw anguish.

"Yes," she began, her voice shaking with pain, "it's true my father asked me to commit treason. Yes, he expected me to betray my country in order to please him. But I didn't. I couldn't."

The cold, analytical part of his nature sneered that she was a consummate actress, and that tears were a woman's favorite weapon. "Go on," he said, ignoring the way his stomach was churning.

"From the moment I read his letter, I knew he was forcing me to choose between England and him," she continued, bravely holding his gaze. "I also knew that once

I'd made that choice there would be no going back, no way I could have both. So I made my choice. I chose England."

"What did you write?"

"I wrote that I loved him; that I always had and always would. And I wrote that as much as I loved him, as much as I respected him as my father, I couldn't do what he wanted. America might now be his home, but England was mine, and I would not betray her. I wrote to tell him good-bye." Her voice broke on the last word.

Adam beat down the urge to go to her side and dry her tears. "Have you proof?" he demanded harshly.

"Only my word," she said, wiping the tears from her cheeks with an unsteady hand. "And you've made it plain how much my word means to you. You wouldn't believe anything I say, would you?"

Because he so desperately wanted to believe her, he gave a harsh laugh. "My dear, you could go down on your knees and profess undying love for me and I'd not believe you."

She jerked as if he'd struck her, and the expression on her face shocked him into an awareness of his vile cruelty. He took an impulsive step toward her, his hand held out in mute appeal.

"Elizabeth—"

She took a stumbling step back. "Then it's as well I never said it," she said, her slender body trembling. "I should hate to have wasted such words on the likes of you."

Her expression of pain shattered him, and he felt literally sick with shame. "Elizabeth, wait," he pleaded, taking another step forward. "Please, let me—"

"No!" she cried, backing toward the door. "Don't come any closer! You've hurt me all you can ever hurt me. Arrest me, hang me, do whatever it is you feel you must, but keep away from me!" She turned and ran from the room, as if fleeing from the devil himself.

Adam stared after her, a whirlwind of violently clashing

emotions roaring through him. He'd been so hurt by what he viewed as her treachery, he'd deliberately closed his heart to everything save the coldest and hardest of facts. But in his pain and anger he'd overlooked the only fact that mattered: Elizabeth was no traitor. A wave of icy horror shuddered through him as the full scope of his sins overwhelmed him. What had he done? he wondered in sick despair. God in heaven, what had he done?

"Elizabeth!" He shouted her name and tore off in pursuit, his heart pounding with a fear he could not name.

Elizabeth had no idea where she was going; she only knew that if she didn't get away, she would shatter into so many pieces she'd never be whole again. Pulling open the French doors, she ran out onto the terrace, glancing frantically about for some avenue of escape. The conservatory lay to the right, but since Mr. Colburt's murder it had been kept shut up. The gardens lay to the left, but at this time of day it was likely she would encounter guests strolling amongst the pinks and blooming roses.

She was trying to decide which path to take when she heard Adam calling her name. Without pausing to look behind her, she made for the conservatory, praying she could reach it before he caught her. She made it inside, but before she could close the door he was already there.

"Go away!" she sobbed, pride and decorum forgotten as pain overwhelmed her. "Go away, Adam. Please."

"I can't," he said, his voice raw and his face pale as he advanced toward her. "We have to talk, Elizabeth. I want you to listen to me."

She sent him an incredulous look, furious he would dare ask such a thing of her. "What more could you possibly have to say?" she demanded bitterly. "Haven't you insulted me enough already?"

"I didn't mean it," he told her, continuing toward her until he was inches away. "Upon my honor, I didn't mean it. I was mad; I must have been utterly out of my mind to say such things. But I never believed them. Even when I was saying them, I didn't believe them." He held out his hand again, the gesture both commanding and pleading. "Forgive me, Elizabeth, please."

Her tear-filled gaze went from his hand to his face. "Why?" she asked, tears spilling out of her eyes to flow down her cheeks. "Why should I forgive you? How do I know you aren't pretending to believe me so you can trap me in a lie?"

This time he was the one to jerk back, but he kept his hand held out to her. "You can't know," he replied quietly. "Any more than I can know you are innocent of any wrongdoing. But I do know, Elizabeth, because I know *you*. I know I don't deserve it, but I am begging you to find it in your heart to forgive my ridiculous accusations. I cannot bear to know I have hurt you as I have."

Now she did shatter, undone not by his anger but by his humility, and by the unshakable sense of honor compelling his heartfelt apology. Without being aware of having moved she took his hand, offering no resistance as he pulled her into his arms.

"You destroyed me," she whispered brokenly, laying her head on his chest. "When you didn't believe me, you destroyed me."

"Elizabeth." He held her to his heart, pressing desperate kisses to the top of her head. "I am sorry, my dearest. I am so sorry."

"How could you think that of me?" she cried, striking his shoulders with her fists. "How could you think I would ever betray my country? That I would betray you?"

"I didn't want to think it," he whispered, his arms tightening about her and drawing her against his shaking body. "God, my sweet, I didn't want to.

"Why do you think I was being such an ogre?" he added, gently cupping her face between his palms and tilting her head up to his. "My heart and my mind were at war, and the battle was destroying me. I know I hurt you. I meant to. Forgive me." He bent his head, his mouth seeking hers in a kiss of desperation and desire.

The press of his lips on hers was almost brutal, but it was its very intensity that made it so sweet. Adam was the most controlled man Elizabeth had ever met, and that he could kiss her with such a lack of restraint showed her more eloquently than words the true depth of his emotions. The knowledge should have terrified; instead it reassured, as nothing else would have done. Closing her eyes, she lifted her arms to circle his neck, pressing herself against his hardening body and eagerly offering him every particle of the love she felt for him.

As if he'd been waiting for just such a response, Adam gave a low groan. His fingers buried themselves in the thick fall of her hair, tilting her head back even farther as he deepened the kiss with hungry ferocity. The sensual intimacy of the kiss shattered Elizabeth's reserve, and she gave a soft cry of pleasure.

"Adam!"

"Elizabeth." He breathed out her name in a voice ragged with passion, sliding his mouth down her neck in a string of sizzling kisses. Unsteady hands slid down her shoulders to cup the undersides of her breasts, and audacious fingers teased the throbbing nipples to hardened peaks.

Elizabeth had never known so bold a caress, and she was helpless to disguise the pleasure it brought her. Her fingers dug deeper into the velvet covering his broad shoulders, and she trembled with an intoxicating blend of excitement and uncertainty. Adam must have felt her shivering because he lifted his head without warning, his eyes glittering like faceted topaz as he stared down into her flushed face. He studied her for several seconds before drawing a ragged breath.

"We have to stop, my sweet," he said regretfully, brushing a final kiss across her trembling mouth. "This is neither the time nor the place for lovemaking, and we've much to discuss."

Feeling somewhat bemused, a silent Elizabeth allowed Adam to capture her hand in his and guide her across the conservatory. She thought he meant to lead her back into the house and was surprised when he led her to the stone bench located in the far corner of the room. A bubbling fountain carved in the shape of a capering Pan and a veritable forest of palms and broad-leaf ferns shielded them from the rest of the room, keeping their presence hidden from anyone who might casually glance inside. The effect was like being in a secluded glen, and Elizabeth wondered what Adam might have in mind. She was weighing several intriguing possibilities when he scooped her up in his arms and sat on the bench.

"Now," he began, settling her across his thighs and keeping his arms looped companionably about her waist, "tell me about your father. This time I promise I will listen."

The sudden shift of conversation had Elizabeth hesitating, and then she was leaning her head against his shoulder, her voice soft with sorrow as she told him of her mother's unexpected death and her father's furious response.

"You don't know my father," she concluded, tears of regret in her eyes as she kept her gaze fixed on the folds of his starched cravat. "You don't know what my mother's death did to him. He hates England with all that he is, and now he hates me as well."

"But why should he blame England for her death?" Adam asked curiously, stroking a gentle hand through her curls. "You said she died of the fever."

Elizabeth shuddered as she recalled those terrible days when her mother had hovered between life and death. "She did. There was a great deal of sickness in the city at that time, and Papa hoped to get us out on the first ship sailing for home. It was a military transport, and the captain refused to take us, even when Papa offered him a bribe. Mama caught the fever while we were waiting for the next ship and died in less than a week. It was only when we were under sail on the other ship that we learned the captain refused us because he'd already been bribed by a British lord to ship his household furniture back to Portsmouth. It filled an entire cabin; a cabin we might have taken had it not been for the captain's greed and the other man's selfishness. Papa kept saying Mama died because of a sideboard, and he vowed never to forgive or forget that fact."

Adam uttered a furious imprecation beneath his breath. "All right," he said after a few moments. "I suppose I can understand why he might hold some resentment against his country. But why should he hate you? You were only doing what you thought right, as he was doing."

"Papa doesn't see things so clearly," Elizabeth replied, tears spilling from her eyes to trail down her cheeks. "In his view I chose England over him, and that he cannot forgive. I am dead to him, as he is dead to me. I will never hear from him again."

He tilted her face up to his, an expression of infinite sorrow on his handsome features. "I lost both my parents when I was not yet fourteen," he said, brushing the tears from her cheeks with a gentle thumb. "It is a pain that time neither dims nor soothes." He pressed a soft kiss to her lips. "I'm sorry, my love."

The simple words soothed her pain and she laid her head once more against his shoulder, listening to the reassuring beat of his heart. They sat in silence for several seconds before she spoke.

"Why were you so convinced of my guilt?" she asked curiously, tilting back her head to study him. "Was it the letters?"

"They certainly didn't help the situation," he grumbled, his arms tightening about her. "Where did you have them hidden, if I may ask? I can't believe they escaped discovery."

A spark of mischief had Elizabeth's lips curving in a reluctant smile. "They were in my writing desk at first," she admitted. "But after I thought someone might have been reading them, I hid them in the band of the hatbox. That's how I smuggled them into the house," she added, unable to resist the temptation to tease him.

He didn't disappoint her. "Devious little devil," he muttered, administering a playful slap of admonishment on her curving thigh. Then he frowned. "What do you mean, when you thought someone else had read your letters?" he demanded. "You never told me that!"

"You never gave me time!" she reminded him, a feeling of incipient indignation rising in her. "You were too busy measuring me for a rope to bother!"

He ignored that. "Well, I am bothering now," he said, his voice taking on the hard edge of command. "Tell me everything."

Elizabeth was too intelligent to waste time pouting, tempting as the thought might be. Instead she told him of discovering the letter and suspecting it had been opened. She thought he would give an indulgent laugh or roll his eyes in masculine impatience and didn't know what to do when he did neither.

"Bronyeskin was in your room?" he asked when she finished.

"Yes," she said, giving his chest an annoyed poke, "and if you're thinking he has aught to do with this, you may think again. Alexi would never do anything to endanger either my reputation or my life!"

"I realize that," Adam responded, tightening his arms about her and drawing her closer against him. "But that doesn't mean I am pleased at the thought that he feels free to visit your room whenever he desires. I shall have to have a word with him, I see."

Elizabeth froze. Alexi hadn't said his departure was to be kept secret, but neither had he given her leave to discuss it. Still, the thought of keeping yet another secret from Adam was not to be borne, and after giving herself a moment to consider the matter she gazed up into Adam's handsome countenance.

"If you wish to speak with Alexi, I fear you shall have

to wait," she said, striving for a nonchalant tone. "He has returned to London."

Adam's jaw clenched, but other than that he gave no outward sign of his emotions. "When?" he demanded starkly.

"This afternoon," she said, relieved to have the matter out in the open. "He received an urgent missive from the Grand Duchess and left almost at once. He said he was going to speak with you," she added, frowning at the memory.

"I was away from the house for most of the afternoon," Adam responded cryptically. "But it is of no moment, I suppose. I never seriously thought him to be a part of all of this, despite strong evidence to the contrary," he added, sending her a censorious scowl.

"What evidence?" she asked, concern for Alexi making her wary.

"The day Colburt's body was discovered, I heard you scolding him for taking too many chances," he reminded her. "A rather poor choice of words, considering."

Elizabeth remembered the conversation. "I was referring to his penchant for insulting people in Russian and then demanding I translate," she said, also recalling Adam's churlish behavior after he'd joined them. She'd wondered if his ill temper had aught to do with her; it would seem she had been right.

"What of the day he arrived?" Adam pressed. "I saw you leaving his rooms, and he was promising to keep your secrets if you would keep his."

Elizabeth flinched, knowing her answer would anger him but accepting the fact that a lie would anger him even more. "I told him I was writing Papa," she said, meeting his gaze with what bravery she could muster. "He was a friend. I couldn't lie to him."

"Yet you could lie to me," he challenged, the soft words containing a wealth of hurt.

She refused to prevaricate, even to spare him pain. "Yes."

He was silent for several seconds before reaching up to gently cup her face between his hands. "And his secrets?" he demanded softly, tracing her trembling mouth with the pads of his thumbs. "If I asked you to tell me about them, would you?"

She shook her head, tears stinging her eyes. It was just like with her father, she thought bleakly, desolation filling her heart. Only instead of being asked to choose between her father and her country, she was being asked to choose between the man she loved as her brother and the man she loved with every fiber of her being.

"I can't, Adam," she whispered rawly, steeling herself for his fury. "I would do anything for you, but I can't betray Alexi. His secrets are for him to share, and if you want to know what they are, you must ask him. Only know they have nothing to do with all that has happened here."

She thought he would push her away, shout at her, and was surprised when instead he drew her even closer. "I know that, my sweet," he said, his voice as gentle as the kiss he pressed to her lips. "But it was something I had to ask." He kissed her again, deeper, but just as Elizabeth raised her arms to embrace him, he was setting her away from him.

"Will you be at the services tomorrow?" he asked, his demeanor changing from that of soothing lover to imperious lord.

The sudden change of topic had Elizabeth's senses whirling. "For chapel services, yes," she replied, struggling to keep pace with him. "Will you?"

"I shouldn't miss it," he replied, his voice assuming the familiar hard edge of command. "In the meanwhile, I don't want you haring off on your own. I have enough on my plate just now without worrying about what new mischief you may be falling into."

Elizabeth gave an aggrieved sniff at what she considered an unfair accusation. "You make it sound as if all of this is somehow my doing," she muttered.

To her surprise he gave a low chuckle. "And so it is,

my love," he murmured, smiling down at her. "Only think of the trouble you might have spared us all if you'd come to me from the start. Now come," he added cajolingly, flicking his finger across the tip of her nose, "give me your word you'll behave sensibly."

Elizabeth's heart gave a painful flutter at the casual endearment. "I thought you didn't believe my word," she said, saying the first words to pop into her head.

The laughter in Adam's eyes died, replaced by a look of raw anguish. "I lied," he said, his voice rough with emotion. "God forgive me, I lied." And he swept her up against him, his lips taking hers in a kiss that sent all Elizabeth's senses reeling with delight.

It was a day well suited for a funeral. The sky was dark and swollen with clouds, and a chilling rain lashed against the leaded windows. Over the murmur of conversation Adam could hear the ominous roll of thunder, and he saw more than one person casting a nervous glance over his shoulder. Both Carling and Derwent seemed particularly affected by the Gothic atmosphere, and Adam's eyes narrowed as he studied each man in turn. He was deciding how best to approach them when Lady Barrington drifted over to join him.

"You're looking properly somber, my lord," she murmured, her blue eyes coolly assessing as she studied him over the rim of her glass. "How surprising; I didn't know you were so fond of Mr. Colburt."

Adam's first reaction was to administer the scandalous widow a sharp set-down, but upon reflection he thought better of it. He'd spent a great deal of last evening and this morning subtly interrogating the other guests, but he'd yet to question her grace. Deciding now was as good a time as any, he took a careful sip of his cordial before responding.

"One needn't be fond of someone to mourn his death, your grace," he said, knowing the duchess would mistrust any sudden show of friendship on his part. "Especially when that death comes so violently and unexpectedly as did Mr. Colburt's."

Lady Barrington gave a light laugh. "Perhaps," she conceded with an indifferent shrug. "But I would hardly think Mr. Colburt's death could be termed *unexpected.* He was such a villainous wretch, it was only a matter of time before someone had enough of his nonsense and killed him."

The unfeeling pronouncement had Adam's eyebrows arching in speculation. "You sound as if you believe Mr. Colburt to blame for his own demise. That seems rather harsh."

"Is it?" She gave another shrug. "I don't believe so. The dolt had only to mind his tongue and his childish temper, and he might have survived into his dotage. But that was Charles; he was never quite as clever as he thought himself to be."

That struck Adam as decidedly telling, but he was politician enough to keep his thoughts to himself. Instead he and the duchess spoke idly of the brief funeral service for Colburt, which had been held a few hours earlier, and after a few minutes her grace drifted off to speak with the other guests. Adam watched her go,

He spent the rest of the afternoon drifting from guest to guest, gleaning from them what he could. He also kept a sharp eye on Elizabeth, and was considerably ill pleased to see her being run ragged by Lady Derring and her friends. When all of this was well behind them, he vowed grimly, he would see her removed from beneath that harpy's claw.

He'd write St. Jerome, he decided. The viscount had proven quite successful in placing his former comrades-in-arms in a variety of positions, and he would best know how to go about securing Elizabeth employment. Or he could even appeal to Elinore, he thought, his brooding gaze sliding in the aloof beauty's direction. Although she'd not had a companion before, there was no reason she couldn't hire one now. She seemed genuinely fond of Elizabeth, and he was certain she would prove a good and kind employer. It was the perfect solution to his problem.

Yet even as the solution presented itself, Adam found himself rejecting it. He wouldn't wish Elinore on his worse enemy, and in any case, she and Elizabeth were both so stubborn and willful, they were certain to be pulling caps within a fortnight. And fobbing her off on any other lady he could think of was equally repellent. Elizabeth was a lady in her own right, and the idea of her in a succession of subservient positions was an anathema to him.

"Good afternoon, my lord."

Mr. Carling's quiet voice interrupted Adam's dark musings, and he glanced up to find the younger man standing before him. To his surprise the lad's fleshy face had lost its usual expression of sullen petulance, and there was a new air of dignity and purpose about him that lent him a quality that had previously been lacking. Mr. Carling, it seemed, had grown up at last.

"Mr. Carling." Adam inclined his head graciously, showing him the respect he'd previously withheld. "Pray accept my condolences. I am sure Mr. Colburt was a very good friend to you."

"Thank you, Lord Falconer," Mr. Carling replied, further surprising Adam by holding out his hand with commendable maturity. "It is kind of you to say so."

More impressed than he ever thought he'd be with the dandy, Adam accepted the proffered hand. The lad's handshake was so firm, it took a few seconds for Adam to notice the piece of paper Carling was pressing into his palm. Their eyes met, and in the younger man's gaze Adam saw both fear and determination reflected in his pale eyes. Adam's fingers curled protectively about the note before he stepped back.

Assuming it likely they were under observation, Adam took pains to conceal the note while he lingered at Carling's side. He waited several seconds before drifting away, and then allowed another ten minutes to pass before slipping quietly out of the drawing room. His own chambers were too far away and he slipped into the hallway, making certain he was alone before unfolding the note.

"I know who took the papers and then killed Charles," he read. *"Meet me in Papa's study after dinner, and I shall tell you all. Tell no one, or I am dead."*

Decidedly Gothic and more than a bit dramatic, he thought, tucking the note back into his pocket. But if Carling had any information he was willing to share, he was more than ready to accommodate him.

He returned to the drawing room and spent the next hour drifting from group to group and keeping a sharp eye on Carling. He noted that the lad kept strictly to tea and hovered protectively near his parents, a sight he viewed with considerable satisfaction. Geoffrey Derwent, on the other hand, seemed as hell-bent on mischief making as always, and was making considerable inroads into the earl's decanter of brandy. Remembering how the idiot had blurted out his suspicions and innuendoes while in his cups, Adam began making his way toward him. He'd almost reached his side when disaster struck. It was no small surprise that Elizabeth was the source of the disaster.

"How dare you, sir!" she exclaimed, her hand lashing out to strike Derwent across the face with enough force to send him staggering back. He fetched up against the tea cart, sending it and its contents spilling to the floor in a cacophony of shattering porcelain and piercing feminine shrieks.

"What the devil?" The dandy lay sprawled amongst the broken dishes and smashed cakes, his hand cradling his cheek as he blinked up at her in drunken indignation. "What on earth is wrong with you, you bitch? You're mad!"

The slurred oath had even more women shrieking and swooning, and several more were glaring at him in outraged disgust. Adam reached him in a few strides, hauling him off the floor and giving him a sound shaking before setting him on unsteady feet.

"Mind your tongue, puppy!" he warned, fixing him in a murderous glare. "I'll call you out if you say one more word."

"But it was a compliment!" the younger man insisted, his humiliation and temper obvious in his flushed cheeks. "Presumptuous doxy; she ought to be grateful for what I offered."

Adam didn't waste any more time with words; he simply doubled up his fist and struck the idiot across the jaw with as much power as he could muster. Derwent went crashing to the floor again, and this time Adam didn't bother picking him up. Carling and two other men came dashing up to help, and Adam gave them each a stern look.

"Take this piece of dung to his rooms and make damned certain I don't clap eyes on him again," he ordered curtly. "I've had all of him I can stomach."

Without waiting to see if his orders were being carried out, he turned to Elizabeth only to see her slipping out of the room, an attentive Elinore at her side. Ignoring the calls and demands of the others for explanations, he turned and gave chase.

"Dearest, are you all right?" he asked, hurrying toward her.

"Of course I'm fine, you dolt!" she snapped, glaring at him in what could only be termed annoyance. "Now get back in there and keep an eye on him before he is killed!"

Adam's jaw dropped in astonishment. He knew Elizabeth too well to think he'd find her near collapse from nerves, but neither had he expected to find her barking orders at him like a top sergeant. Concern gave way to male bafflement and he turned to Elinore, who was also regarding him with a singular lack of appreciation for his heroic efforts.

"What the devil is going on?" he demanded in bellicose tones.

"Mr. Derwent was bragging that he knew the identity of Mr. Colburt's killer," Elinore answered, her gray eyes frosting over with displeasure. "He then offered to share the information with Elizabeth in exchange for her favors. Thank heavens she had the presence of mind to slap him before he said anything more."

"It sounds as if he said quite enough to me," Adam muttered, wondering if he should kill Derwent and be done with it. "How dare he presume to insult you in such a manner!"

"Adam, will you stop brooding over my honor and pay attention to what is important here!" Elizabeth retorted, fisting her hands on her hips and casting him an annoyed scowl. "I didn't slap Mr. Derwent because of his crude innuendoes. I slapped him because it was the only way I could think of to stop him from blurting out the truth without tipping our hand to the enemy!"

Adam's anger faded as the enormity of her observation sunk in.

"Who heard him?" he asked, furious with himself for failing to have grasped the significance of the matter sooner.

"Lady Bealeton, Mrs. Deville, and a few of the others," Elinore replied, ticking off the names with a frown. "And the vicar, Mr. Smithing, was nearby, as I recall, but he is so deaf I doubt he would have heard a brace of cannons if they were shot off next to him. I can't think of who else might have been about."

"Lady Barrington was there talking to Miss Harewood," Elizabeth provided, looking thoughtful. "But judging from the way she jumped when Mr. Derwent upset the tea cart, I'm certain she wasn't paying him any mind."

"Pray to God everyone else was equally inattentive," Adam responded, thinking quickly. He glanced at Elinore. "Lady Elinore, do you know where your footman might be?"

"Taking his turn at passing biscuits, I shouldn't wonder," Elinore replied, eyeing him with her customary coolness. "With the household at sixes and sevens, Lady

Derring has bespoken his services. Do you think I should offer to have him stand guard over Mr. Derwent?"

"Please," Adam said, although privately he thought it would be no great loss if the unknown assassin succeeded in doing away with the drunken Derwent. "In the meanwhile, I want the two of you to continue keeping your eyes and ears open. Report to me the moment you learn anything of value."

Elizabeth opened her lips as if to offer argument, but when Elinore gave a discreet shake of her head, she quickly closed them.

"Of course, my lord," she said, dropping a graceful curtsy. "Will there be anything else?"

Adam cast her a sharp look, strongly suspecting sarcasm. "No," he said between clenched teeth. "There will not."

"In that case, I wonder if her ladyship would be so good as to help me to my room?" She turned to Elinore with a speaking look. "I am sure you will understand that I am quite overwhelmed by all of this and need to seek my bed."

"Of course, my dear," Elinore responded, her dulcet tones making Adam's suspicions grow even sharper. "I shouldn't care to have you swooning in the hall. Come now," she said, and led Elizabeth up the stairs with studied attentiveness.

Adam watched them go, his jaw clenching as he fought the urge to go after them. He hadn't time for Elizabeth's temper now, he told himself, turning back toward the drawing room. He had a murderer to catch, stolen papers to recover, and a potentially ruinous political scandal to avoid. The moment he was done with that, however, he would deal with Miss Elizabeth Mattingale. The recalcitrant companion had walked away from him for the last time.

Twelve

"Odious, overbearing tyrant!" Elizabeth wasted little time in letting her annoyance be known. "Telling us to keep our eyes and ears open as if we were a pair of eavesdropping schoolgirls! Who does he think he is?"

"A man, of course," Elinore replied, surprisingly sedate as she reclined on her chaise longue, calmly sipping her tea. "And a marquess in the bargain. There is no more overbearing species on the planet, I do assure you. Why do you think I refused him?"

The wry observation brought Elizabeth up short, and she blushed to think what she had said and to whom she had said it. Elinore had in a matter of a few days become a very dear friend, but not so dear that Elizabeth could afford to forget the disparity in their stations. She cast the other woman a guilty look over her shoulder.

"I beg pardon, my lady," she began hesitantly, "I didn't mean to—"

"Oh, nonsense, Elizabeth!" Elinore snapped, her complacent air vanishing as she sat up and set her cup on the table. "Don't 'my lady' me! I should have thought we were far beyond that."

The genuine hurt she heard in the other woman's voice and saw reflected in her light gray eyes had Elizabeth feeling immediately contrite, and she returned to her chair with a sheepish smile.

"We are," she said, reaching out to briefly squeeze Elinore's clenched hand. "Forgive me for implying otherwise. It is just that his lordship has me so vexed, I vow I cannot seem to think."

"Falconer has that affect upon some women, I have noted," Elinore replied after a moment, studying Elizabeth in her disconcertingly keen manner. "Thankfully he never had that affect upon me; another reason I refused him, by the by. How long have you been in love with him?"

The cool question had Elizabeth leaping from her chair, her face blazing and then paling as she met the other woman's assessing regard. She sat back down with an unladylike *plop*.

"Is it so obvious?" she asked, praying Adam hadn't guessed the truth she thought she'd taken such pains to hide.

"Only to someone who cares for you both," Elinore assured her, and this time it was she who gave Elizabeth's hand a gentle pat. "But don't worry, I shan't tell a soul, and his lordship is far too thick-headed to notice. Unless he chooses to do so, of course."

Elizabeth decided it would be wisest to ignore that cryptic observation for the moment. "What now?" she asked, forcing herself to concentrate on more immediate concerns.

"Now we wait," Elinore replied, settling once more against the plump cushions and looking thoughtful. "Papa is returning in a few days, perhaps as early as tomorrow, and he writes that he is bringing us news that will finally settle this unpleasantness once and for all."

"That is good," Elizabeth said with a relieved sigh, feeling much of the weight easing from her shoulders. She knew both Adam and Alexi were working diligently on her behalf, and although she appreciated their efforts and had complete faith in the outcome, she was also unwilling to sit by and do nothing while others cleared her name. That was why she'd gone to Lady Elinore to ask for her help.

Since the day of the murder, she and the other woman had spent several hours debating the mystery of the missing papers and Mr. Colburt's death. Their plotting sessions sometimes involved Lady Barrington, and she was deeply touched by both women's willingness to be of assistance. Of course, lately their talks had only been between Elinore and herself, but that was because Lady Barrington was occupied with a new lover. Or at least that was what Elinore had told her, lifting her eyebrows with a worldly acceptance Elizabeth couldn't quite bring herself to emulate.

"He also writes that your friend Bronyeskin has been breaking hearts and causing scandal everywhere he goes," Elinore was continuing, her full lips pursed in disapproval. "Rather swift work on his part, don't you think, considering the wretch has been in London but a handful of days?"

Elizabeth smiled, thinking of Alexi. "His highness could create a scandal in under a minute, if such was his intent," she said, and then frowned, wondering if indeed a scandal of some sort *was* Alexi's intent. It made for an intriguing possibility.

"Perhaps." Elinore gave an irritated shrug. "At least we shan't have to worry about his returning to plague us. With everything in place for the Czar's fête, he will be far too occupied to come to the country."

They continued talking and planning for the next half hour before Elizabeth excused herself and returned to the drawing room. Since Lady Derring had yet to give her her *conge,* she still considered herself to be in the countess's employ, and she was determined to carry out her duties until the end. Her ladyship might still give her the sack, but she was hanged if she'd let her have the satisfaction of claiming it was because she'd not given proper service.

Elizabeth wasn't surprised to find the drawing room all but deserted upon her return. Less than half a dozen guests remained, Lady Barrington among them, and when she saw Elizabeth hovering in the doorway she gestured her forward with a graceful wave.

"Dear Miss Mattingale, are you quite all right?" she asked, her blue eyes bright with concern as they studied Elizabeth. "That pestilent beast! I cannot imagine why the Derrings allow him to remain. He is the outside of enough."

Although she more than shared the duchess's assessment of Mr. Derwent's character, the presence of the other guests had Elizabeth holding her tongue. "I believe they allow him to remain because of Mr. Carling," she said at last. "Mr. Colburt's death has been quite hard on him."

"I cannot think why," the duchess opined with a sniff. "He was as big a fool as that tedious fop Derwent. Which reminds me," she added, sliding Elizabeth a quizzing look, "do you really think he meant it when he said he knew who killed Mr. Colburt? I own I find it difficult to believe."

"As do I," Elizabeth agreed. "Mr. Colburt was also his friend. One would think if he had any useful information of the crime he'd have told the earl at once."

"That is so," the duchess responded with a nod. "Doubtlessly he was bragging for effect; a dangerous thing, considering the real killer could have overheard him and be moved to silence him. How fortunate for his health that he is as ignorant as he is vicious."

Elizabeth started to agree and then stopped, frowning as a sudden memory shimmered to life in her mind. "I hope the same might be said of Mr. Carling."

Lady Barrington's gaze sharpened. "What do you mean?"

"The night of the murder, Mr. Derwent seemed to be hinting that Mr. Carling knew more than he was telling," Elizabeth replied, lost in thought. "I remember Mr. Carling seemed quite upset and was trying to hush him even before Lord Falconer intervened." Then she shook her head.

"But that's nonsense," she said, feeling decidedly foolish. "It makes even less sense than if Mr. Derwent had some knowledge of the crime. Given his devotion to Mr. Colburt, he would certainly have shared whatever he knew with his father so that the killer could be brought to justice. Keeping quiet would make no sense, unless he was doing so to hide his involvement with the theft of his father's papers."

Lady Barrington gave a startled gasp. *"Mr. Carling* took the papers?" she demanded incredulously. "But that is infamous!"

Elizabeth blanched in horror at what she'd inadvertently let slip. At least the duchess had kept her voice low-pitched, and a frantic glance about showed that the other guests seemed oblivious to the outburst and were deep in their own conversations. Vowing to be more circumspect in the future, she leaned toward the other woman in a confiding manner.

"I have no proof, you understand," she whispered, once she'd finished sharing her suspicions. "But Lord Falconer agrees with me. He says it's precisely the sort of prank they would pull."

"And so it is," the duchess agreed, her lips tightening in outrage. "A malicious schoolboy trick that not only put you in danger but the earl as well. His career in the government would be ruined if it ever became known that his half-witted son was helping himself to the contents of his dispatch box. Indeed, I daresay there is nothing Derring wouldn't do to keep that bit of gossip quiet. How interesting."

Elizabeth was about to ask what her grace found of such interest when Lady Derring reentered the room. Her employer's return put an end to Elizabeth's freedom, and after murmuring her apologies to Lady Barrington, she made her way to the countess's side.

She spent the rest of the afternoon and evening biting her tongue and catering to the older woman's increasingly peevish demands. Her ladyship seemed determined to make her lose her temper, and by night's end Elizabeth was more than of a mind to oblige her. Adam and the others had best solve the mystery of the missing papers and Mr. Colburt's death soon, she thought with an irritated scowl. If they did not, she'd likely end in the docket for strangling her irksome employer.

Her duties kept Elizabeth working through dinner, and it was approaching midnight before she was done. Usually the guests would be up and indulging themselves, but the funeral and dreary weather had cast a decided pall over the household and everyone retired early. Elizabeth never thought to miss their noise, but as she lit her candle and began making her way toward the front of the house, she couldn't help but find the oppressive silence disconcerting.

The darkened hallway seemed full of shadows and shades, the meager light cast by her flickering candle scarce piercing the stygian blackness. When she drew even with the door leading to the earl's study the long clock in the hall began tolling out the hour, and she almost dropped her candle as she gave a start of fright. She was mentally cursing herself for her foolishness when an arm snaked out of the darkness and a hand clamped over her mouth.

"It's me," a familiar voice whispered in her ear, and then she was free. She whirled around, the flame of her candle dancing as she glared up at Adam.

"Adam!" she gasped, clutching her candle even tighter. "You frightened me half to death! What are you doing skulking about at this hour?"

"What am I doing skulking about?" he demanded incredulously. "What about you? Why aren't you in bed? And set that candle down before you drop it. You'll set your skirts aflame." And the candle was plucked from her fingers and placed on the hall table.

With her hand free she doubled up her fist and struck him on the arm as hard as she could. "If I had dropped it, it would be all your fault, you wretch!" she hissed, her heart hammering with fear and rising temper. "And you haven't answered my question. What are you doing creeping about like a housebreaker?"

For a moment she didn't think he would answer her. He looked coldly furious, and there was a grimness about his eyes that she'd seen the day of Colburt's death. She was wondering if she should repeat her demand or take her leave when he suddenly reached out to take her hand in his.

"It's just as well you're here," he said, turning her toward the study. "You're a sensible sort, and I am in need of help."

Elizabeth had to hurry to keep up with his longer stride. "What sort of help?" she asked, aware of the tension shimmering about him like a halo. "Adam, what is going on?"

"I was to meet Carling," he said, pushing open the door to the study. "He was going to tell me who took the papers and killed Colburt. Unfortunately there has been a complication."

"What sort of complication?" she asked, and then gave a horrified gasp at the sight of Mr. Carling sprawled facedown on the floor of the study, blood seeping from his head.

"This sort," Adam said calmly. "Ring for the footman, would you, and ask him to ride for the doctor? We seem to be in need of his services."

"He will live," the doctor pronounced, wiping his hands as he rose to his feet. "He'll need to be watched but, God willing, he should make a full recovery."

The earl sagged at the news and his wife began sobbing piteously into her kerchief. Adam paid them no heed, his concentration fixed on the still figure lying against the pillows.

"When will he regain consciousness?" he asked, staring at Carling as if by the sheer force of his will he could make the younger man open his eyes and begin speaking.

"Oh, not until morning, perhaps even later than that," the doctor replied with a wave of his hand. "Wounds to the head can be quite serious, don't you know, and there is no predicting how the patient may respond. 'Tis best to wait and allow the brain to recover in its own good time."

Adam's lips thinned in annoyance, but he accepted the doctor's diagnosis. Carling had roused slightly while they were carrying him to his rooms, but his slurred mutterings made little sense. However ill it pleased Adam, there was nothing to be done but wait until morning and hope to heaven Carling would still retain what few brains he possessed when he next opened his eyes.

The Derrings lingered at their son's bedside until the doctor gently but firmly ordered them from the room. The countess paused on her way out to whisper something to Elizabeth, and Adam's eyes narrowed in speculation. His suspicions were proven correct when she walked over and sat on the chair beside Carling's bed. A quick glance at the physician showed the older man to be deep in his discussion with Carling's valet, and Adam wasted little time in hurrying to Elizabeth's side.

"What do you think you're doing?" he whispered, taking care to keep his voice pitched low despite his fury.

She glanced up at him, her expression making it plain she considered him hopelessly dull-witted. "Sitting with Mr. Carling," she said, using the tone usually reserved for the very young or the very old. "Her ladyship wants me to sit with Mr. Carling and—"

"To the devil with what her ladyship wants!" Adam interrupted angrily, and then lowered his voice when both the doctor and the valet glanced avidly in their direction.

"To the devil with her ladyship," he repeated, his jaw clenching in determination, "you're not sitting up with Carling, and that's the end of it. Not only is it improper, but it's dangerous as well. There's a killer at work in this household, and I won't leave you unprotected. What does she think you'll do if he comes back to finish what he has started?"

Elizabeth blanched, her aquamarine eyes going wide with horror. "Just so," he said, giving a grim nod. "I'll speak with the countess tomorrow and explain things, and in the meanwhile I'll set my own man to watch over Carling. He'll be fine, I promise you. Now go to bed, Elizabeth. You're exhausted."

"Very well," she said at last, rising gracefully to her feet. "But first I believe I'll look in on Lady Barrington. She seemed quite upset."

Adam grimaced, thinking *upset* was as good a word as any to describe her grace's performance. She'd appeared with the rest of the guests when they'd come dashing out of their rooms, summoned by the countess's screams, and her own shrieks rivaled Lady Derring's in shrillness and volume. She'd been dressed in a diaphanous peignoir in violet silk, and he was fairly certain he wasn't the only man present to note the lush feminine breasts visible through the sheer silk. Certainly Lord Stoughton seemed to appreciate the sight, and he heroically carried the duchess back to her room after she collapsed in a graceful swoon. He hadn't been seen since, and Adam could well imagine the reason for his absence.

"You needn't bother yourself with her grace," he said, imagining the scene that would follow if Elizabeth caught the trysting couple in flagrante delicto. "I'm sure she'll survive without your ministrations. And in any case, I am surprised to find her behaving so squeamishly," he added ingenuously. "I shouldn't have thought her the missish sort."

"Any lady is certain to be missish when two men are attacked so viciously in under a week," Elizabeth said, defending the other woman spiritedly. "Besides, I'm not certain she has recovered from Mr. Colburt's death. She spoke of seeing him lying facedown in his own blood, and you could tell it upset her."

Adam stopped, his hand resting lightly on Elizabeth's back. An image of how he first saw Colburt lying on the stone floor of the conservatory flashed in his mind.

"She said he was lying facedown?" he said, taking care to hide his acute interest.

"Just like we found Mr. Carling, I should imagine," Elizabeth agreed, patting back a yawn as he guided her from the room.

Adam said nothing, although his mind was racing with speculation. He couldn't remember whether the duchess had been one of the many people crowded into the conservatory that day, but if she had been, wouldn't she have seen Colburt lying face up? It made for an interesting theory, and he tucked the information away for further consideration.

The hallway was deserted when he and Elizabeth emerged from Carling's chambers. The door to the upper sitting room was standing open, and it occurred to him that he'd been granted the perfect opportunity to steal a few private moments with Elizabeth. Casting a quick glance about to make certain they were alone, he pulled her into the room and closed the door behind them. Leaving her only long enough to light a candle, he returned to her side and began kissing her with long-suppressed passion.

When he lifted his head Elizabeth was gazing up at him, her expression languorous. "Finding wounded men would seem to have an odd affect upon you, my lord," she teased, winding her arms about his neck. "How shocking."

Her boldness delighted him. "Imp," he replied, placing another kiss on her soft lips. "It's you who has the affect upon me, and there's nothing in the least shocking about it."

"As you say," she agreed, smiling with shy pleasure. "And as it happens, you have the very same affect upon me."

The lure of her was more than he could resist, and he

gave in to the need to taste her again. Their kisses grew ever more heated, and it was with greatest reluctance that he forced himself to call a halt.

"Elizabeth," he said, reaching down to tenderly brush back a wisp of blond hair from her cheek, "I want you to listen to me. Things are rapidly coming to a head, and that means it is certain to become quite dangerous. I'd send you away if I could, but since I cannot, I want you to exercise the greatest care. Trust no one, and make certain never to be alone with anyone other than Elinore or me. Promise me."

The lambent glow in her eyes died and her expression grew somber. "Very well," she said, laying her hand against his cheek and gazing up at him in concern. "But what about you? Won't you be in danger as well?"

"Perhaps," he conceded, smiling down at her, "but I'm more able to protect myself than you."

"Why?" That chin he adored came up a notch. "Because you are a man? Both Mr. Colburt and Mr. Carling are men, if I may remind you, and it didn't do either of them a whit of good."

Despite the seriousness of the situation, Adam felt his lips twitching. Trust his Elizabeth to argue to the very end, he thought, and silently opened his jacket, revealing the pair of pistols tucked in the waistband of his trousers.

"There, you see?" he said, smiling as he rebuttoned his jacket. "I'll be fine, I promise you."

Her scowl lessened, but she still looked far from convinced. "But what about—"

Adam silenced her the quickest way he could think of, taking her mouth in another kiss. When he next raised his head, his breath was coming in heavy rasps. He wanted Elizabeth more than he'd wanted anything in his life, but there simply wasn't time.

"Go to bed, Elizabeth," he ordered, frustrated desire making his voice sharp as a blade. "And mind you do what you're told. I won't have you risking your life out of sheer stubbornness."

"And I won't have you risking yours out of sheer masculine bravado," she shot back, fiery as always. "Although heaven knows why I should worry; your head is so thick, there is no denting it!"

Again Adam was aware of the urge to smile, but he ruthlessly suppressed it. "Just remember what I said," he ordered. "Trust no one, and whatever you do, don't be alone with any of the guests. Is that understood?"

Her reply was a haughty sniff, but to his relief she offered no further argument. Instead she turned and walked toward the door, her shoulders stiff with temper. Her fingers closed about the handle and she pushed the door open, but instead of walking out, she hesitated and then turned back to face him. Adam braced himself for more angry words and was stunned when he saw tears shining in her eyes.

"Elizabeth"—he took an impulsive step toward her— "what—"

"Be careful," she interrupted, her voice soft and husky with tears. "Please be careful. I could not bear it if something were to happen to you." And with that she was gone, slipping from the room before he could find the words to stop her.

Elizabeth rose from her bed the following morning, wooly-headed and exhausted. The thought of Adam in danger had filled her with such terror she'd been unable to sleep, and had spent the better part of the night staring up at the ceiling and trying desperately to solve the ever-deepening mystery swirling about them. She'd been on the verge of dropping off when a sudden thought occurred to her; a thought so extraordinary it had her popping up in bed, her exhaustion vanishing as if it had never been.

She passed the rest of the night developing the thought into a theory and marshaling arguments sufficient enough to convince Adam that she had the right of it. But as dawn was creeping over the horizon she had a change of heart and decided to discuss the matter first with Lady Elinore. The duke's daughter was as cool as they came, and Elizabeth knew she could rely upon her for sage advice and counseling. She also knew she could count upon her discretion; on the outside chance she was mistaken, the fewer who knew of her outlandish theory, the better.

After splashing cold water on her face to revive herself, Elizabeth dressed for the morning and set out in search of her friend. She found her ladyship in the morning room, taking her breakfast in solitary splendor. When Elinore saw her standing in the doorway she gave her a welcoming smile.

"Ah, Elizabeth, there you are," she said, raising her cup in a toast. "Come join me. I was about to expire from loneliness."

Elizabeth hurried forward, waving the footman away as she took her seat. When the other woman caught sight of her wan features, her smile quickly faded.

"Good heavens, my dear, what is wrong with you?" she exclaimed, studying Elizabeth with marked concern. "You'll forgive my bluntness, I am sure, but you look dreadful! Are you ill?"

Elizabeth shook her head, too weary to prevaricate. "No, no, I am fine," she said, and then turned to the hovering footman, who was also regarding her with a great deal of alarm.

"Thank you, Henry," she said, relieved to have remembered his name. "You may go now. Lady Elinore and I can serve ourselves. I am certain you must have a great many other chores in need of doing."

The footman cast Lady Elinore a questioning glance, and at her silent nod he picked up the coffeepot and took his leave. Elizabeth waited until she was certain he was gone before leaning toward her friend.

"I must speak with you," she continued, taking care to keep her voice low-pitched in case Henry had a propensity for listening at keyholes. "I wish to ask you something, but first you must give me your word you'll not breathe a word of what I am about to say to anyone."

The brunette's eyebrows lifted in silent query, but that was her only sign of interest. "You have my word," she said quietly. "What is it you wish to say?"

Elizabeth drew a shaky breath, suddenly uncertain of what she was about to ask. But then she thought of Adam, and the knowledge of what he was risking had her straightening her shoulders in determination.

"What do you know of Lady Barrington?" she asked at last, deciding it was wisest to be as blunt as possible.

Elinore's shoulders jerked as if in surprise, but her manner was as impeccably cool as always as she lifted her cup to her lips for a dainty sip. "What do you mean?"

Again, Elizabeth decided only the blunt truth would serve. "Is she to be trusted?"

Elinore was quiet a long moment before replying. "No," she said carefully, setting down her cup and meeting Elizabeth's gaze with narrowed eyes. "I would have to say she is not. May I ask how you came to this conclusion?"

The cool question had Elizabeth frowning in confusion. "You don't sound very surprised," she said, thinking her friend remarkably sanguine, considering the fact that they were discussing treason.

Elinore shrugged and picked up her cup again. "We've known for a long while that her grace has been selling secrets to the French," she replied, settling back in her chair. "It was never anything vital—that is to say, of military or diplomatic importance—and so it was decided to leave her in place and keep watch on her. We were more interested in discovering her contacts than in stopping her. That is, until Lord Knolton."

"Lord Knolton?" The name wasn't familiar to Elizabeth.

"You wouldn't know him. It all happened while you were out of the country, and the matter was hushed up as much as such matters could be. Suffice to say the viscount was one of Lady Barrington's many paramours, a member of the Privy Council who slit his own throat last October. At the time it was put out that he'd done so over his debts, but in truth there was another reason."

"A reason involving Lady Barrington?" Elizabeth asked, going green at the thought of someone so driven by despair he would cut his own throat.

"Indeed, although we didn't tumble to that until one of our men in France revealed that Napoleon's agents had a draft of a letter to the Americans offering peace," Elinore continued. "The original letter was known to be in Knolton's diplomatic pouch, a pouch that went missing shortly before the viscount took his own life. We decided he realized that his mistress had been helping herself to his dispatches and killed himself to avoid the scandal."

"And then Lord Derring's papers went missing," Elizabeth said, easily making the connection. "That's why you came, isn't it? Your pretending to be reconsidering Adam's proposal was a sham."

Elinore gave a delicate sniff. "Indeed, haven't I already said no woman of sense or spirit would have him? But that is neither here nor there," she added, before Elizabeth could protest. "We've no time to be pulling caps over the wretch now. Only tell me how you came to decide her grace was involved. Papa will be arriving at any moment, and he'll be wanting a full report."

"It was the attack on Mr. Carling," Elizabeth replied, magnanimously electing to overlook the slur to her beloved's character. "Her grace and I were talking about Mr. Derwent and his stupid boasting, and I commented that while I didn't think Mr. Derwent knew much about anything, I rather thought Mr. Carling might. Her grace agreed with me."

"And then Mr. Carling was attacked just as he was about to reveal what he knew to Falconer," Lady Elinore concluded, nodding. "Yes, it all fits. Now all we need to do is to find some link between Lady Barrington and Mr. Colburt, and we shall have her. Have you any theories to put forth?"

"Perhaps," Elizabeth said carefully, thinking of the other part of her theory that had kept her up for most of the night. "It occurred to me that if I was making use of the local gentlemen to send my letters abroad, then perhaps Lady Barrington might have similar resources. How else could she get the information out of the country with no one being the wiser?"

Elinore looked much struck by this. "It's possible, I suppose," she conceded, tapping her foot. "The smugglers hereabouts are generally held to be loyal subjects, but who is to say they aren't adverse to a touch of treason? Any ideas how we might make contact?"

Elizabeth hesitated. Adam had given orders that they were to keep to the house, but if she and Elinore had any hopes of stopping the duchess, she didn't see they had a choice. However much she disliked the idea of going behind Adam's back, she disliked the idea of a traitor going free even more.

"Elizabeth?" Elinore was regarding her impatiently. "Did you not hear me? Have you any ideas how we can contact the local smugglers?"

Elizabeth shrugged off her troubling doubts and sent the other woman a slow smile. "As a matter of fact, my lady, I have. How would you like a new bonnet?"

Thirteen

"It was Lady Barrington," William said, his resolution obvious despite his weak voice. "She killed Charles; I am certain of it."

"And yet it never occurred to you to inform anyone of this?" Adam demanded furiously. "Why the devil not?"

When he'd been informed that the earl's son had regained consciousness and was asking to speak with him, he'd been prepared to give the lad some degree of latitude. His congenial attitude hadn't lasted above five minutes, however, when he learned the magnitude of what the bloody fool had been keeping from him.

"Because we had no proof to offer!" It was Derwent who answered, his sulky manner only slightly subdued. "Barrington's a duchess, for all she's no better than a whore, and we dared not speak against her. *You* weren't so quick to cast aspersions, I note," he added, his lips curling in a sneer.

Adam considered knocking him out again but decided the fop wasn't worth the bother. He turned back to Carling. The lad seemed determined to make a clean breast of things, and Adam wanted to learn all he could before the duke arrived from London.

"When did you suspect her of taking the papers? I know the three of you took them initially," he added, in case they should think to escape blame. "But when did you know it was she who had them rather than Charles?"

"When Charles told me that he didn't know where they were," Carling said, his eyes level as he met Adam's gaze. "And I was going to tell you we took the papers. I've already told Papa."

"Did Charles tell you he'd given them to her grace?" Adam did him the courtesy of believing him without demanding proof.

Carling shook his head cautiously. "No, but when the papers weren't found where they should have been, Charles told me to stop fretting. He said 'she' must still have them, and that he'd get them back by morning."

"Did he name her directly?" Adam pressed, realizing how delicate the situation was. As Derwent had unfortunately pointed out, Lady Barrington was a duchess, one with powerful lovers in very high places. The case against her would have to be ironclad if they had any hope of succeeding.

"No," Carling admitted with visible reluctance, "but he did say enough to let me know they were lovers. Charles was a poor man without connections or funds; there could be only one thing he had to draw that viper's notice: the papers. He stole them for her, and when he asked for them back, she killed him."

The lad's acuity took Adam aback. Carling had more bottom to him than he first supposed, he decided, and then turned his thoughts back to more pressing concerns. "We'll go into that at another time," he said, giving each young man an icy glare. "Just as we shall pursue the matter of your stealing Crown secrets. But for the moment, tell me of last night. Who struck you? Was it Lady Barrington?"

"I was struck from behind," Carling said, choosing his words with the greatest care, as if standing in the witness box. "At first I didn't see who had hit me. But as I was lying there I heard the rustle of skirts, and when I looked up I saw a woman slipping out the side doors and into the garden. There was a brief flash of moonlight, and I saw her quite clearly." His lips thinned, and for a brief moment Adam saw evidence of the man he was becoming. "It was Lady Barrington. I shall swear to it in a court of law."

A pleased smile touched Adam's lips. He might have preferred the lad tell him the truth right away rather than making him pry it out of him, but he wasn't about to quibble when the end result was so much to his liking. They had their traitor, and that meant Elizabeth was out of danger.

He rose to his feet, but before he could say anything the door to Carling's room burst open and the Duke of Creshton rushed in.

"What the devil are you doing standing about?" he demanded, his hair standing about his head like a snowy halo. "Why aren't you going after Elinore and Miss Mattingale?"

"Elizabeth and your daughter are upstairs, your grace," Adam replied, staring at the duke in confusion. "But first, sir, I must tell you that we have some good news for you. Lady Barrington is our murderer. Carling can identify—"

"Of course Barrington is the murderer, you dolt!" Creshton interrupted, clearly distressed. "We've known that from the first. But what I want to know is what you mean letting that she-wolf ride off with m'daughter and Miss Mattingale? Have you taken leave of your senses? She will kill them!"

All of the blood drained from Adam's head in a rush that left him feeling faint. He heard a roaring sound in his head, and for a terrifying moment he feared he would disgrace himself by swooning. Instead he drew a deep breath and met Creshton's wild gaze. "Do you know in which direction they are headed?" he asked, his manner so cool he might have been asking about the weather.

"To the bay on the other side of town, we think," the duke replied impatiently. "Several boats are at anchor there, and we assume she is making a run for it. Are you with me, or are you going to sit here and debate the matter for the rest of the day?"

Adam didn't have to think. He was already moving toward the door, his expression impassive and his thoughts centered on just one thing: getting Elizabeth to safety before it was too late. "I'm with you," he said, and walked out into the hall.

"How fortunate I was able to catch you before you'd started for town, my dear," Lady Barrington murmured, her polite tones at odds with the pistol she held trained on Elizabeth and Lady Elinore. "Otherwise I should have had to ask that my own coach be brought about. This is much cozier, don't you agree?"

"As this is the first time I have been held at gunpoint, your grace, you will forgive me if I appear less than delighted," Elinore said coolly, her gaze never leaving the duchess.

"This?" The pretty blonde gestured casually with the pistol. "A necessary precaution, I fear. In my profession one learns to prepare for any eventuality. But you needn't worry overly much," she added, her gaze shifting to Elizabeth. "I shan't kill you. Unless I have to, of course."

"As you had to kill Mr. Colburt and Lord Knolton?" Elizabeth challenged, taking her cue from Elinore and refusing to let her fear show. They had been alone with the duchess for less than a quarter hour, and she knew if they had any hope of surviving until Adam was able to rescue them, they would have to be very, very careful and very, very lucky.

Lady Barrington had appeared out of nowhere, pushing her way into Elinore's carriage before they even knew she was there. At first Elizabeth simply thought her incredibly rude, but the pistol in the other woman's hand had soon put paid to that.

"So you figured that out, did you?" Lady Barrington replied in answer to Elizabeth's question. "I always did say you were a clever creature. And I wouldn't have had to kill poor Frederick if he hadn't been so tiresomely burdened with morals. He was going to turn me over to the Crown, can you imagine? The ungrateful wretch; and after I endured his ham-fisted attempts at lovemaking. Men. What a sad and useless lot they have proven to be."

"What do you mean to do to us?" Elinore queried, picking up the conversation coolly. "You're bound for France, I gather?"

"France?" The duchess sent her a horrified look. "Heavens no, my dear! With the Bourbons back in power, I shouldn't dare show my face in case they know of my association with the little Corsican. I am far too fond of my neck to risk it with Madame Guillotine. It will have to be the Continent for me.

"Or perhaps I shall travel to America," she drawled, her bright blue gaze resting on Elizabeth with malicious glee. "Richmond seems to have a great deal to recommend it. I thought it sounded quite delightful from your father's letters."

Elizabeth didn't so much as blink. She'd already suspected the duchess of being the one to read her letters, and she refused to give her the satisfaction of showing her fury at the violation.

"So you did read them," she said, sounding bored when what she wanted to do was scratch the other woman's eyes out. "I rather thought you had."

The duchess frowned, clearly uncertain what to make of her hostages' cool responses. "Well, I must say I was properly shocked by your father's demand that you commit treason, and without so much as a farthing for your trouble," she continued, clearly determined to provoke some sort of response from her captives. "If a woman is going to betray her country, she should at least be well paid for her pains. Do you not agree?" Her smile was as poisonous as her tone.

This time, Elizabeth made no attempt to disguise her

reaction, her loathing plain as she met the other woman's gaze. "I would never betray my country."

Her grace laughed unpleasantly. "No, I don't suppose you would. You are too virtuous. How Charles laughed at you. He wanted you, you know, but he was too afraid of Falconer and that delicious Russian prince to make a try for you. But of course, even if it hadn't been for your knights-errant, I couldn't allow him to dally with you. Men are so much more biddable when they are focused only on one woman."

"I am sure you would know, your grace." Elinore's words were as cutting as her tone.

The duchess turned next to her, clearly delighted to have drawn the other woman into a verbal battle. "And you, Lady Elinore, I must say you have come as a bit of a surprise. The daughter of a duke *and* an agent; how extraordinary. A pity there is a peace on just now; otherwise I should have been tempted to turn you over to the French. You'd have fetched a pretty penny, I am sure."

"I would like to think so, thank you, your grace," Elinore replied drolly, and the duchess gave another laugh.

"On the other hand, you'd likely have proven too difficult to control, and I would have had to kill you," she said, with what might have been regret. "And that would have been a pity as I have actually grown quite fond of the pair of you. I find most women tedious, don't you?"

"I find *some* women tedious," Elinore agreed, her gaze fixed on Lady Barrington with cool dislike. "Especially the obvious ones."

The laughter died in the duchess's eyes and her lips thinned in displeasure. "You grow impertinent, Lady Elinore," she said, tightening her hold on the pistol. "*I* am the one holding the gun, a fact you would do well to remember. Now be quiet; you are no longer amusing."

Elinore shrugged negligently and leaned back against the squabs. Looking at her cool expression, one would think her indifferent to her fate, but Elizabeth knew better. Sitting beside her, Elizabeth could feel the tension emanating from her, and she realized Elinore wasn't nearly as sanguine as she pretended to be. As if sensing the direction of her thoughts, Elinore reached down and gave Elizabeth's hand a comforting squeeze. Her lips scarcely moved, but Elizabeth caught the urgent command in her soft whisper.

"Be ready."

"Remember, lad," Creshton warned, his blue eyes cold as he studied Adam, "no heroics. At the moment Lady Barrington has better reason to want them alive than dead. So long as she believes that, Elinore and Miss Mattingale should be safe enough."

Adam gave a distracted nod, although he barely heard the duke's words. Since learning that Elizabeth had been taken prisoner he'd gone cold inside, his emotions locked behind a wall of ice. He refused to accept the possibility that she could already be dead, knowing if he did so, he would go mad. Elizabeth was alive, he told himself grimly, and once he had her safely back he'd ring a peal over her head that she'd not soon be forgetting.

He loved her, he admitted rawly, his head still spinning at the thought. It was an emotion he'd avoided since the death of his parents, too afraid of risking his heart to open himself up to anyone. Yet from the moment he'd met Elizabeth he'd been drawn to her, unable to stay away from her despite the risk of scandal and ruin. He wasn't even certain when he had come to love her. It was as if the emotion had always been there, and was yet newly born. He'd admired her from the first, desired her soon after, and had been both possessively jealous and protective of her, wanting to keep her safe at any price.

He supposed he should have known he loved her when the mere possibility she'd betrayed him had made him mad with pain. He'd never have been so furious if his heart hadn't been so thoroughly engaged, and he wondered that he could have been so blind. Or perhaps not so blind, he admitted, his lips tightening in a bitter smile. What he'd been was terrified, and now there was every chance his cowardice could cost him his love. He broke into a cold sweat at the very thought.

"I'm sure they will be fine," the duke continued, not seeming to notice Adam's brooding silence. "Elinore's pluck to the backbone, and your Miss Mattingale's got a good head on her shoulders. We'll have 'em back by luncheon, I daresay."

"Yes, your grace," Adam agreed, his stomach twisting with fear. He had to believe Elizabeth was unhurt, he thought, his hands tightening about the reins of his horse. If he believed otherwise, he would go out of his mind.

"There they are," Creshton said as the elegant carriage rumbled over the crest of the hill. "Are the others in position?"

Adam turned in his saddle and glanced toward the woods, where half a dozen men, led by the redoubtable Henry, were waiting.

"Yes, Lord Creshton," he said, turning back, his jaw hardening. He pulled out his pistol and held it in his hand, the trigger already cocked. If worst came to worst, he wanted to be prepared for immediate action.

The duke saw him, and a bleak expression stole across his fleshy features.

"Falconer, listen to me," he began, his voice surprisingly gentle. "Even if we learn the duchess has harmed the girls, we must still make every effort to take her alive. Do you understand? She is too important for us to risk. Will you give me your word not to fire unless there is no other choice?"

Adam gave him a long look. Since obtaining his majority he had done all he could to serve his country and his king and never doubted the cost. He would willingly die for his country, if need be. But this . . . he slowly shook his head.

"No, your grace," he replied, his voice as dead as his

soul would be if aught happened to Elizabeth. "I will not."

Lord Creshton studied him for a moment before heaving a weary sigh. "I thought as much," he said, not sounding particularly upset by Adam's defiance. "Ah, well; we can only pray her grace is as practical as she is greedy. It is our only hope."

Adam didn't trouble with an answer, his attention centered on the carriage that was rolling toward them. He and the duke had their mounts situated so the road was blocked, leaving the driver no choice but to stop. Since the carriage was Creshton's, the coachman was familiar with the duke, and Adam saw his surprise as he pulled the carriage to a halt.

"Yer grace, wot the bloody devil—" he began, his gruff voice a mixture of annoyance and confusion.

"Get off the carriage, Kelmont, if you will," the duke said, his voice as steady as the pistol he trained on the door of the coach. "Maneuver three."

The coachman wasted no time with words. Both he and the tiger riding behind him scrambled down from the box with considerable dexterity and ran to the cover offered by the hedgerows. When they turned back the coachman had a pistol in each hand.

Before Adam could comment on this amazing sight he heard a pistol shot ring out, and his heart stopped when he realized it had come from the carriage.

"Elizabeth!" He roared out her name, dismounting and running toward the coach on unsteady legs. Before he could reach it the door opened, and a flurry of skirts and women came tumbling out. He saw Elizabeth and Elinore struggling with Lady Barrington, but because they were locked together it was impossible for him to get off a clean shot without risking the lives of all three women. He tucked the pistol back into his waistband and dove into the pile, emerging with the duchess in his grip. He rolled to his feet, hauling her up with him and unceremoniously thrusting her into Creshton's waiting arms. When he was certain the prisoner was secured, he turned back to Elizabeth.

His heart pounding, he gently helped her to her feet, his gaze sweeping over her as he checked her for any sign of injury.

"Elizabeth! My love, are you all right?" he demanded, and then went icy with terror when he saw the blood staining the front of her cloak.

"Oh, God! You've been shot!"

"It's not me, you idiot," she snapped, shoving him back with surprising strength. "It's Elinore!" And she dropped back to her knees beside her friend.

"It's all right," Elinore said, clasping her hand to her forearm. "The bullet merely grazed me, that is all."

"Here, poppet, let me see." The duke was kneeling beside her, his big hands shaking as he gently moved her hand to one side so he could examine her wound.

"There now," he said, his voice breaking with emotion. "It's not so bad; a mere scratch, as you say. Although how I am to tell your mama about this, I know not. She will have both our heads."

"I am sorry, Papa." Elinore smiled weakly in apology. "Perhaps you could say I was injured in a carriage accident?"

"And risk her learning the truth?" His blue eyes were filled with tears as he brushed back a lock of hair that had fallen across a dust-stained cheek. "I am not half so brave as that. Lie still now, dearest. We'll soon have you home."

"Yes, Papa," Elinore murmured, and fell immediately into a swoon.

"Really, such dramatics." The duchess gave a pretty laugh, and Adam and Elizabeth turned around to face her. She was standing between the coachman and Henry, her beautiful face wearing its customary expression of cool amusement. Despite the fact that her bonnet was crushed and her cloak was torn and bedraggled, her air of insouciance was such that she might have been still in the Derrings' drawing room. When she saw him glaring at her, her lips curved in a mocking smile.

"You needn't cast daggers at me, my lord," she purred in her cultured voice. "Lady Elinore getting shot is more her fault and Miss Mattingale's than mine. They attacked me, you know."

"Only because it was the only way to stop you, you unprincipled witch!" Elizabeth snapped, shooting the duchess a furious scowl. "I hope they hang you!"

The duchess merely gave another laugh. "Oh, I daresay they will try." Her gaze moved next to Adam. "I suppose appealing to your chivalry as a gentleman would be quite useless?" she queried.

Adam thought of all the harm caused by the duchess's greed and treachery. "Quite useless," he agreed coldly.

"I thought as much," she said, clutching her reticule to her chest. "Pity. It was for money, you see. My old fool of a husband left me all but destitute, and I refused to live on the paltry sum his clutch-fisted son offered me. When I learned what the French were willing to pay for the tid-bits of information I could gather, I saw no reason why I should not oblige them. And really, is it my fault my lovers took such delight in prattling in bed? If they had kept their precious secrets to themselves, I would have had nothing to sell."

That she could blame the men she had ruined and be-trayed with her greed disgusted Adam, even though he could see the truth in some of what she was saying. "That may be," he conceded reluctantly, "but that doesn't excuse the way you used Elizabeth. You pretended to be her friend even as you betrayed her."

A sad smile touched the duchess's lips. "That is what is so odd," she murmured softly, "for toward the end I did come to think of her as a friend." Her gaze went to Elizabeth.

"I knew you would be accused," she continued, her blue eyes filled with genuine regret, "but I also knew Falconer would never let you be charged. He is quite besotted with you, and if you are half so clever as I think you are, you'll be a marchioness before the summer is ended."

"That's nonsense!" Elizabeth sputtered, going white with shock.

"Is it?" The duchess lifted her shoulders in a shrug. "Perhaps. And perhaps I like to think so, merely to ease my conscience. Just as it eases my conscience to think that had you truly been clapped in gaol, I would have done the honorable thing and come forward. I suppose there is no way we shall ever know." And she pressed the reticule to her chest.

Understanding dawned and Adam rushed forward, knowing even as he began moving that he was too late. "Your grace, no—" His protest was drowned out by the report of a pistol shot, and the duchess fell to the ground.

Adam and Elizabeth reached her together, and they rolled her gently onto her back. The front of her cape was already soaked with blood, and Adam knew there was nothing anyone could do to help the traitorous duchess now. He glanced down into Lady Barrington's face and saw by her expression that she knew it as well.

"It is better this way," the duchess said, struggling for the words as she gazed up at him and Elizabeth. "I would not have enjoyed being hanged. What—what should I have worn?"

"The papers?" Adam pressed, hating the necessity of hounding a dying woman "What did you do with Derring's papers?"

"I—I sent them to London," she replied, blood coming to her lips as she coughed weakly. "There was a Russian prince with very deep pockets willing to pay for whatever I could send him. I can't recall his name, but he is with the Czar."

"Zaramoff?" Elizabeth bent lower, the duchess's hand held in hers. "Was it Zaramoff?"

An ominous rattle came from the duchess's chest as she struggled to speak. "That—that sounds right. He had

the coldest eyes . . . like death. He made me afraid . . ."
She coughed again and closed her eyes, her breath and
her life leaving her in a soft sigh.

"And you are not to leave that bed until the doctor says
you may," Elizabeth scolded, her expression stern as she
tucked the bedclothes about a sullen Elinore. "If you do,
your papa has given me leave to write your mama."

A genuine pout had Elinore looking surprisingly
young. "He would," she said, sulking. "And you would
do it, too, I've no doubt."

"If I must," Elizabeth replied, smiling despite the sadness tugging at her. A week had passed since Lady Barrington's death, and she was still struggling to come to
terms with all that had happened. There had been so many
changes in her life, there were days when she felt like a
bit of flotsam in the middle of a stormy sea. Even her
position had changed; instead of working for Lady Derring she was now employed as Elinore's companion, a
change that pleased both her and Elinore very much.

Her place of residence had also changed, as instead of
carrying Elinore back to Derring Hall they had taken her
to one of the duke's many country houses, located in a
nearby village. Elizabeth had remained at her friend's side,
nursing her through the inevitable fever that followed her
injury. The duke had remained only until he was certain
his beloved daughter was out of danger, and then he and
Adam had departed for London. The duke had written to
let them know that he would be arriving within a few
days, but of Adam there hadn't been so much as a word.

"Well, once we are in London I refuse to be coddled,"
Elinore said, drawing Elizabeth back to the present. "If
what you have told me about this odious Zaramoff person
is true, we shall have a great deal to do. Any man who
would support Napoleon against his own people is clearly
a villain of the first water."

"He is that and more," Elizabeth assured her, relieved

to turn her thoughts to something other than her foolish longing for Adam. "And I do wish you would reconsider and let me contact Alexi. He is already working to uncover Zaramoff's treachery."

As it always did, mention of Alexi's name had Elinore muttering decidedly unladylike sentiments. "I'd as lief contact the devil himself," she said, her eyes flashing. "The devil would no doubt prove a great deal less trouble."

Elizabeth started to defend her good friend when the door opened and a heavyset lady swathed in fur and silk swept into the room, Adam trailing in her wake. Elizabeth scarce had time to register his presence before the unknown lady was swooping down on the bed and Elinore.

"You wretched, ungrateful child!" she scolded, tenderly embracing Elinore. "I let you assist your papa in his work, and this is how you repay me!"

"Mama." Elinore wrapped her good arm about her mother and gave her a reassuring hug. "I'm fine, truly I am. Whatever did Papa say to upset you so?"

"That you had been wounded by that awful Barrington woman," the duchess said, settling on the chair Elizabeth had vacated upon her entrance. "But why should I believe a word that wretch says? He also tried fobbing me off at first with some ridiculous fiction about your being hurt in a carriage accident." She glanced up at Elizabeth and smiled.

"Hello, my dear, you must be Miss Mattingale. As you may have gathered, I am this hoyden's mama, and I have a great deal to thank you for, it seems."

Elizabeth made a clumsy curtsy, her brain suddenly unable to function. "It is kind of you to say so, your grace," she said, her gaze drawn helplessly to Adam. "But I assure you I have done nothing deserving of your praise."

"Have you not?" the duchess asked, her gaze going from Elizabeth to Adam. "Well, we shall see. In the meanwhile, would you be so kind as to leave Elinore and me for a moment? I mean to read her a thundering scold, and I really can't do that with his lordship present. Oh, and ring for some tea, will you? Traveling always makes me dreadfully thirsty. There's a dear."

Elizabeth gave a start, realizing that she'd been dismissed. She felt oddly ill at ease, longing to be with Adam and yet afraid. This would be the first time since their meeting in the drawing room that they would be alone, and she was suddenly terrified of being private with him.

"Yes, your grace," she said, hiding her reluctance as she dropped another curtsy. She glanced at Elinore, only to find her friend regarding her with what could only be termed smug satisfaction.

"Shall I see to the packing, my lady?" she asked, hoping to put some sort of distance between herself and Adam any way she could. Reminding him of her position as Elinore's companion seemed the best way, and she could only hope he would take the subtle hint.

Elinore's smile widened. "That would be fine, Elizabeth," she said, inclining her head graciously. "Thank you."

It was evident from the black scowl that immediately settled on his handsome features that the little byplay between her and Elinore had not gone unnoticed. But her hope that he would withdraw behind the rigid lines of class distinction were dashed when he grasped her firmly by the arm and marched her from the room. Ignoring her struggles and indignant protests, he led her to the upper parlor and unceremoniously thrust her inside.

"What was that business of your calling Elinore *my lady?*" he demanded, the moment the door had closed behind them. "You're not her blasted servant."

Elizabeth could only gape at him in astonishment. "Of course I am her servant!" she exclaimed. "Her ladyship was kind enough to hire me as her companion, and—"

"The devil she did!" Adam interrupted, his gold eyes flashing with temper "That little witch! I *knew* she would do something like this." He folded his arms across his chest and cast her a burning look.

"Well, you may just forget it, do you hear me?" he commanded, his arrogance making her teeth grit in fury. "I didn't save you from being executed as a traitor just so you and Elinore can run about playing at being spies."

"We are not playing!" Elizabeth denied, furious that he could be so dismissing of her and her friend when Elinore had almost died performing her duties. "Elinore *is* a spy, and I mean to help her in any way I can."

"You most certainly will not!" he shot back, dropping his arms and stepping forward until they were all but nose-to-nose. "Spying is an occupation best left to a man, and by heaven, that is what you shall do! A woman has no business risking her life!"

Elizabeth treated this pronouncement with the contempt she felt it deserved. "Why not?" she challenged, too incensed to be cautious. "Or do you think patriotism purely a man's prerogative? You believed quick enough that Lady Barrington was a traitor. If you could believe a woman capable of betraying her country, why should you find it so difficult that a woman could be equally capable of defending it?"

Adam opened his lips and then closed them, clearly at the end of his tether. "We are not going to argue about this," he said firmly, placing his hands on her shoulders and drawing her against him. "My marchioness is not going to go tearing about the countryside courting danger, and that is final."

"I am not your marchioness, nor shall I ever be!" Elizabeth cried furiously. "I will do as I please, and there is nothing you can do to stop me!"

"Isn't there?" He pulled her into his arms and took her lips in a kiss of unmistakable passion.

At the touch of his mouth on hers, Elizabeth's hurt and temper melded into a desire so strong, she was helpless to fight its pull. She loved Adam, and she wanted nothing more than to be in his arms. Right or wrong no longer mattered; there was only she and Adam, and the powerful magic they created together.

"Elizabeth, my darling." Adam breathed the words in a ragged sigh as he lifted his mouth from hers. "I adore you. Don't go away from me. Please. I could bear anything but to lose you."

His plea brought a sheen of tears to Elizabeth's eyes, and she tightened her arms about his neck. "I won't," she promised softly, clinging to him as tightly as she could. "I'll never leave you. I love you, Adam. I love you."

"And I love you." The admission was made on a groan of need. "Marry me, Elizabeth. Be my wife."

Her legs collapsed as if she had been poleaxed. *"Marry you?"* she repeated, staring up at him in wide-eyed disbelief.

"Of course marry me," he replied, frowning down at her in disapproval. "Didn't I offer to make you my marchioness?"

Elizabeth thought about that for a moment. "Actually," she said, her lips curving in an amused smile, "I believe you commanded it."

He shrugged and kissed her again. "Command, offer, call it what you will, so long as the end result is the same, I don't care. But if it will make you any happier"—and he dropped to one knee, her hand held tightly in his hand.

"Elizabeth," his eyes were eloquent with love as he gazed up at her, "will you be my wife? I love and adore you, and I give you my most solemn word that I will cherish you all the days of my life. Will you marry me?"

The tears Elizabeth had held at bay filled her eyes, and she was unable to blink them all back. "Are you certain?" she asked, knowing it would kill her to marry Adam and then to disappoint him in some way. "Knowing what my father is—"

He rose to his feet to take her in his arms once more. "I don't care what your father is!" he told her fiercely. "I care only what his daughter is! You are a brave, wonderful woman with more honor than any lady I have ever known. I'd never thought to find anyone like you, and I won't give you up now. I won't! You will marry me, by heaven, if I must cause the greatest scandal to rock this kingdom since Prinny married his second wife!"

His angry words reassured her in a way nothing else could have done, and she pressed another kiss to his lips.

"A scandal isn't necessary, my lord," she said, her heart overflowing as she smiled up at him. "Especially one of such monumental proportions. I'll marry you.

"But," she added, stepping back when he would have swept her into another kiss, "I want it plain that I still mean to be of assistance to Elinore. You are not the only one who can serve his king, you know."

Adam looked far from pleased at her demand. "I don't like it," he declared, every inch the haughty lord.

"I am sure you do not," she returned, accepting his disapproval. "But I promise to take no more chances than you do. Agreed?"

He was quiet a long moment, long enough to make Elizabeth wonder if she had pushed him beyond what he could accept. Yet as much as she loved Adam, she loved her country, and Alexi, if it came to that. She could not sacrifice one for the other. Biting her lip, she held her breath and waited for his reply.

"Agreed," he said at last, his lips curving in a smile so complacent, Elizabeth was instantly suspicious. "And since usually the most dangerous thing I undertake is a speech in front of Parliament, I think I can guarantee we shall both look forward to a long and happy life. Agreed?"

Elizabeth smiled again. "Agreed," she said softly, surrendering to the kiss that was but the first in a lifetime yet to come.

More Zebra Regency Romances